RISING ON THE ROAD TO FREEDOM

WILLIAM KLEIN

Cover photo: iStock.com/CampPhoto

Printed in the United States of America
Published by Braughler Books LLC., Springboro, Ohio

First printing, 2020

ISBN: 978-1-970063-44-8

Library of Congress Control Number: 2019919201

Ordering information: Special discounts are available on quantity purchases by bookstores, corporations, associations, and others. For details, contact the publisher at:

sales@braughlerbooks.com
or at 937-58-BOOKS

For questions or comments about this book, please write to:

info@braughlerbooks.com

"Remain true to yourself, but move ever upward toward greater consciousness and greater love! At the summit you will find yourselves united with all those who, from every direction, have made the same ascent. For everything that rises must converge."

Pierre Teilhard deChardin, SJ

Dedicated to the people who
taught me how to "stay together."
My family (Mom, Dad, Jimmy, Carol, Kathy,
Susie and Jane) and Warren A. Miccio

PART 1

1

Every soul who has ever graced the face of this earth has met a circumstance beyond control. The stories of our lives traverse the landscapes of our imagination on a quest to satisfy our hunger for freedom and quench our thirst for understanding. The realities and illusions of life can make or break a person. Travis' misfortune was extraordinary for a 16-year-old boy.

No one could know the trouble he would meet when he was asked to be a messenger on behalf of his grandfather. The message to be delivered was to a priest, Father Paul, who was helping refugees escape political persecution and certain death in their country; crossing the US-Mexican border. *Their* predicament was even more harrowing in light of this reality, and Travis carried this in his heart as he ducked and shuffled through the channel to the daunting world of the unknown. Eben Manning, Travis' grandfather, built the tunnel, but his wife, Eleanor, an unwilling co-conspirator would shoulder much of the blame and her grandson's circumstances haunted her more than anyone. Fear has a way of paralyzing even the bravest and boldest, and Eleanor's trepidation in entering the tunnel and delivering the message herself stemmed from avoiding cramped and closed spaces at all costs.

A reminder of life's fragility interrupted the calm of the evening when Travis emerged from the tunnel carrying a loaf of bread and a flashlight. He was dismayed when he saw the warning flares of the fireworks his grandmother shot telling him trouble was in full swing on their side, and he paused as the significance of this moment settled in his bones.

He explored the area to look for Father Paul and his guests but stayed close to the tunnel. A small breadbox filled with supplies and locked was busted open. Wrappers lay strewn in the sand and rough. The boy listened closely as the dead quiet of the desert hills was disturbed by a sound of gravel splashing to the foot of the knoll and the emergence of a slow scratching of rock to find footing in the loose stones and pebbles. He was anxious to meet Father Paul and the migrants, but was none too happy when the expected visitors turned out to be an unexpected beast of prey searching for food.

Travis couldn't quite make out what the beast was at first, but any four-legged animal with a quest for survival could startle a boy stranded on his own doing the same. It wasn't going to be a fair fight as the beast moved with stealth and caution. The animal frightened him from his toenails to the hairs on his head when it came into view and aged the teenager thirty years in a matter of seconds. Travis didn't bring a gun, as he thought he'd only be there a short time. Now he was regretting it and vowed he'd carry one with him in the wild wherever he went if he came out of this alive. His heart jumped out of his chest and pulsed into his throat as the beast's menacing presence presented him with images of youth he'd forgotten, and his short life flashed before his eyes.

"What would Grandpa do here?" he thought to himself. He could hear his grandpa telling him "to respect the power of nature and never underestimate how it could touch you."

The beast's head dipped as it sought clarity in the shadows of twilight and moved from side to side to catch a better view. Travis' shadowy silhouette caught the beast's eye as it witnessed a sudden movement from its potential prey and quick stop. The beast peered into the area of Travis' direction where it thought it saw the movement. The beast bowed back on its hind legs, positioned itself for optimal support, its mouth gaping and dripping saliva, as this was a glowing prospect of food supply after a futile hunting day. Travis and the beast played a game of cat and mouse as neither one moved and both waited for the other to draw first. Travis was paralyzed with fear, and his mind tripped the wires of options and a thousand thoughts at once. He felt as though he stayed still for an hour, though just two minutes had passed. He wondered that it might have been the beast that had rummaged through the small pantry box.

The animal flinched and boldly took the first step forward into a cascade of gentle light displaying all the features of an adult 200-pound mountain lion. The large cat's ears were erect at attention. It was light brown all over with a streak of white on its underbelly and bore a silly looking moustache under its nose. Long whiskers with fangs in a wicked snarl, the lion hissed its intentions that it would wage any battle any animal brought.

There were short hedges of brush, no trees to hide behind but a clear path between the foot of the knoll and the open tunnel. If Travis made it to the tunnel, it didn't guarantee his safety, as the lion could follow him, trap the boy in the narrow den of darkness and have its fill with a cool place to rest. Travis was caught between the mountain lion and the tunnel, so he hoped to stay close and cling to the hill not tempting fate if the animal hadn't seen him. Travis decided that to make a move to the tunnel might be deadly. He kept quiet and calm, hoping that the lion hadn't seen him, but his thoughts were dubious. This was just a form of denial that comes with desperation.

Travis was reluctant now about making this journey. He felt as though he was over his head and this was way more than he expected. Grandma's concerns were legit and the lesson was learned. He was uncertain about everything in life and the whirl of chaos inspired deeper thoughts of regret, which only made him more anxious. His desperation inspired him to rethink his situation over and over again, but all thoughts trailed back to survival and there was no good answer or satisfaction to the quandary he faced. *"Stare in the face of death and hope for the best in standing strong,"* he thought to himself. These were potent thoughts for a boy whose greatest concern in the past was whether or not he should talk to a girl of interest at school. He could picture himself back in the comforts of his room or with his horses in the stable. Life and death situations have a way of inspiring the deepest convictions and counting the blessings of comfort.

"Maybe he didn't see me," he thought, just as the next movements from the lion drew consternation from the boy. The animal looked lost as it moved its head to and fro like it was searching the land for something more. It stopped, moved back and straightened as if it was fooled by its own senses and looked away to see if it could get a better vantage point from another angle. It walked away from Travis' line of sight and looked in a different direction. Suddenly it came back into view. It behaved like a distressed cat at a zoo, walking back and forth, as if it were trapped or working out its next move; it was as if it were trying to orient itself and reclaim a piece of territory from another animal and marking off its territory with its paces.

"No chance for Father Paul if he comes here now. Ain't likely that a priest is good with a rifle and probably doesn't have one

anyway," thought Travis. The animal could catch him by surprise. The young man was afraid to make a noise.

The beast growled a low burly growl and showed its yellow fangs as if it were keenly aware of another intruder in the area but didn't know exactly where it was. It was erratic as it suddenly jumped up to a higher plane on the hill to see what might be up there. After a harrowing minute of checking out the higher part of the landscape, it reclaimed its poise and went back to sniffing low to the ground for what it initially came for — food. It rested on its haunches. *"It must've been aware that there was food in the area before and a smart animal knows where to get it,"* thought Travis. *"He clearly didn't see me,"* he thought to himself. *"If he moves away far enough, I'm gonna high tail it to the tunnel."* Then his worst thought came to pass.

The lion was discreet as he recognized Travis' presence and slow movement while the boy determined it was time to make a move to the tunnel. It crept closer to him. Inch by inch it became evident to Travis he'd now most definitely been discovered by the lion. He thought about using the light to distract the cat. He thought about how his dog Groucho would chase the light, and thought it might work here while he could slowly work his way to the hole and disappear. This was no time to test animal behavior on a lion, and he thought better of it as it might just agitate it more. He found his fingers flipping on the light anyway. The cat stopped a second in wonder at what the boy was doing. It looked to the light, but its interest was clearly set on him, the source of light. The cat crept towards him, and that distinct low growl tumbled from the beast's neck to his belly and reverberated into a gravel purr like it was ready to attack. It was twenty feet away.

Travis pitched his head back in terror, closing his eyes and reminding himself how this petrifying episode came to be in the first place. It all returned to him in the tornado of a moment swirling around his mind while his heart quickened the flow of blood and adrenaline poached his breath and a cold sweat of uncertainty blanketed him.

2

Travis took a deep dive inside the heart to see and understand people in a new way. He took another look at the place where he grew up and the people who made up the town because of the incidents that happened in the fall of 2017.

For the most part, Travis grew up in Jacaranda Hot Springs, Texas. Home can be an oasis and a harbinger of hope for some, but for others it's a place to wait and painfully mark time until the death knell chimes. Jacaranda Hot Springs is just such a place, a fact that Travis learned faster than most on account of his mother dying when he was just five. That's when he moved to the Hot Springs to live with his grandparents. Unfortunately, he understood this in an even deeper way through the story about to be told.

Eben Manning, Travis' grandfather, was content to stay planted in Jacaranda as much as possible, whereas his grandmother Eleanor hailed from Louisiana and was reluctant at first. The French Quarter of New Orleans always held a life of excitement and luminous possibility for her. The romantic tangles of vibrant creative quests became the very lifeblood of who she was, so if you told her that she would make a life here in the desert she would've said, "You're a fool." Devotion tends to confuse things when one settles on dedicating one's self and one's destiny to ineffable love and there is artfulness in pursuing the act of love. It is here in the Hot Springs that she learned the art with flair and distinction. Her husband's family had a ranch in this quaint, provincial corner of the world. It is here in the Hot Springs that she learned to accept circumstances in the name of love. Deep down the country girl in her thrived and found its peace in these quarters, and she had no regrets about that.

There had been a drought this summer. It wasn't obvious by looking at it, but when the Hot Springs did get good rain, the land's rich with loamy soil, so it's good to plant onions, tomatoes, radishes and the like. The silt, sand and clay are good for long growing plants, but for the last couple years the yield was scarce and hopes of a good harvest equally so. Farmers and ranchers set their sights on looking for other opportunities to supplement their wages. That's why they were using the land to rent out to a company that manufactured wind turbines and solar panels.

The town is a character all its own. It has enjoyed certain respectability in the past but hasn't aged gracefully. It used to be a nice resort for tourists who bathed in its purifying hot spring spas on weekend getaways, but now the spa looks like a rickety cathouse badly in need of a renovation, and other unused buildings next to it are boarded up. The old Woolworths, Lopez's Hardware Store and Bordanaro's Butcher Shop used to be there when the Mannings moved here some fifty-eight years ago, but they've gone the way of the other mom and pop shops these days being replaced by bigger more efficient entities. As the population dwindled in town so did the need for these stores. Like other border towns, it has its share of squares and roundabout turns with adobe architecture that indelibly etched mythic lore and mysterious enchantment of the "Western frontier" in its roads — the very roads forged from the limestone quarry and brick of its nearby mountains.

It holds its idyllic past close to its heart but meets the present-day concerns for safety and security with truculent authority and watchfulness.

In the past it was a place to rest on the journey, but nowadays it's a place where passers-by keep on moving. It enjoyed a past where man and animal alike roamed free, but since the nineties it's marked by a strong, imposing fence firmly rooted in its dirt stretching for miles caging folks in their respective countries of Mexico and the US. Up close, the fence looks like a rusted train of dominos as it snakes its way up and down the hill into valleys working its way into the landscape of cacti, brush and craggy cliffs of mountain. It runs the length of Jacaranda with walls and other barriers to keep people out like Mexicans, Guatemalans, Salvadorans, Hondurans and any other poor souls "they" don't think deserve to be here. It's an imposing thing, the fence. It's composed of tall girders six inches apart and rises to about twenty feet high. The fence is heavily guarded and the Border Patrol station is just down the road apiece with checkpoints and radar stations for additional support to CBP agents. For better or worse, it's been a fixture in the town and locals have learned to live with the eyesore.

Travis and his friend Merk used to hang out around the famous fence. "Merk" was short for Merkel. Sometimes locals got lazy in addressing people by their full names. One day the boys were playing catch by the fence and the ball landed in "No Man's Land." It has a small patch of land behind the fence where a barbed wire demarked Mexico from the US.

"Who's gonna get it?" Travis asked.

"You threw it."

"You're the idiot whose glove it bounced off. Hits your glove, you shoulda caught it."

"Well, I ain't gettin' between those things," Merk said pointing to the iron girders.

"Yeah, I guess you're about two sizes too big. Let's see if I can reach it." Travis was getting lanky in his adolescence, so he pulled himself close to the fence and stretched in futility nowhere near able to get it. He thought he might be able to reach it with his feet, so he tried to angle his legs. He put his feet between the slats, scooched his body as close as he could, pointed his toes and tried to take a swipe at the ball. He just missed it and tried to get back, but he was stuck between the slats.

"Well, it looks like that was a dumb idea. I ain't goin' anywhere fast," Travis said.

"You stuck?"

Travis looked at him and his idiotic question with disdain as he tried to wriggle out. "Of course I'm stuck."

"Uh-oh," Merk said pointing to the car kicking up dust down the road. It was a white SUV with a large green swoop on the side and read "Border Patrol" on it. "I'll see you later."

Merk ran into the thickets to avoid getting caught while Travis called to him.

"Get on back here, you scallywag! You ain't gonna leave me here…I'm gonna tell them what a sucky catcher you are and you'll never play another game a catch in this town again," fumed Travis. Merk ignored him and ran away. The man in the patrol car called to him from the loud cracking speakers in his car as he pulled up to them.

"Hey, where you running to, son?" the voice droned.

Merk stopped dead in his tracks for a second but continued on his way. "I gotta get on home," Merk replied trying to save himself and his marked embarrassment.

"Don't you take another step," the officer admonished. Merk stopped, put his hands up in the air in surrender and slowly walked back towards the patrol car. "Whatchoo doing there?" the officer asked Travis as he exited the car.

"I'm just tryin' to get my baseball and got myself stuck." Travis lay helpless as he gazed up at the officer.

"You Mexican?" the officer asked with a straight face. "You tryin' to escape Mexico?"

"No sir. I'm American. I swear I am."

"We both are," added Merk. "I ain't no illegal alien."

"I don't know if I believe you," the officer said with a smirk on his face. "I get you outta there, I'm gonna have to take you in for questioning. You go and sit in the back of my car," said the officer to Merk. The tag on his shirt read "Cruz." He made it known in no uncertain terms to not cross a "Cruz."

"Yes sir," Merk replied as Cruz opened the door to his car and escorted him inside.

The officer helped Travis out of the predicament and pulled him to safety. Travis thanked him, and Cruz took him by the shoulder and led him back to the car where he joined prisoner Merk. "You lost that baseball. I ain't gonna be able to reach that. Bummer, ain't it?" Travis was silent. Cruz looked at the baseball laying there in the sand and the profile of a dust angel swing Travis created with his leg in the dirt. He could've used his club or a pole in his car to get it, but he wanted to teach the boys a lesson. "That's the way life goes sometimes. Sometimes the things we love are right in our reach, but we just can't get them. We've gotta leave them behind." Cruz said as he slammed the car door shut and wrote something. "You boys know you're not to be going through that fence," Cruz said as he drove them away. They remained quiet in the back of the car. "Anything could've happened to you. What if I were to come up there and just shoot you dead thinking you're someone you're not? You've got animals out there that'll eat you up and spit you out as fast as they kill ya'." There was a long pause of discontent. "You're lucky I believe your story. You know it's not good for you to hang out and play around here, don't you? You think if I let you go you'll learn your lesson?"

"Yes sir," the two boys blurted out in unison.

Not listening he continued, "Huh? Orrrrr, do I have to take you to the station, and we can fingerprint you, stick you in jail, call your parents and do this right?"

"I think we learnt our lesson," Merk said. "Don't you, Travis?"

"Yes sir," intoned a frightened Travis. "We didn't mean no harm, I swear." Cruz drove to Main Street and let them out.

"You two go on and get home," said officer Cruz pulling the car over.

The boys got out of the car and walked away when Travis saw Eben Manning, his grandfather, turn the corner and start coming down the road in his broken down '72 blue sun-faded Chevy truck. Manning hadn't seen that they were just in the patrol car.

"Hey, strangers. You want a ride home?" Manning asked his grandson.

"I'm just 'round the corner, sir. I'm gonna see you, Travis," said Merk as he ran off down the side road.

"See ya'," Travis said as he hopped into the truck.

Manning was headed to the Feed and Supply Store to get some supplies for the ranch.

• • • • •

The truck sputtered along as they drove by the ranch houses and two bedroom shanties with rusted fences that lined the side roads of Main Street. It would pass Border Patrol agent Guy Stillwell, and the two drivers acknowledged each other with a slight wave. That's the way they do things in Jacaranda — even if you don't like your neighbor.

"Been a good day, Wiz?" Manning liked to call Travis "Wiz" to inspire him to recognize his own wisdom, and because he was a "wizard" at video games and computers.

"Yeah," Travis replied discreetly, not wanting to hedge his bets on how his grandfather would respond to his connection to the police.

The dry heat of the noon hour was becoming oppressive and as hot as a sauna. A light air kicked up dust and dry tumbleweeds this fall day but it wasn't enough to help a man who sweats easily. The old man wiped his forehead with a red paisley headband marking up his round face with soot, but it didn't do much good, as he'd soon be wiping it with his dusty rag again in about ten minutes time. Eben Manning had a reflex habit of smiling through everything in life, so he smiled right through the heat with no cares or concerns, and his squinty eyes glistened with optimism.

The Feed and Seed Supply Store was quiet this day, but there were a few people milling around. Today Manning was buying some feed for his horses and cattle when he wandered into a conversation between another farmer, "Dingy" Walters and the manager. Dingy, the town comedian, got his name from his marksmanship in "dinging" cans with a 22 shotgun. "Dinged that one," he'd say. "Dinged that one, too…" even if he didn't. Later he saw that he was just as good a marksman with his car and the dings that mysteriously popped up on his bumpers, hoods, doors and side mirrors. He didn't claim those, though. It looked like someone took hammers to parts of the rusted-out machine. Dingy just seemed to have a knack for destruction.

The air conditioner rattled and the store smelled like a mix of turpentine and well-oiled leather, as Travis meandered and casually listened to the exchange between Dingy and the manager. He stuck his nose into the leather satchel taking a big sniff like he was inhaling his asthma medication inhaler. The smell of tannery goods was euphoria for him. He was more concerned with checking out the latest editions of bridles, tacks and other horse equipment in a display nearby rather than bothering with his grandfather's business and the business of others.

"How much you done need?" asked the bucked-toothed manager.

"I think we should git by for now with about fifty tons a' concrete. I think I can stretch it. You think you can git me dat?" Dingy asked.

"That's gonna be a purdy penny, Dingy. Long as I have an order, I can put in for it," the manager said.

"That's all right. It's my new investment."

"What the hell kinda project you fixin' to do?" gruff old Manning asked.

"I'm gonna make a big wall over that fence," Dingy said as he examined his list.

"That's a perfectly good fence. It's a mix of iron and steel fabricated in it with tall slats. Ain't nobody getting through there. Why you wanna build a wall instead?"

Dingy was unsettled in his skin and unconsciously picked up a product even though he didn't want to buy it and quickly set it back. "I don't know. I guess too many have been getting through the fence. Anyway, it's my land, I can do what I wan' do. They gonna pay me for it too. Better than the crop we got this year."

"To each his own and to own his each," Manning said under his breath. Travis continued to mind his own business. Although he was aloof and off into his own world like any kid his age would be, he could tell by the tone of the two men that it was an important conversation.

Still pondering the subject old man Manning smiled and posed another question. "How they do that? There's barbed wire on the other side of the fence just five, ten feet away. I guess they can cut through that and catapult over that fence. I just wonder how they still get through it. You ever seen one do that? Catapult?"

"Yer ridiculous, Manning. They build a wall they ain't getting through it."

"Many ways to get over a wall. It better be tall, that's all I can say," interjected Manning.

"It'll be tall. It'll be beautiful. Watch and see how nice it's gonna be. They want a prototype wall to look at and I'm gonna make it. They gonna use my wall all over this country. Ain't nobody craftin' things like me. It's gone be the nicest wall they ever done seen. It's gone be real purdy."

"Hmm," Manning scratched his five-day beard and smiled a skeptic's grin. "Creative types can always figure out ways to make things happen. If someone wants freedom enough, they'll figure out a way to get it. I reckon you better take that into account, Dingy."

"I'm sure the brains at the top got that one figured out," said Dingy.

"Yeah? Those brains ever been down here? They ever met some a' the people we seen?" The manager remained silent and embarrassed, as he didn't want to get involved.

"They don't got da' time."

Manning laughed. "I reckon they don't. I just like to see 'em come down here and face the problem head on. They don't get the creativity of some of these folks. I seen one with a rocket belt once. Just floated over to play with the authorities. He went up and down, up and down, up and down."

"They shoot 'em down?" Dingy was curious now, drawn into Manning's whimsy.

Noting the ridiculous nature of the statement, Manning spoke with probity, "Hell no! Cause a national incident? He did it to prove a point. He landed, made his point and went right back after they seen him. He was a rich immigrant. He could afford it. They got a kick out of it, just laughed it off. They like the rich ones but can't stand the poor ones."

"Of course they don't like the poor ones. They taken food from our mouths."

"Stop that. They ain't takin' your food, Dingy. When was the last time you seen one a them takin' food from you and your table?"

"Tommy Cassidy caught one stealin' clothes from his line."

"That ain't food," objected Manning.

"I heard about one sneakin' into one of those onion crates. They tried to sneak on one a' them trucks."

"I heard about that. Driver heard 'im in the back, drove right to the border patrol. Patrol leveled their guns thinking they had a hot one and it wa'nt nothin' but a lil' fat raccoon hissin' at 'em. They saw the raccoon getting fat and sick with all them onions," Manning smiled amused at the thought of it.

"That ain't the one I'm talkin' 'bout!" Dingy said throwing up his arms in frustration and waving him off. "I'm talkin' 'bout the time before dat. Ah, you ain't even worth it, Manning."

"I'm gonna see if I can get some more feed for you, Manning. I think I had some of that corn feed you were looking for last time. It's in the back." The manager went off.

"You know what your problem is, Dingy? You believe everything that's told to you. You watch that damn TV, listen to those fools givin' you what they need and buyin' what they sell ya'."

"Not me. I don't believe nothin' the news says. It's all fake news. I'm with the Donald on that one."

Manning was maintaining his composure but made his point with conviction. "That's what I'm talkin' 'bout. First thing an autocrat wants to do is undermine the press. You don't believe the press, you don't believe nothin'. Then they can tell you whatever they wanna tell you and do whatever they wanna do."

"You don't know what yer talking 'bout, Manning."

"You gotta think for yourself. Discern what's true and false and why it's true and false. You gotta consider why someone's doin' what they're doin' and walk in the shoes of their understandin'."

"I know what I know. You're just full a hot air."

Manning paused exasperated and knowing there was nothing more to say. "Ain't hotter than the air I'm feelin' here," said Manning with a smile and easing the tension as he looked up and around.

Dingy was suspicious but thought he was referring to the weather. "Well, I guess you got that right."

"Someone took that corn feed, Manning," said the manager returning. I thought I had it back there and I'm just not seeing it."

"That's all right," said Manning. "You take care of yourself, boys. Have fun with that wall, Dingy."

"Taker easy, Manning," said the manager.

"Yep," replied Dingy. "I don't know when dat guy's serious and when he's jokin'."

Manning and Travis checked out their items up front and moved along.

3

Manning and Travis rode back to the house and talked about the usual things grandfathers and grandsons talk about. Manning tried to get him to talk about the girls he liked and playfully chided him for being secretive. They got to work trying to feed the animals and chickens in the coop, but settled indoors for the most part to keep cool.

"You going out there tonight?" Eleanor called to him.

"Yep, I guess I'll go for a few. I wanna bring some water there. Looks like we're short. Should be coolin' off by then," said Manning. She wasn't happy about it, but learned to accept it. She still banged a pot or two in the kitchen to punctuate her anger.

"Grandpa where you go at night?" asked Travis.

"I go to my bar and grill."

"You own a bar?"

"Kinda." He looked back at the kitchen and spoke in hushed tones, so she wouldn't hear. "You wanna come see my place?" Travis was excited by the prospect and nodded yes. "Meet me out back after dinner. Just between you and me," he said with a wink.

That evening just before sunset Manning carried a few bottles of beer and a coke and placed them in a small ice cooler along with a canister of nuts and walked to his truck. "Hop in." The boy hopped in, and they were on their way. They drove down the quiet road of Main Street Jacaranda Hot Springs. They drove past the large rusted out striking snake sculpture that was twenty feet high with gaping mouth and fangs on display. They drove past Travis' old elementary school with the screaming red hawk on the front of the building. Manning stopped the car on the side of the road in front of two signs that were back to back of one another. "Ever see those signs?" Travis shook his head. "Read it out loud to me." He read it carefully and full throated.

The sign read:

"SMUGGLING IS A FEDERAL FELONY:
PUNISHABLE BY UP TO 10 YEARS IN PRISON
VIOLATORS WILL BE PROSECUTED BY LAW
TO REPORT SUSPICIOUS ACTIVITY CALL 555-766-3000
US BORDER PATROL"

"What do you think they're implying there?" asked Manning.

"You're gone to jail if you're sneaking things."

"What they teaching you at that school? They teaching you to put two and two together?"

"Well, yeah," Travis said with hesitation.

"Whatchoo think it means, Wiz? You think people smugglin' furs?"

"I was thinkin' of drugs."

"Well, that's good and logical. I'll give you that one. What else you think they wanna get in this country?"

"I don't know. Looks to me like they're worried about illegals coming here. They smugglin' people?" Travis spoke as if he didn't want to say it. There was something innocent about not saying it and now that it was out in the open that innocence was destroyed.

"Bingo! That's my Wiz," said Manning. "By the way, we Mannings call 'em 'immigrants' or 'migrants.' Everyone has a right to live, that don't make them 'illegals.' I hate that term," Manning hastened to add.

They drove further to a distant location off the beaten path. Manning told Travis to get the case of water out of the back of his truck and Travis obliged. As they walked, there was a small sign that said "Beware of Rattlesnakes." Manning smiled as he saw the fear in Travis' face. Manning played with him, as if there were rattlers close by. "Tssssssssssss…" but it was only him making the hissing sound with his tongue between his two front teeth, as he grabbed Travis in play. "Gotcha!"

"Stop that, Grandpa!"

"I'm only havin' fun with you. I ain't gonna let anything get you."

The land was rocky and seemingly the only area where one could hide from the sun. There were a few pinyon pines scattered throughout along with some short palms, a few Joshua Trees and sprawling brush and cacti. There were more warnings of dangerous terrain and coyote country signs scattered throughout. "Don't mind that. I use that to keep people outta here." Another sign about snakes was seen as they approached the bombed-out car that was wedged between a large rock and some brush. A small rickety lawn chair was next to it. Manning popped the cap of a beer as he sunk into the unsteady chair, grinned a wide grin and looked around the area. He tossed a big case of nuts in the bombed-out car. "Here, gimme those bottles, please." He broke open the case of water bottles and tossed them in a pile next to the nuts by the old steering column that was mangled with cords and wires.

"What is this place?"

"It's my happy place," said Manning with pride. Travis looked around and didn't think much of it.

"Why you do that, Grampa? Why you leave those there?" as he examined the car by hopping inside while Manning tossed bottles.

"'Cause Jesus tole us to."

"You always say that," said Travis.

"Well, he said, 'to feed the hungry, clothe the naked, give drink to the thirsty…Whatsoever you do unto the least of these you do unto me.' It's what we call welcoming the stranger. That's good enough reason, ain't it?"

"I guess so." Seeing he wasn't satisfied with the answer," he continued. "I let you know more when you're a little older. Okay? Now, get outta there and comere." Travis climbed out walked up to him. Manning put his hand on his shoulder and led him away, pulling him in close embrace. "You know I'm good for my promise."

"I know. So you mean people're coming here," said Travis.

"Yeah, people come here." Letting him go from his grasp. "Refugees find their way here. That's why I leave this here, so they have a place to rest, have a place to eat and drink. Look at that sign." He pointed to a rickety artfully painted sign that said, "Manning's Bar and Grill" and smiled with pride. "It's a cantina. Know what a cantina is?" Travis didn't know. "It's a Mexican bar." Travis was even more confused. "I'm doing my duty as a farmer. I'm harvesting a crop of people for our land." Travis looked at him bewildered. "Look, I'm planting seeds for people."

"I don't get it," said the boy looking dumbly at his grandpa.

"What's a plant need to survive?" asked Manning throwing his arms back with a slight turn of the head and an inquisitive look.

"Water, sun, plant food…"

"Good soil, too. Don't forget that. That's what people need. I'm leavin' this so people can eat like plants and grow. They get this good American soil, they grow and prosper...we all grow and prosper. This is just 'tween us. Right?"

"Is this all our land?" asked Travis.

"Yes siree, this is our land! I own this land. That's why I can do whatever I want. I can put whatever I want out here. You didn't answer my question," said Manning with a stern rebuke. "This is just 'tween us, Wiz."

"I know," said Travis.

"Scout's honor?" Travis held out his hand with three fingers perched and crossed his heart.

"Good. I may get in trouble otherwise." Manning said, grabbing his arm to punctuate his point.

"Why?"

Manning stopped, bent down and gave him a serious look. "'Cause some people don't like people helping others. That's just the way it is."

"How do those migrants know to come here?" asked Travis.

"They just do," Manning replied with a wink and grin.

The boy was intrigued more than ever. Manning walked away. The boy looked over at the beverages and food again. "Let's get on the go," said Manning cheerfully as he quick-stepped forward. "I got more to show you." Travis trailed behind him. "From that tree there to that fence is our land. The government has a right of way. That means they have a right to come on this property at the fence. They can patrol the border here." he said indicating the plot of land recognized by the government. "But this here is mine." They walked up to the barricaded fence that stretched for miles in both directions. Manning picked up a rock and pinged it against the fence, but the rock made it through the other side. "That over there is Mexico. People would do anything to get over here. You know why?"

"'Cause of freedom."

"They got freedom there, too, don't they?" Manning posed hypothetically as he pulled out a cigar, lit it, took a puff and waved the blue-smoke away as it mingled with the desert air.

"Yeah, I guess so. But we got things better here."

"Exactly. You can't know how much better till you been over there, but I guess you could say that's the case."

"Why don't they just come over like other people? Legally?"

"It's a lil more complicated than that. Ya' see, in that country they live in what's called an oligarchy. An oligarchy is when a few people control the power and wealth of a country. They determine who lives and dies. They determine who works and doesn't and ultimately, who succeeds and who doesn't. A minority determines what is right for a country. What's the Golden Rule I taught you?"

"Do unto others as you would have them do unto you," Travis recited in a rote manner with confidence.

"Not that one. The other one, the one this world lives by," interjected Manning.

"Oh, 'He who owns the gold, makes the rules.'"

"Bingo. Get it?" grinned Manning as he jutted his cigar at him to punctuate the point.

"I think so," Travis said with a vague look.

"Let me help you a bit. The process for people getting over here is difficult. Some people who try to get here have roadblocks set up to stop 'em. Some of those people are political refugees, controversial figures. If they try to cross and the government doesn't let 'em in, they're sent back and done for.

There's so many things blocking their way, it's almost impossible to get them a fair shake. Even when people try to migrate here legally there's a lotta blocks standing in their way," Manning walked away. "Our economy depends on these people. People running companies in California and Florida depend on them. They're doing jobs for lesser wages that others won't do. Undocumented people contribute over eleven billion dollars in taxes between sales taxes and property taxes. That's a hefty sum for our government. Some businessmen and women speculate the economy would collapse if they were all kicked out. They wanna get 'em a path to citizenship, so they can keep providing for their families. Comere, Wiz." He motioned to Travis. "See that other shack over there. There's a secret compartment over there that could take you into another world. It could take you right into Mexico." They walked to the shack. Manning opened the creaky old door and stepped inside. It was dark inside but the room had a table and one chair and Manning navigated the darkness and turned on a light. He wandered over to a part under an old stove, and they looked under the floorboards. "No one knows about this — just you and me and your grandma. We gotta keep it that way. Understand?" Manning had that serious tone. Travis only heard this tone when his grandpa needed him to fully understand.

"Yes sir," Travis said. He always responded this way when he heard that tone in his grandpa's voice.

"Good. I don't need you messing around here. I didn't want to tell you about this place, but I don't like keepin' secrets from my loved ones, either. That ain't my way. I confided in you and trust that you're a man of your word."

"This is cool…I never let you down before, Grandpa," Travis reminded him as he hopped down.

"No, no you haven't."

"Then why would I start now?"

"I don't reckon you would.

"Don't go too far now. There ain't nothin' more to see here. We gotta get on home to Grandma. Come on, let's go." Manning closed up shop and they walked back to the truck as the sun set over the range.

4

Travis took great pride in the area knowing that it was his family's, and he was intrigued with the old shack and bombed out car. He often hung out in the area and a part of him deep down inside hoped he'd see someone. Such is the life of a boy and his curious call to adventure that beckons in his bones having been read great adventure stories in childhood at bedtime.

The mystique of a foreign land and its inhabitants whirled in his imagination and he thought maybe one day he'd be able to learn more from the land. It was like the land was whispering stories, and he could sit and hear them whistling to him, wanting to share more with him. The desert is funny that way. In its quiet, it speaks of the sacred past and you can see it, hear it, and even feel it. The locals all find their vortexes of energy that catch them in their glow. It's palpable when it's found and this was Travis' special place right from the moment it was introduced to him by his grandfather. He understood his grandfather's intrigue with the place.

When Travis got tired from the heat, he would go have a drink of water from there. He figured it wouldn't harm anyone to have a drink. *"There were plenty of bottles for everyone,"* he thought. One day when he was out and about playing catch with his friend Merk again. They stayed clear of the fence this time, but they still roamed the farms playing catch as they moseyed along. The two boys got thirsty and they were close to the Manning plot. In his haste for thirst, Travis misspoke not even considering what might come as a result of his actions. This too seemed to be a dilemma for a brain that is still trying to connect to its senses.

"I know where to get some water," posed Travis. He brought Merk to the bombed out car and handed Merk some water.

"How'd you know this is here?" asked Merk.

"My grandpa told me about it. I reckon it wouldn't harm us to have a lil drink a' water."

"That's pretty cool. You got nuts here?" He saw that the canister had been opened, but he hadn't opened it.

"Yeah, but we can't eat those. They're for someone else."

"Who?" asked Merk.

"That ain't none of our business. I don't know who. It just ain't for us."

"Your granddaddy harboring fugitives?"

"I didn't say that," said Travis with a stern rebuke and kicking the flattened tire.

"Why the hell you got food and water in the middle of nowhere then?"

Travis pretended to not hear the question and remained cool as he jumped on the back of the trunk. He tried to think fast on his feet. "My grandpa likes to come out here and shoot his guns." The boy bought this line but was still curious. "Let's go. I shouldn't have even showed you. We ain't supposed to be here," said Travis. "My grandpa doesn't want us hurting ourselves on this thing."

Suddenly they heard a rustling in the rocks. Merk stopped, wrinkled his brow and squinted his eyes in attention. He saw a beleaguered raggedy looking man leading a woman trying to keep a child quiet, but to no avail. The man looked out and saw the boys about twenty yards away. He scooped up his child and darted as fast as he could with his wife in tow.

"Wetbacks!" cried Merk.

"What the hell you talking 'bout?" asked Travis calling from a distance.

"Lookey there. Dey ain't supposed to be here," said Merk running after them. Travis sprinted at the boy and grabbed him by the shirt.

The migrants tried to disappear into the brush, but there was no hiding in this barren land, so they sprinted as fast they could to find a place for cover. They looked frail, bewildered and scared like deer caught in the sights of a hunter and cornered in a pen.

The boys stopped to watch but lost track of them. "We gotta tell someone."

"What are we gonna tell 'em. We seen some people climbin' the fence? That ain't what we seen," said Travis.

"How'd they get here then?"

"Maybe they're new in town."

Merk giggled with excitement. "I seen one wetback, I seen 'em all. Them were wetbacks." Travis tried to consider a new line, but he knew in his heart Merk could not be fooled. He went along. "Wow, I guess they were migrants. They're gone now. I imagine they'll get caught somewhere down the line," said Travis.

"I wanna look for 'em," said Merk. "Come on. I gotta get home," said Travis. Merk talked nonstop about the treasure he'd found. Travis was mostly quiet on the walking and guilt slipped in to his stomach and his head spun with worry. The boys parted ways and Merk ran home.

* * * * *

Merk's father and Dingy were in the basement workshop skinning rabbits he'd just killed the day before and stretching out their furs on a drying rack when Merk ran into the house excited. "Dad?!" Merk said as he bounced from room to room looking for someone to tell.

"Hey, hey, we're down here," said his father. Merk skipped steps and jumped down the stairs into the basement. "Whatchoo all excited about?" asked his father in a measured tone as he examined his work.

"You ain't gonna believe what I seen," said Merk.

"What's 'at?" inquired his father as he continued to skin a dead rabbit.

"I seen some wetbacks!"

"Is that right?" Dingy said with piqued interest as he sat on an old cabinet.

"Where you see 'em?" asked his father as he slowly ran the blade through the carcass.

"I saw 'em on the Manning's land out there by the fence," said the boy.

"I didn't know he had land by the fence," countered his father.

"He's gotta lotta land, that one," said Dingy.

"Yeah, he's done all right for himself that's for sure. He's a wily business man and knows how to make a buck, that's for damn sure."

"Me and Travis was out there screwin' around and they come from outta nowhere and scared us. They was starin' us down and makin' like they done gonna make us quiet."

"Where you think they headed?" Dingy asked.

"I think they gotta be in that part of town by the old hitchin' post and water tower," said Merk with pride that an adult was interested in what he said.

"Manning's land," said Dingy. "I tell you that guy's not right.

I tole you once, I tole you a thousand times he's up to noooo good, that one. I know you like 'im 'cause he's a veteran and he's always doin' right by our boys, helpin' with funerals and stuff, but he ain't right. He's prolly helpin' them out. I wouldn't be surprised if that guy helped 'em over the fence."

"Well, he's an ornery guy that's for sure. He's got some funny ways, but I don't see him doin' that," said Merk's father.

"Travis said it's a cantina. He's got his own bar out there where he goes off and shoots his guns."

"A cantina. You got food and water in the middle of nowhere. What's that tell ya?" reasoned Dingy.

"Yeah, but I got food and water in middle of nowhere when I go huntin'. I got me some duck blinds. That ain't nothin' special."

Dingy would have none of it. "I was talkin' with Joe Ford at the store and he butts into my business talking all smart with me, objectin' to me building a wall. I tell ya' I just don't trust that guy. He's so smart, that one." Dingy's sarcasm was radiant.

Merk's dad stopped skinning the rabbit and focused his attention on his son. "You sure about all this?"

"Travis was all like we shouldn't be there," said Merk.

Dingy was getting angry. "These illegals are bad news. They drain our resources and take money from us. They don't pay no taxes. They take our jobs."

"You're right, but not around here, though, too close to the fence. I ain't never seen an illegal take a job here, but sounds like they got millions of 'em in places like California and Arizona."

"I gotta cousin... They're out there picking cotton up in Mississippi, too. One of 'em took a job taking care of his mother as a home health aide. They call the cops on her; sure enough, she's one of them. She don't have no papers, taking money under the table. They kick her out the country." Dingy was talking so fast he just kept on talking without taking a breath. The train of thought just kept rolling along. "See, they know the laws…They have babies here, so their babies can be citizens and then everyone's like 'Don't break up the family, don't break up the family.' They should just kick 'em all out. Even if their children were born here! They make their beds when they wanna come here. Think of it this way. I'm in the hospital and I need a doctor. You get an illegal in there and they're taking attention away from me. I have a right to all the attention I need. Those are my tax dollars paying for that doctor."

"If you're right, we gotta do something. Nice goin' son," said his father wiping the blood off his hands."

Dingy took out his phone and dialed the police. "I'm already on it," said Dingy. "I'd love to see that old fogey get his. If this is true and he's one them people helping those people, I would just love to see him get strung up." He turned his attention to the call as he dipped his finger in a pool of blood from one of the rabbits and swirled it around making a design. "Hey, Phil? Yeah, it's Dingy. I got some information that may be of interest to you." Dingy told him everything he heard and even put Merk on the phone to confirm it. Travis was right. He shouldn't have showed Merk the place. Manning would question whether he should've shown Travis, too.

Travis wanted to say something to his grandpa, but didn't know what to say or how to broach the subject. He went into his room and hid as he tried to figure out what to do. There was nothing he could say to his grandfather, as he saw the Looming County Sheriff's police car slowly roll up the driveway. He knew he was in trouble.

Eleanor greeted the officer at the door. "Can I help you?" she asked with a genteel charm as southern hospitality dictates.

"Well, I was wonderin' if I might talk with your husband for a few."

"Sure, come on in," said Eleanor throwing open the screen door wide. "Let's get you something to drink. Have a seat."

"No thanks, I'm good, ma'am," said the officer. "I been sitting too long already."

Manning entered the room and shook the officer's hand. "What can we do for you?" asked Manning.

"The Merkel boy tells me your grandson run into some illegals in town."

"I haven't heard anything about that," said Manning. "Hey, Wiz. Can you come out here a minute?" Travis was scared and tried to make peace with his fear. He moseyed in the room looking tired and frazzled, as if he'd just awakened from a deep sleep.

"Travis, this man says you seen something on our land," said Manning laying it out like he was a child. Travis knew he was in trouble because he called him "Travis."

"Yes sir. Me and Merk were out just hanging around. We got thirsty and I thought we might've left some water on the land when we were out there. I'm sorry I didn't get to tell you. I just got home."

"I understand, son," Manning said putting his mind at ease.

"The Border Patrol caught a man, woman and child near your property. The boy said they come from your property there," said the officer as he took out a pen and wrote in his notebook.

"What fault of that is ours?" countered Manning.

"Now, now…hold on here, I'm not saying there's fault. It's just suspicious."

"Someone said they seen another one coming off your property a few weeks ago. That's a popular place to be for illegals. They seem to like your place there," said the officer.

"Well, I like that place, too. It's got some jacaranda trees, some aloe plants, a few avocados and some lemon and lime trees growing on it. Seems to me like those are good sources for food and medicine. Hell, what can't you do with an aloe plant?" said Manning.

"Yeah, well, I guess so," said the officer.

"I mean, if I 'uz looking to take care of myself, I'd look for a good tree. Seems like a logical place to be."

"Well, I'd like to take a look on your property to see what's happening there."

"I have no problem showing you around. Any more than that, I don't know if I can help you. You're gonna need a warrant."

"You mind if we take a ride out there?" posed the officer pleasantly with a calm demeanor as he slipped the pad into his pocket.

"Sure. Let's go," Manning said with a matter of fact air.

The officer walked out to the car.

Travis was sorry, but Manning was preoccupied. "I was gonna tell ya', Grandpa…I swear I was, I jes…"

"I know, I know. You taker easy, Wiz. It's okay. This woulda happened with you or without you." He directed his attention to Eleanor who was leaning against the sink watching the officer outside. "Eleanor, I need you to call Smialek and let him know what's goin' on here. I gotta feelin' this could be trouble brewing, maybe a long night. We might need to talk with Father Paul, if you know what I mean?" She understood implicitly. "See if we could get word to him somehow.

Know what I mean? I don't know. Let's see what goes down." He hurried out the back and hopped in the cop car. Eleanor watched as the men drove away.

She was none too happy with Travis and Travis knew it as he escaped into his bedroom. Eleanor bee-lined to his room banged open the door. "You have no business being there! Understand?"

"Yeah." It was the tone that always made him sit up and listen. He hated it but this time it was even more stern and full of conviction and fire.

Eleanor made her point and knew it. "Your grandpa told you about the land."

"Yeah," said Travis, nervously flicking the curtain by his bed with his fingers and trying to look away.

She straightened up his room and folded his clothes. "I was opposed to his hare-brained schemes to save the world. It's right up there with starting a military for peace…a military that goes out and does nothing but spreading peace in the world. I won't even go out there myself. I don't want any part of that craziness. I'll support him any way I can and love him to the tilt, but I don't want any part in that business and you shouldn't either." She picked up a shirt off the ground, whipped the chair, and cleaned up the room. Ordinarily she would make Travis do it, but she was reordering her anger and Travis was silent. She needed to vent and stormed in and out of the room to let him know her anger wasn't subsiding. It was her way of taking it out on the world and her grandson. He'd witnessed this strength before. Travis was fidgety and couldn't stay in his room, so he eyed his grandma and joined in the cleanup, organizing papers to appease her and let her know he was on her side. He knew she would eventually simmer down, and he thought his effort might help the cause. The anger dissipated with the profundity of his next question.

"Grandma, where are they gonna take those people?"

She witnessed the guilt written across his face and the concern he bore in his expression. Her heart broke for the boy. "They'll probably process them in a place near El Paso. I think there's a detention center there. They'll give them some food and shelter. It's probably a public shelter like an army barracks, but they'll have a place to stay tonight."

Travis went to bed that night with it on his mind. He grabbed his baseball and glove and pounded his concern into his mitt as he thought about what she said.

• • • • •

The ride out to the land for Manning was tense though there were a few early pleasantries exchanged enough to make it bearable. The discomfort wrought banal small talk that was about the weather and things that were happening in town. The officer talked about his plans to clean up the town and alluded to a "new element" coming into town and his pleasant sing-song voice suddenly had a menacing tone to it. Manning just nodded and wouldn't play into what he was saying. Aside from this, the two men just didn't have anything to say to one another and neither one made any bones about that.

Once they arrived at Manning's parcel, the officer was slow as he meandered around the lot. Manning stayed back by the car and waited with arms crossed in defiant conviction. The gruff old man figured if the man had any questions he could come to him. The officer was curious about the bombed-out car and rocked it a bit and leaned against it with a slow speculative look, like he was ready to buy it and kicking the proverbial tires. "Why you got a bombed-out car in the middle of nowhere?" he called to Manning.

"It's sentimental. I'm hoping to fix it up one day for my grandson." Manning moved a bit and walked towards him with his hands on his hips like he was ready for a showdown.

"It looks like that thing's beyond fixin' ain't it? I mean that's just collecting dust and rodents. Seems like all it's doing is becoming a health hazard for the area. I don't know if it's legal to have a trash heap here on your property," asserted the officer with a staunch judicious twang in his voice as he wiped his hands with a hanky.

"It's one car. I don't see how one broken down car in the middle of nowhere and ain't running's gonna be a big hazard to anyone. I don't view this place as a trash heap."

"Oh yeah?" the officer said as he picked out a bottle of water and helped himself to it, guzzling it down and throwing it on the ground. "That's not how I see it," he said with smug conviction.

"I guess we have a difference of opinion there," replied Manning.

"We got a difference of opinion on many things." He walked a little further and kicked the ground a bit like he was dissatisfied with the whole situation. He then surveyed the land, noted the shed, and waved Manning to come to him. "That shed out there...that come with the land?"

"Yes sir, I believe it was there when I got it. That was one of the first structures in town. I think it belonged to old man Farley who owned this place. That's a landmark."

"Uh-huh," said the officer not buying what Manning was saying. "You got a sentimental attachment to that rickety place, too, huh?"

"Yeah, I guess so."

"I don't reckon we might be able to take a look inside there."

"I didn't bring the keys. I didn't think we're gonna be more than a few minutes."

"Uh-huh," the officer said with skepticism. "You ain't hidin' something in there? are you? I mean, you're hesitant for me to take a look in there."

"I ain't hiding nothing from you. You're on my land, I'm showin' you the land like you asked me."

"Now, you gonna get snippy with me?" said the officer standing like Superman with his hands on his hips. "You gonna assert yourself to the law with a tone like that, boy?" Manning knew it was time to shut up and not say anything. He knew the game and refused to be provoked. "Well, you don't seem like you're being too helpful neither. You could show a little respect when I ask for it," the officer snapped at him.

"Look, I ain't looking for trouble," replied Manning. "I'm doing what you're asking here."

"You ain't doing what I'm asking, and I ain't appreciating how you're making my job hard on me. Maybe we need to talk about this back at the station. Seems to me you know we're coming out here, you'd show me a little more hospitality on your land like you do other people."

"I don't know what you're implying," said Manning sternly.

"Sure, you do. You know exactly what you're doing. We both got a pretty good idea of what's gone down around here, don't we? Why don't we cut the bullshit?"

"I ain't bullshitting no one."

"Now you're using profanity against me," said the officer smiling sweetly.

"I'm quoting what you said."

"Illegal dumping, acting belligerent, using profanity. Well,

I guess it's your word against mine." Manning was chilled to the bone and shuddered. His mind grappled with conclusions as he considered what might happen next and remained silent as the officer continued. "No, I don't like this. I don't like this one bit," said the officer taking out his notepad again and writing. They walked back to the car and he opened the door to the back seat. "I think we need to talk about this a little more back at the station." Manning paused a moment weary and unsure, and the officer wore a stupid grin as he held open the door for the old man, but Manning got in the back of the car. The drive back to the station was silent, but the tension was loud.

The prosecutor's office was informed of what was going on with the Manning's land but couldn't reach the judge given that it was the weekend. The officer wanted to make sure that Manning wasn't able to contact anyone while they worked on getting the injunction, so he kept him in the holding pen overnight. It was a restless night for Travis and Manning, both working out what their actions had brought them. Eleanor went to visit Manning at the correctional facility the next day. Manning looked tired as he met her behind a Plexiglas window. He was wearing black and white striped jail fatigues.

"How'd you end up here?" Eleanor asked. He could read the fear in her eyes through her frightened glare, but he always knew how to tickle her heart to lighten things up even in these times.

"Don't this look nice," presenting his wardrobe. "I like the stripes. They make me look skinnier."

"You okay?"

"I'm okay. It's hot in here, though. The air conditioner's on the fritz. It's hotter than a dragon's spit. They said I wasn't cooperating, which is bull cookies! They just didn't want me gumming up the works, so they fixed a complaint on me and are trying to make it stick. I talked with Smialek. He said they could be fixin' to impose eminent domain and take over the place. Want to go onto my land to see what they can find there. Take it over. They find something, they're gonna send me away for a looong time, he says. I got my lawyers working on it now, but they don't know how long we can hold them off. I guess all we can do now is pray, get Father Paul to pray for us," he said with a wink. He examined her face to see if she got the message. "Let him know that we need all the prayers we can get. I was supposed to meet with him tonight. I guess I can't make that appointment."

She understood the code and grew uncomfortable and mouthed the words. "I told you I don't want any part."

"I need you. Please. Lives are depending on this," he whispered and straightened with earnest zeal.

She was jarred by the stinging solicitation and slow to respond as she thought through what he was asking of her. It was a slow-going reality check that bit her in the neck, and she chafed at the stress he'd just imposed. Manning knew her answer. She was becoming a reluctant participant, but he knew he could count on her and watched her manner change as reality sunk in and she grew accepting of it. She hung up the phone gently. He kissed his two fingers and placed them on the glass, and she imitated him and looked stoically into his tired, sad eyes.

5

Eleanor was wrapped in haunting sorrow as she drove home and ran through the horrors of everything that could go wrong. She unconsciously ran her fingers nervously through her hair, pulling out threads from her bun. She glanced in the mirror and her gentle wisps of gray were splayed, giving a frazzled look to what she once considered a gracefully aged face. She looked haggard with indecision and worry as she turned the corner that led to their long driveway. She tried to put up a good front for Travis, whom she spied riding his horse bareback.

"You're riding that one pretty good. Whatchoo call him, Zeus? Two weeks ago, he wouldn't even let you on him."

Travis had just finished a few tricky moves and the horse lowered its body to let him off. He gave the horse a scratch behind the ears and a little feed. "What's the story with Gramps? He gonna be all right?" Travis said, running to hear the details.

"Well, let's just say they're keeping an eye on him for now. He's gonna be all right, though. You know your grandpa he sticks to his convictions like gum on a shoe. I have to go out there tonight. Your grandpa was expecting someone at the grill."

"Can I go with you?" Travis spoke with excitement and urgency.

"Did you hear me the other night?" She scolded him with a fiery stare.

"Yeah, it's just that…"

Eleanor spoke before he could complete his sentence. "I meant what I said. I say what I mean. You understand that, too. I know you do."

"Yeah, but you always say, 'We make things right by taking the right path to the right.'" She hated when he used her wisdom against her and paused not knowing what to say. "I know you don't want me there, but I think I need to make this right."

"Now, I don't know if that's wise. There's more to it than that." She walked away.

Travis persisted and trailed behind her like a duckling trying to keep up with his mama. "Grandma, I feel responsible for all this. Please let me help. I need to do this for Grandpa."

She sighed. "Ahh, your grandpa, he's got us both in a heap of trouble." She paused on the step and grabbed the rail. The weight of the situation making her slump, and she grabbed a potted plant that was dying. She weaved her hand through the flower and stem stroking it as she contemplated her next move. "I just don't think we need to get you involved in this," she said wearily.

"You don't know how bad I feel. This is all my fault," Travis pleaded with her.

"Now, stop that. This could've happened at any time. It's a chance your grandpa took when he asserted himself in helping." She placed the plant on a stand and grabbed another pot to repot it. "Get me that scooper over there, will you, please?" Travis abided but continued to make his point.

"No, I mean it. I don't know if I can live with myself if I can't help."

She saw the sincerity in his face as he handed her the trowel. He had a way of working his way into her heart just like his grandpa when he needed to, and he knew the look that worked the best. "I need to think about that."

"I ain't never been in the tunnel, but I'm fast and squirrelly. I can get in and out like none other."

"That's true. You are a spry one." *"We gotta make a plan. Damned if I do, damned if I don't,"* she said to herself as if thinking aloud. "Let me think this one over," she told him. "Please go check the chickens for eggs and give them some feed." He was dismissed for now and walked away moping. *"I'll be damned if I can get in that tunnel. Last time I was in a small place I nearly died from hyperventilating,"* she thought to herself. *"He'd only have to be there until Father Paul got there."*

She thought it over the next two hours and tossed a jacket to him while he was working on his computer. "Finish homework?" He nodded. "Come on. Time to go." She gathered her keys and made for the car. Travis was enthusiastic, as he grabbed his phone and a pack of gum, and he lowered the top on his computer. He was proud of himself as he plopped himself in the car. They drove to the site and she spoke to him like a concerned parent — she had a tendency to do that. "As hot as it is during the day, it can get cold at night. You make sure to take that jacket now. You get in there and get outta there fast as you can. You hear me?"

"I got it."

"You tell Father Paul that they can't come this way as they got an eye on us. If I shoot off a firework, there's trouble, and you stay with him until we can figure it out. If I don't, we're good to go and you get on back. You hear me?"

"Why can't you call me?"

"It's terrible reception here. The radar jams the signal. You take care, you hear me?"

"I hear you. I'll take care, Grandma. Don't you worry about me," said Travis.

"You're all we got, of course I'm gonna worry 'bout you. That's my job. Ever since your momma passed, I've been thinking more and more about what we need to do for you."

"Grandma? Grandpa told me he'd tell me why he does this when I get a little older. Why's he feel so passionate about helping these people?"

"Your grandpa had someone very close to him in WWII. His sister's husband was a Jew, and she met him when she was living in Europe. When the war broke out, she made it back all right, but they were separated. He was sent on a ship that docked right outside this country in Jersey. Because they were Jewish, they didn't want to keep them. They thought they'd be too much trouble politically, so they turned that ship around, sent him back to Europe. He was a refugee and a man without a country. The Nazis found him, shipped him to a concentration camp at Buchenwald and never made it home. Your grandpa was with the 6th Armored Regiment with General Patton and liberated Buchenwald. He said liberated prisoners were like 'ghosts running at them in striped pajamas — emaciated with vacant stares in their eyes, mustering every last ounce of breath to greet their liberators, crying and bellowing away in sublime gratitude for life and liberty.' Horrible what another man can do to his fellow man." She shook off the image as the truck turned a corner and the realization of worldly horrors burrowed into her thinking, leaving her half engaged. "The things he saw there. When he found out his brother-in-law died there, well, it made him feel like a helpless baby. Those images stayed with him. Haunted him to think one of his own was there and he couldn't do anything to help. Your grandpa felt bad we didn't do more for his sister and her husband. He felt like his hands were tied. 'Never again,' he said. 'I got the wherewithal to help a righteous man, I'm gonna do it.' When Father Paul was looking for help, he thought he might make up for it by lending him a hand. He made up for his misfortune in spades. I think that's the one he was gonna tell you about at some point. He's got some stories about that concentration camp."

Travis reflected deeply on this as his grandmother drove. She threw her arm over her head as she often did when she doubted herself. She was rethinking her plan even as she was telling him the story. When they arrived at the site, she had him bring more water and some bread. "I'm pretty sure he always takes water over there no matter how much he thinks there is. One can never have enough water. I just made the bread. They may like that. They're gonna be hungry. You're gonna need a flashlight, too. Take this one." They walked to the shanty, and she revealed the spot underneath the old stove. She removed a plate in the floor and revealed a hole with a small ladder leading down a short shaft. "There's air down there, so you should be all right. You get in and get out as fast as you can now and you give Father Paul our best." She gave him a kiss on the head and hugged him close. He disappeared down the hole. She climbed down too, looked for the switch on the wall and hit it. Eleanor stopped and listened and heard the motor kick in soon followed by a breeze of white noise that was pleasing to her.

The tunnel was cool with a crisp smell of cold cement in parts but had a rancid odor of death in other parts like an animal had died there. It was dark, and he used his flashlight to navigate but didn't see any dead animals. The channel was lined at the top with an aluminum accordion duct that rattled against the hastily cemented ceiling as air circulated to small vents scattered throughout. The tunnel was in the shape of a tube, and Travis felt like he was part of a sewer canal or a bunker like he'd seen in an old war movie with his grandpa.

He could see why his grandmother would not want to go in there. He knew she was claustrophobic and probably wouldn't have made it halfway through the tunnel. As for him, he had no intention of going back. He was intent on his mission to get the message to the priest.

Travis was riveted at the thought that he might be helping in a big way. He was excited that his grandparents let him in on their secret and now let him help with their mission. In a strange way he felt more connected to them. It was like the experience was linking them in a more meaningful way. His heart raced as he ran through the hole crouched down. His throat was cold and he could taste the blood of fear in his throat. He heard a few squeaks from what sounded like mice and paused. They were getting closer. He continued on his way and waved his flashlight as if to warn them he was coming and to get out of his way. He wasn't afraid of a few mice, but rats — rats were another thing.

As he neared the end of the tunnel, the guardian mice were, in fact, rats. He paused and waited for them to move. Then he kicked some dirt at them, snarled in frustration and tossed a bottle of water to force them to move. They took their time but scurried out of the hole. They were nibbling on some food and the smell of his bread didn't make them move any faster.

Eleanor sat and waited for a bit, but something told her to

take a walk down the road to see what was happening in the area and if anyone was around. Two sets of headlights emerged from the distance and another set was behind that. She knew it was odd to have more than one group of cars out there and hid in the brush. She saw that it was the Border Patrol and they were parked outside their land. One of the officers got out of the car, took out a pen and paper and made notes on her car like he was giving a ticket. She made her way to the shanty, closed up the hole and walked off about fifty yards away. She fired off a set of fireworks and they screamed through the air like blistering missiles. Shhhhhhhhoooooeee-pop!

Meanwhile, Travis emerged from the hole and sat tight. He noticed the little box that looked like it had been broken into by an animal with the lock ripped clearly off it. It was empty of food and wrappers were strewn around the ground like wrapping paper at Christmas. He saw the peel of the fireworks and the short lived but beautiful plume of reds, whites, and blues, which alerted him to the trouble on the other side. All he knew was it wasn't safe to go back there, so he sat and waited for the priest and the new arrivals.

Eleanor did not want the patrol to go near the shed, so she walked out of her way and called to the visitors. One of the officers dressed in green border patrol fatigues and a green cap approached her. "It's a little early for the Fourth of July isn't it?" he asked.

"Not around here. Good ole' boys shooting fireworks all the time," Eleanor quipped. "Y'all must be new around here. We love our guns and fireworks."

"Relatively. But I know the law here. You can't shoot them here. You need a license to do that. Besides, you're firing in Mexican airspace."

"I didn't know we're at war with Mexico. I didn't think they'd mind. That's desert over there. Ain't nobody gonna see them for seventy miles."

"You don't know the laws, do you?" the officer said.

She remained cool. "Fireworks are prohibited in the city limits. It doesn't say anything about out here."

"That's right. But the law says 'you can *transport* fireworks, but you can't shoot them off.'" He said this as he was filling his gums with tobacco.

"What kinda sense does that make, officer? You think good ole' boys and girls gonna buy fireworks and *not* shoot them off? You think those store owners who are selling that illegal act ascribe to that?"

"Just stating what the law says, ma'am. I'm gonna give you a warning on that. You ain't supposed to be out here anyways."

"Well, this is our land," She proclaimed standing firm with her lighter in hand like Lady Liberty ready to raise the torch.

"Not anymore, it ain't. Judge slapped an injunction. Don't want anybody out here. I'm here to close it off."

"What judge is that?"

"Judge Smoolls," the officer garbled as his lip was full of tobacco and spit.

"What? Smoolls?" she retorted.

He spit his tobacco to be clear. "Judge Smalls," he annunciated as clear and plainly as he could. "S-M-A-L-L-S. Smalls, not 'Smoolls.'"

"Oh, I thought you said 'Smoolls.' Can I see that injunction?" He handed her the paper. "Looks like everything's in order here. You are correct. It is 'Smalls.' There's our Fourth Amendment at work. When did they issue this?" She asked as kindly as she could.

"This evening, ma'am."

"Well, I'll be damned. They didn't tell me about it. When were they fixing to tell us?" she said as she read over the document, stalling for time to ensure Travis was in the clear.

"I don't know, ma'am. I guess they're telling you now. Point is you can't stay here." The officer said with great glee at one-upping her.

"That's fine, officer. I don't mean any harm anyway. You have a good night," she said calmly as she handed him back the injunction.

"You too, ma'am," said the officer, spitting again.

The border guards were posting signs telling people to "Stay out by order of the government." Eleanor was cool and collected as she sauntered off and got in her car, but her heart was racing with uncertainty. She wondered how they might get Travis back now. As she drove home, Eleanor thought about new possibilities. She hoped he remembered to bring a gun, but everything happened so fast, she was worried he had not. She would get on her phone and call Travis to let him know what was going on. She would do it well out of earshot of any prying ears. Although there were dead spots in this range, she figured she could leave a message to let him know what was happening and the sticky situation that was about to haunt her and keep her from a good night's sleep for the next week or so.

6

Travis was face to face with the reality of life and death again, jarred in a harrowing quagmire of survival. The past no longer mattered as he was alive to the present. He knew there was no going back as he faced off with the mountain lion and the hungry beast was ready to pounce. The boy was alarmed and raised the loaf of bread like a quarterback and was about to throw the loaf to distract it and get back in the hole when a gunshot rang out. The shot hit the animal in the neck and hurled it ten feet like it was violently pulled by an invisible rope. Travis ran for the tunnel as a knee-jerk reaction to be safe. It was a dumb move, as his quick movement could have startled the gunman and a shot could've been leveled at the boy. He just responded to the fear and sought safety. "Don't shoot me!" cried Travis, emotionally trapped in the liminal space between the tension of near death and the elated feeling of safety.

The animal was shocked and screeched a piercing cry that shivered the night's air. After a few seconds it became disoriented and couldn't make a vocal sound. It just gurgled for dear life and lay on the ground pawing and trying to reclaim its feet. When it would get to its feet it would fall again, falling again and again like a drunk trying to find his feet. A second shot rang out and the animal lay still.

A figure emerged from the shadows holding a rifle. He slowly walked over to the animal and kept his distance as he watched the lion murmur to its death. When the animal took its last breath, he walked over to see his work. He blessed himself and kissed his hand as the eyes of the beast stared off into nothingness. More figures reticently emerged from the darkness. They were cautiously looking about them both concerned because the lion may have had a partner and also due to the unsure footing of the ground.

"You got him good," said one voice, but the man remained silent as he watched the animal for movement.

Travis saw two kids walk over to the animal in curiosity, but the mother called to them in Spanish. "Vengan aqui'… Vengan." (Come here. Come.)

One child said, "Virgo!" (Cool!" in Guatemalan)

The other child said, "Los leones tienen que cazar para comer." (Lions have to hunt to eat.)

And the man said, "No va a comer esta noche." (He's not eating tonight.)

"Is Father Paul with you?" inquired Travis as he walked from the safety of the tunnel toward the man.

The man with the rifle turned to Travis. "I'm Father Paul. And who are you?"

"I'm Travis, the Mannings' grandson."

"Nice to meet you." He extended his hand and Travis shook it.

Travis was taken aback as the priest was in plain clothes. He wore jeans and a short-sleeved t-shirt with a shirt tied around his waist. "All due respect, you don't look like a priest," said Travis.

Paul laughed. "Thank you. I'll take that as a compliment."

Travis spoke up. "You're handy with a gun. Thanks for killing him. I don't know what I would've done. I left my gun at home."

"Don't mention it," said Paul. "We didn't see you there. We were watching him for a few minutes from the ledge. We had to wait for the right moment to do it. I'm glad we got him when we did. You've got a message for me?"

Travis said, "We can't go through the tunnel. The Border Patrol's there and my grandma said it's not safe."

The priest looked forlorn at hearing the news, but tried to keep a stiff upper lip and nodded. "That *is* a message. Thanks." The man asked Paul what happened and he looked dejected, like the wind that held him up had been taken from him, but Paul assured him not to worry. "Is that for us?" he asked pointing to the bread.

"My grandma made it." He handed it to him and Paul gave it to the family. He blessed it and they prayed in Spanish. "Bless us oh Lord for these thy gifts, which we are about to receive from thy bounty through Christ our Lord, Amen." As hungry as they were, they were reverential. After the blessing they devoured every crumb as fast as they could. They were starving and looked like they hadn't eaten in days. "We'll have some meat to go with that shortly," said Paul, as the priest pulled out a large knife and walked over to the lion. He wrapped his shirt around his mouth like a bandit to block the smell of death and cut open the animal. The man helped him.

"Any other Americans with you, Father?" Travis innocently asked.

"We're all Americans," said Paul. "They may be more American than you," he joked.

Travis was embarrassed that he had asked the question. He meant to ask was he the only citizen? Father Paul playfully punched him, feeling bad that he made the point. Travis felt good about himself as he handed each one of them a bottle of water and introduced himself. "My name's Travis. No habla Espanol."

The Hispanic man laughed. "Hola, I speak English. My name is Francisco, amigo. This is my wife and children. Thank you very much for the brea…." his voice trailed off with emotion as he took a bite. His accent, as the others Travis spoke with, was exotic, but his English was fluid.

"Can you make a fire, Francisco? I think the Mannings left some wood by the hole over there? We'll save the Bunsen burner stove for when we need it," said Paul. Francisco gathered up the wood for a fire.

"Hola, it's okay, we all speak the English," said the mother. "My name is Angelina. These are my children, Sancho and Juanita." The children gnawed on the bread while their father started the fire. Angelina told them one bottle each, as she knew they might need more later.

"Oh, we got some more of that, ma'am," said Travis.

"We still gotta be conservative with them," asserted Paul.

"You see any *coyotes* out here? They keep stealing our water."

"No sir, only animal I seen is that one you took down."

"I'm not talking about animals. I'm talking about people. They call people who transport humans across the border '*coyotes*.' It's big money smuggling people. Some of those *coyotes* make between five thousand and ten thousand dollars a pop. And that doesn't guarantee you're gonna make it across."

"They must've been the ones who broke into our box and stole the food," said Travis.

"I wouldn't doubt it. They're ruthless on this side of the fence."

"See this?" said Travis pointing to the busted lock on the box.

"That looks like the work of a *coyote*," said Paul. "Dammit! I had whiskey waiting for me in there."

"How much you get for bringing people?"

Paul laughed. "I get about as much as your grandpa gets. About enough joy and satisfaction as a man *can* get. Can't put a price on saving a life, son, remember that. No amount of money can give you that kind of satisfaction. I'm hoping I might get a nice smile from God in heaven."

Father Paul was a renegade and staunch liberation theologian who made it his life's work to serve the poor. He came to this ministry via Central America in the mid-1980s having visited in the 1970s as a seminarian. He put in a request to serve there, and he was assigned to a church in El Salvador. He thought he would one day be a diocesan priest in America, but he fell in love with the Salvadoran people. A devoted follower of Archbishop Romero, he memorized the legendary bishop's homilies. Paul was a friend of Rutilio Grande, an associate of Romero's who was equally courageous in fighting for the rights of the poor and land reforms and was martyred for the cause. Father Paul came to this ministry in a roundabout way, as he hoped to help the poor establish reforms in their countries. When he saw that there was no hope for that to happen and the greed of the oligarchy was standing in the way, he brought awareness of the problem to America by discreetly finding ways to get the attention of the government to intercede and hold the Salvadoran government responsible. It was a calling for him. "I met them through their cousins who are Salvadoran. Francisco and Sancho here are wanted by their government for treason. They're political refugees."

"What'd they do?"

"They came from Guatemala. They had the temerity to ask for basic human rights. They had the indecency to request a dignified job that supports and sustains a family. They had the nerve to ask for livable conditions that should be guaranteed under the Declaration of Human Rights. They organized the poor, that's what they've done. You organize the poor in his country and you're recognized as a rabble rouser, a traitor and enemy of the state." A coyote howled in the distance. "That's a real coyote," said Paul lightening the mood.

Travis became more interested. "You came from Guatemala?"

Francisco wouldn't look him in the eye, as it was a sign of respect in his culture. "Si, senor. We had no choice. We traveled over 2,267 miles, but who's counting — hey, Padre?" he said nudging Paul.

"I wasn't with them the whole way. I was just on the last trek, a few miles," interjected Paul.

"You walked?" Travis asked Francisco riveted by the conversation.

"We walked across the desert, yes. But we made it across the border to get here and had help by boat, cars, trains, whatever we could do. This was the hardest. The desert is merciless. We walked seventy miles under the brutal blistering sun. No cars, no trains, no help. Pure will and desire got us here," said Francisco.

"Not everyone made it. We lost a few back there," interjected Paul. Travis thought deeper about this. *"What kind of person would put his family's life in jeopardy to make it to America?"* Paul could read it on his face. "You don't risk the lives of your family to travel across the border if you aren't desperate. Some of those *coyotes* take advantage of this vulnerability. They rape the women, steal food from the mouths of their children and take their money. Evil is real, son," Paul didn't mince his words. It wasn't his way. "Welcome to the battle of good versus evil."

He turned his attention to cutting the animal and showed Francisco a piece. The blade slithered along the side of the animal's potbelly and blood ran out as the fur mingled with the animal's innards like a carpet being torn off a hardwood floor. Francisco monitored Paul's progress — his hands at the ready if he needed him. Travis' interest was bathed in the surreal quality that death inspires as it dances with the fleeting gift of life in such a magnificent beast. "There's good meat. Look at that, Francisco," Paul said.

"My mouth is watering, Padre," Francisco said.

Travis looked like he had cold water splashed in his face. "Ever had mountain lion? How you want yours cooked?" Paul asked.

"I could eat it raw, Padre," Francisco said.

Travis slowly walked to Angelina and the other kids. He didn't want to know anymore. He'd heard enough.

"What grade you in?" asked Travis.

"I haven't been going to school," said Sancho. "I was in tenth and my sister was in ninth." They were about his age. Travis gave him a smile. "Maybe I could show you my school sometime." Travis didn't know how realistic this was, but he wanted him to know that they were close to freedom and inspire hope in them. "It's right across the border there."

"I'd like that very much," said Sancho.

"We are close to freedom?" asked Juanita.

"We are close to freedom," echoed Angelina. "But God knows when we'll see it."

"We gonna do everything in our power to make that happen

for you," Travis said, as he picked up rocks and sorted through them for good looking stones.

"Tonight we sleep, tomorrow we walk," Angelina said.

Travis appreciated the lack of pretense in eating by the crackle and pop of campfire. Everyone ate with their fingers, scarfed the meal with few if any pleasantries exchanged but plenty of ecstatic "aahs" and "oohs" of sublime gratitude of which his grandmother shared previously about his grandfather's experience at a concentration camp in the war. They licked their fingers clean and ravaged every morsel feasibly consumed. Paul noticed Travis' hesitance and reminded him by speaking to Francisco, "Eat everything you can, we don't know when we'll eat next." Between the tough gristle and lack of seasoning, the feast was adequate on nutrients and low in delectability for Travis. The family's bellies were full for the first time in a long time, and the guests enjoyed their time at the campfire. Travis gave Sancho and Juanita a piece of gum for dessert, which they both gobbled up in a few bites, as they were hungry and couldn't resist this reflex action. They chewed the second one after Travis told them not to eat it. He gave them the whole pack and their mother took it from them for safekeeping.

Father Paul thought about what they were going to do with Travis. He considered bringing him to the fence and turning him over to the authorities, so he would be safe. But he reconsidered, thinking it would compromise the chances of getting the family across. It was a no-win situation.

7

The night came and one by one the travelers lay their weary heads down to sleep. As Travis looked up at the stars, he thought about his grandparents and wondered how they were doing. The stars inspired a connection to them along with a connection to nature. The stars were tens of thousands of light years away, but if his grandparents were looking at them and he was looking at them at the same time, he thought, they were both present to the immediacy of their beauty. "You look at them and I look at them, we're there together," his grandfather once said. The poetry wasn't lost on his grandfather who took him camping and taught him the constellations. He looked for what his teacher had taught him — the Big Dipper, the Little Dipper, Orion's Belt, the signs of the Zodiac. He thought of the stories his grandfather taught him by the campfire and about how the universe was formed. They were grand stories with mythic realities. He leaned on those mythic realities to help him dream. He understood his grandparents in a new way. Once he was connected to them by nature, now he was connected to them through the service of others and helping to save lives. What a powerful and noble inclination. It was all starting to ring true for him. He may be away from them, but he still shared the sight of the stars and the mythic realities that connected them and the power of the universe to dream and serve.

He wondered if the kids knew the meaning of the stars. He thought it might be a nice way to connect with them and share his understanding at some point. He hoped he would remember it. But life has a way of forcing us to dream new dreams and distract us from such noble ambitions.

He took his finger to see if he was viewing stars or satellites when suddenly there appeared a small cross of red and blue lights scanning the scene in the vicinity. It was a mini UFO as it dove and darted with a swirl of light and illumined streaks as it made its way. "What the...?" He sat up and watched as the small cross of light circled the area and hovered over their fire. "*That looks like a drone*," he thought to himself. The red-blue streaks shimmered and a flash of light splashed across the sky. It vanished as fast as it arrived. Travis thought about calling out to see if anyone saw it but they were all dead to the world in sleep.

The base of the mountain covered the light of the campfire like a ship's mast. It was peaceful as the high moon and the burning fire were the only light and crickets the only music singing in harmony with the deep breaths of sleep. Travis could see the swirl of the Milky Way curling into unfathomable space when he heard someone get up in the middle of the night. He followed the footsteps of the person down the gravel path past the hole and was curious to see who it was and where he was going. He thought he'd see if he could help in some way.

Travis watched closely as he saw that it was Francisco. He walked around the rocky base to the edge of the wire that separated Mexico from the US and stepped under the wire. Travis didn't know what to do. He was nervous that the border patrol cars were there, so he slowly followed him and eyed him. On the other side of the fence he could see flickers of light in the distance. He didn't know what to make of them. Slowly the light got brighter and it was clear to him that headlights were trained in their direction of the fence. Both were as quiet as dead men in limbo. Travis watched Francisco gingerly climb through the wire and the boy was unsettled. *"What was he doing?! Was he trying to escape? Was he trying to blow their cover?"* Travis thought. Francisco slowly walked to the fence and stood there for a minute. Travis walked to the wire and called to him. "Hey, Francisco, you okay?" Francisco was quiet as he turned, nodded and placed his finger to his mouth to keep him quiet. He took his right foot and placed it between the slats of the steel girded fence and hugged the fence. He then knelt down and placed his hands in the earth and pulled up a handful from the other side and brought it through the fence. He gently kissed it. He sorted through it and pulled out a small rock. Clutching the rock, he placed it in his pocket.

A beam of light flashed in their direction and Francisco pulled back and collapsed on the ground. A light scanned the area and voices could be heard coming closer to the fence. Travis was alarmed even more and his heart raced. He placed his hand on his head like a helpless man trying to hold in every ounce of fear. If a border agent was at the fence, their cover would be blown. Francisco gently pulled his foot back and quietly returned from the barbed wire as the flashlights moved down the fence. Francisco slowly retreated and Travis breathed easier when he was over a bluff and out of harm's way of being seen.

Travis followed Francisco back to the camp. Francisco was embarrassed. "It's all right. Good to sleep," said Francisco.

"You all right?" asked Travis in hushed tones.

"I know I shouldn't do that, but I couldn't resist, amigo. I don't know what will come of us. I wanted to be able to say I stepped foot in America, so I'm sorry to have frightened you. I will not do that ever again. I've been there. I've stepped foot in America. Now I will be able to sleep tonight."

Travis' heart broke for Francisco. They both returned to their spots and tried to get to sleep. He looked up at the stars and dreamed about taking down the fence. He thought to himself, *"We share the same sky, the same light of the moon, even the same waters of the Rio Grande that run from the Rocky Mountains of Colorado, to New Mexico, Texas and Mexico. Couldn't we share the same land?"* He welled up with tears.

He thought about the people who were captured as a result of his curiosity. The night his grandfather left, he asked his grandmother where they would take those people? He recalled her telling him that they would be in the States for a little while until they could be sent back. He couldn't bear to think about where they were now. She had told him there was a camp for illegal immigrants somewhere in Texas where they would be processed and fingerprinted before they were deported. He was sad and embarrassed for Francisco, but there was a pinch of broken-heartedness as Travis realized just how desperate Francisco was to claim freedom.

8

When Travis awoke the next day, Father Paul spotted him and told him right away to look in his shoes for scorpions before putting them on. "They like to hide and nestle in the warm toe of a boot," he warned. "One zap and you're done."

"I slept with my shoes on," Travis said as he wiped the sleep from his eyes.

"Like a good cowboy," Paul said.

Travis approached Father Paul who was packing his bag. The buzzards and vultures were already gathering in the area and swooping through the air and circling, fighting for position to pounce on the carcass of the lion.

Travis informed Father Paul of the drone he'd seen last night. Paul's interest was piqued and knew that this further compromised their position.

"So what do we do today?" Travis asked.

"We walk the border along the side of this mountain till we figure out a new plan. I don't know what I'm going to do with *you*, though. We need to get you home. We need to find a live spot where we can talk with your grandmother to let her know you're with me and you're all right. You've got your phone, right?"

Travis pulled out his phone and turned it on. The little display signal in the upper corner indicated there was no signal, so he powered it down. "When we call my grandma, we can have her track us through my phone. I got an app on my computer," said Travis.

"I didn't think about that," said Paul. "That's a good idea. You think you can walk with us?"

"I don't want to leave you, Father."

"That's nice of you, but you don't know what you're asking. It's treacherous out there and a lot of unknowns we're walking into."

"I can handle it," Travis insisted as he helped Paul gather his sleeping bag.

Paul grimaced knowing full well the boy had no idea and didn't buy it. Travis liked that he respected him enough to be honest with him and not treat him like a child. "I don't know," Paul said. He paused and examined the area. "We'll walk west. I have friends who can connect with us there and get us food if we need it. I've talked with Francisco and we both agree any tunnel is dangerous at this point — especially if they're eyeing us now. We'd be walking right into their trap. "Listo?" He called to Francisco.

"Si!" He replied hurriedly as if not wanting to keep the priest waiting and hurrying his wife to be ready.

As they left the area, Travis looked back and could see the birds kamikaze to the ground at the dead mountain lion, attacking each other and pecking for morsels and staying true to coordinating its keep in the web of life. Paul gently prodded Travis to keep looking forward. The kids were distracted by Paul and in good spirits considering that their hopes of freedom in America were dashed the night before. They had learned early to roll with the punches of life and were fully initiated into adulthood having survived some harrowing adventures. Travis wanted to know more. "You got any advice for me? Looks like I'm a refugee, too."

"Do you pray?" Juanita asked.

"Only when I'm told to," Travis replied with a glint of shame in his voice.

"Learn to pray. It keeps the mind busy and fills you in ways you never considered," she advised with an air of erudition.

"In some ways it fills the heart like food," Sancho added.

"You ever lose hope?" Travis asked.

"That's the game we play, amigo. We lose hope, we gain hope, we lose hope, we gain hope," Juanita said in a singsong manner. "We just keep moving and hope tends to win out."

"The mind is a tricky thing. In the desert we were fooled many times into thinking we saw things that weren't there. We get fooled," said Sancho.

"You hallucinate?"

"Si. When you hallucinate, you lose all sense of what is right and wrong. We saw many pools of water that weren't water."

"Mirages."

"Si, mirages," Sancho said nodding his head with one bob. "We need each other to help each other see what's right and wrong. Do you see that mirage? No, I don't see it, or yes, it's there. We get there only to discover it's not there."

Juanita chimed in. "I saw beings."

"Beings? Like what, aliens?" Travis surmised, as he had heard about aliens in the desert and UFOs.

"No, like celestial beings…beings of light. One of our friends was dying and I thought I saw something he was seeing. It looked like a heavy gray smoke that hovered in the distance and trailed behind us, but caught up to us. The sun hit it in a way that made it reveal a sort of face and robe in the smoke. It moved closer to him and called to him. His eyes brightened as he said he saw it, too. We described it together. He took his last breath looking at this being of light," continued Juanita. "You could see it in his eyes. It was more present to him than it was to me. It was like the wonder of the sight pulled him into eternity. It was very beautiful. His last words were 'Wow, beautiful.' I watched as the smoke disappeared. It was like it was carrying his soul, leading him to the sun and greater light and all that was left was the shell of his body. His eyes looked beyond us into the infinite. It was like he was mesmerized into another world."

"In the desert there's like this—how do you say? Cloak?" Travis looked confused and Sancho thought more. "It is the veil of reality and the other world is very thin. There is more here than meets the eye, amigo," interjected Sancho. "You can't know until you have seen for yourself."

Father Paul had been walking behind with Angelina and Francisco. They were deliberating about a course to walk when Father Paul recognized the intense interest in Travis' face. He caught up to them, heard what they were talking about and scolded them. "Hey, we talk about good things."

"We *are* talking about good things, Padre," insisted Juanita.

"Tell him about your art, Sancho," Paul said curtly not having any of it.

"You're an artist?" inquired Travis with a dazed look, still processing the power of the story from Juanita.

"Si. I like to paint. I'll show you some time."

"I like to write," Juanita posed as she danced to a single lavender flower in the craggy rocks and gently pulled it making it her own. "This journey has taught me a lot. There is much to say when I'm free. Isn't that right, Padre? I'll have some tales to weave from this."

"You will indeed," proclaimed Father Paul. "But what have I told you about the tale you'll need to tell and how to tell it?" Juanita paused and scrambled in her mind for an answer.

He prodded her with a curious look and turn of the head and a point of the finger to help her recall.

"About the power?" Juanita confirmed as she quickly concocted an answer to give her more time to find the precise words.

"And the glory," continued Sancho wanting to say more, but giving her the chance to find it on her own as Paul nodded that he understood that Sancho got it. Travis looked confused as she rumbled through the lesson summoning the touch of poetry the priest imparted.

Juanita found the words: "The power and the glory in the heart create the bountiful and beautiful in the art."

"That's it. Aye for the day," said Paul. "Give glory to the presence of God within and the poetry will find its way to the heart," he added. Sancho and Juanita smiled and Travis looked a little lost as he tried to piece together the lesson. It seemed Father Paul always looked for opportunities to affirm life. It kept them all going.

"What do you do?" Sancho asked to include Travis.

"I like horses. You like horses?" Travis countered.

"Si," said Juanita. "They are wise animals. I looooove horses."

"I ride bareback," continued Travis trying to impress them.

"This is very hard," said Sancho. "I can't ride bareback, but I like to ride. We all ride, my whole family."

"Seems to me like if you get on their wavelength, you can talk to 'em. They can do things for you to help you. But you have to gain their trust," continued Travis.

"I know what you mean," chimed Juanita. "It's kind of like finding the place in their hearts and connecting to it," she added.

"What else do you do?" asked Sancho.

"I'm a big computer guy. I like programming. I like soccer, too, though."

"Futbol? I love futbol," said Sancho changing his countenance with a smile."

"Futbol is soccer," said Paul to help Travis understand. "Futbol Americano is football."

The banter continued for miles and though the noon sun baked their skin Travis cherished the walk and talking with his newfound friends. Father Paul gave him an extra shirt to fashion it as head protection like a sheik covering his head and neck. Paul splatted a few drops of lotion, and imitated the noise with a raspberry shot from the side of his mouth and a wink. Travis spread it on his face and hands while he listened to them tell about their culture. He saw fits of lightness in their stride and a dreamy air of deep gratitude for simple gifts their land afforded them. He saw tangible signs of worldliness and supreme understanding of life having clutched the gauntlet of death. Their wisdom touched his heart. Though they were his age, they were much older and wiser having made the journey. The laughter they shared tapped a part of his empathy that made him fuller as a man. He was opening himself up in ways he couldn't imagine, but travel in a foreign land has ways of initiating certain feelings and fullness of life, even if it was just across the border from where he lived. He had a newfound respect for them, their culture, and their survival instincts.

Paul asked him to check his phone periodically to see if there was a signal. After a few attempts, they finally had one. There were just a few bars, but it was worthy of a chance to call. Paul was cautious and posed the possibility that they could be tapped, but he took the chance of calling Eleanor to ensure that Travis' grandmother knew they were safe. Eleanor picked up on the first ring.

"Travis?!" She answered with vim and vigor like a chortling contestant.

"It's me, Grandma. I'm okay, I'm with Father Paul."

"I left a message telling you what was happening. Did you get it?"

"This is the first chance we've had to call," said Travis. "I made some new friends. I'm okay. I don't want you to worry about me. You can follow me on the computer." He instructed her in what needed to do be done. Eleanor was about as good on the computer as a blind man in a crystal shop, but she took good notes and would try to make it work. Paul took the phone and they discreetly discussed possibilities. They both agreed that the authorities would find the tunnel, which would pose its own problems. Then they turned their attention to the safety and security of Travis.

"As long as he's with you, Paul, I feel all right. He's in good hands," said Eleanor.

"It's still very dangerous," Paul said. "I just don't know what we can do without compromising our situation unless we get to a station and turn him over and move on." Travis was listening and shook his head as if it were unacceptable to him. Eleanor asserted that he was a smart boy and could hold his own. "How's Eben?" asked Paul.

"I didn't want to say anything to Travis, but he's been ill. They think he suffered a heat stroke while in detention. Eben's in the infirmary at the correctional facility. God helps us, Paul."

"I understand," said Paul. "We do what we can and the rest is in His hands."

Paul was hoping he might be able to get some rations at a designated point down the line. He thought they might be able to take them through the fence. Eleanor posed the possibility that she may be able to help with that, but they determined that the Border Patrol would have a keen eye on her. She noted that there were more police cars in the area patrolling their land.

As he hung up the phone, Paul was even more confused about what he was going to do. He said a quiet prayer to himself. And then an insight came to him. "I find it interesting that the signal is not always there. Isn't that interesting? There's a vast desert out there and no one's looking to connect with it. It's as if it's not there. We're not there. We only commune with those close to us. We build our borders and shut out those we don't think we need. We don't consider those in the desert. They're on the fringes of society. These are the places that may need connection the most. I wonder who we're shutting out that we could be letting in," he said. "I mean, maybe, just maybe one of us has the answer to a problem in that country. It seems to me we need to consider who we're keeping out. Terrorists and evil cats, obviously, but what about the possibilities we're closed to?" he reasoned. He thought about the gifts of each of them in his group. Francisco was a great agronomist, his wife Angelina a brilliant scientist at the university who gave up time to mother her children. The kids—well, their gifts have already been addressed. He shook his head, dispelling the thought and handed Travis his phone. "My oh my, it's gonna be a hot one."

PART 2

9

It had been a long day of patrolling the sea of nothingness in nowhere land and young border agent Steven Cruz had pulled his "war wagon" over to meet with his buddy Guy Stillwell, a veteran on the force. The scorching sun of the high noon heat radiated fumes from the engine as he looked down the mountain landscape to a blue sky. The US Border Patrol vehicle had been revving nonstop for the past three hours, and Cruz had been on patrol since six in the morning. Cruz surveyed the area and saw that the illusionary rippling waves of the desert heat formed a curtain down the road apiece like it was raging gaseous fumes from a grill, and a small mirage, a puddle lay in the middle of the road. Steve rolled down the window of his air-conditioned cab and placed his olive skinned arm on the burning ledge of steel on the door only to quickly take it off, as it was too hot and burned him. "Man, oh man, it's gotta be one-oh-five today."

Guy checked his dash. "I got one-oh-eight on my dash here. That's nothing. It gets to a hundred twenty and things still move here. You ain't seen nothing yet. I saw a lizard bake in the sun once — catch fire. Got so hot the damn thing near exploded, just internally combusted," he said with a laugh. "Bring your lunch and heat it on the grill of your jeep there. Don't have to worry about microwaving your lunch. Cooks in no time," he continued as the two shook off the heat with a no-never-mind attitude, as it's all in a day's work in the desert.

"Nothing's coming up today. You got anything on your end?"

"It's one of those rare days," countered Guy.

"I thought we get someone every day."

"We usually do. I don't know why nothing's coming up. I followed a tip someone give me on a spot just over the gully over there, but I didn't see anything. That's the way it goes. You get to know the spots around here. You check your spots daily and someone pops up. We just tend to go there and know that's where someone needs to go 'cause they can't go nowhere else. Don't sweat it, we'll meet our quota," he said right on cue grinning like a dog in resigned contentment as he blasted an AC/DC tune from his I-phone in good humor. *"Now you're messin' with a…Now you're messing with a son-of-a-bitch…"* followed by a twanging guitar riff and a bob of his head in heavy metal fashion. Deputy Cruz laughed. Cruz had been on the force for exactly six weeks, five days and twenty-one hours. He'd grown accustomed to the advice of his friend and knew that it would bear fruit this day. "You eat?" Stillwell asked as he took a swig of his Mountain Dew.

"Nah, but I think I need to get something soon. I'm getting dizzy."

"Stay hydrated. It's the key to everything. You go outside, sweat out your calories in a matter of minutes."

A report came over the radio and both men listened intently as the voice on the other end droned out a potential sighting of an "illegal" heading in their direction. They turned their heads in unison towards their respective radios in a monotonous robotic action. Cruz started up his car again. "Roger that," Stillwell called on his CB. "Cruz and I'll take a look. Over." He turned to his friend. "Let's bust it," said Stillwell and Cruz replied with a wide-eyed look of excitement.

The two patrol cars sped off to their destination. When they arrived at the general vicinity of their call, they decided to split up and patrol the area from the crossroad along the border fence. "You take that path and see what you can find down there, I'll go this way," stated Stillwell. One headed west and the other east. The cars dipped up and down the hill and painted the pristine clarity of the view brown with dust kicking up from their radial tires, which formed clouds of smoke in the area. They moved slowly as they gazed over the brush for any sign of movement and tried to pinpoint any disruption of brush and footprints.

Cruz was fidgety. Whenever he became anxious he resorted to finding his way to make the world right. Today he was in such a hurry to get out of the house, that he wondered if he had forgotten to turn off the lights and the air conditioning. He liked his world in a nice orderly fashion. He searched his house in his mind recalling what he did that morning and where he was. He kept a clean house, with a clean kitchen and polished stainless steel appliances, a clean office with file folders neatly stacked in cabinets ordered with bills in order of importance and filed alphabetically just the way he liked it. He wondered if he left his favorite mug at his desk with coffee in it. He surmised that it was right where he left it with the new pencil holder cup near the erasers that were fresh and clean because he rarely made mistakes due to his mindful nature and obsessive-compulsive attention to detail.

He rolled down his window again and the heat powered its way into the cab. He thought he heard an aching cry coming from somewhere, but he couldn't find the place where it was coming from. He called for backup. He hated the idea of getting out of his cool cab, but he turned off the engine for a minute and listened. He kept searching and scouring the land with his eyes. He had to go into the land to find his prey. "Hola?" He yelled but there was no answer, so he walked into the dead coral of snaking bonsai trees and cacti. He could hear a rustling but didn't know where it was coming from. "¡Sal y permíteme cuidarte! Permíteme obtenerte la atención que necesitas. Se acabó!" (Come out and let me take care of you. Let me get you the attention you need. It's over.)

He resorted to cutting sign, an ancient Navajo tactic for tracking. He looked at the cut of the brush and noted that someone had disturbed the land and flora. The deep orange-red ground was discolored a light brown. The ground was wiped away as if someone had covered his tracks, but he found a footprint deeper into the patch of ground.

He calculated the print with his rubber measure. He measured it from heel to toe and the width of the foot surmising that the alien was a young male. It looked like an Adidas tennis shoe footprint, so he speculated that he was about twenty-seven years old and about 160 pounds, so he held his M-4 rifle at the ready. The footprint had a meandering way with a slow drag about it and the brush indicated that he was disoriented and possibly dehydrated.

He got pissed and spit fury. "Yo sé que estás aquí. Puedo sentarme en mi cabina y tú puedes morirte. Podemos hacerlo de ese modo o puedo conseguirte ahora." (I know you're out here! I can sit in my cab and let you die, we can do it that way or I can get you now,) he muttered under his breath. "¿Dónde está?" He called. "Son-of-a…" his voice trailed off. He eyed something moving in the brush, so he ducked low, but as he got closer it was just a jackrabbit. He looked to his right and there he was, a man in a white t-shirt sprawled in the brush. The man suddenly darted to his feet as if to run, but stumbled after a few feet, as Cruz called to him in Spanish, "¡Para! Manos arriba!" (Freeze! Put your hands up!) "Pon las manos en la cabeza." (Put your hands on your head!) The man collapsed and Cruz stayed low to the ground in case he had a gun and was ready to shoot.

Cruz was cautious as he moved toward the man who was wearing a New York Yankees baseball hat, white t-shirt and jeans. The man was fatigued, huffing and coughing the dust he'd kicked up with his attempted escape. The man wore his journey on his face; it was burned by the sun, broken and ripped with scars and peeling dry skin, open wounds, scrapes and scratches with parched cracking lips and bleeding gums; it was a face of surrender that wore helpless eyes and a beard of desperate want; a furrowed brow with an indented river of fatigue in every line and crevice of need; he was sweating and he looked anxious to die in a cool place.

"*There we go,*" thought Cruz. "This is how we do it. We got one for the day. Bet you're a *mule*," he muttered to himself. The man looked up and thought he saw a halo around Cruz's head, but it was only sun glaring into his line of vision as Cruz radioed for assistance. "¿Tienes algo escondido? ¿Tienes armas? ¿Drogas? ¿Hablarás conmigo en inglés? ¿Puedes hablar inglés?" (You got anything on you? You have any weapons? Drugs? Will you speak to me in English?)

"¿De dónde eres? ¿Mexico?" (Where are you from? Mexico?) The man nodded. "¿Eres uno de esos cabrones que me lanzaron una roca el otro día?" (You one of those assholes who threw a rock at me the other day?) Cruz said as he reached down to check the man who had his hands on his head. "Creo que eras tú.... No me vas a lanzar más rocas, hermano." (I think you were.... You're not throwing any more rocks at me, brother.) He cuffed him, took off his belt and the laces of his shoes, brought him to his feet and radioed that he'd captured "an alien."

Stillwell had called for backup when Cruz heard the shots fired from a short distance away. He winced as he threw the man in the back of the car and hurried to the driver's seat and sped away toward Stillwell's car and the line of fire. The UH 60 L helicopter swooped down to assist the agents in their pursuit. More shots were fired.

10

Stillwell was writhing in pain, but they managed to locate the culprit through sky patrol and Steve took him down as they exchanged shots. They transported Stillwell via helicopter to a Medevac station to treat wounds to his eye, arm and chest; from there they rushed him to a hospital where his near-death wounds could receive thorough attention.

Steve stopped by the room to visit Stillwell who was unconscious at the time. He looked at him sullenly and pondered how it could've very easily been him had he decided to take that route. He didn't want to wake him, so he only stayed a moment. He recalled the chase and shootout that ensued as the suspect was able to claim higher ground. He was lucky he was a good shot and disabled the suspect on the fifth shot.

Cruz then walked to another room where the man he captured was awake and had IV drips in his arm. He knocked three times and entered the room. He alarmed the man at first sight, and the man was cold as if he'd been bothered from looking at a nice view outside his window, but the space was windowless.

"¿Me reconoces?" (You recognize me?) The man looked at him for a minute and grunted a yes and continued with a low mumble, "Te conozco." (I know you.)

"Bueno. ¿Harás mi trabajo más facil y hablar en inglés?" (Good. You gonna make my job easier and talk to me in English.) The man agreed.

"Even better. Looks like they pumped some balloons outta your system. Doctor tells me there was a foreign substance that was tested for cocaine. Care to comment on that." The man was silent. "You care to tell me your name?"

"Esteban Cruz," he said quietly.

"Steve Cruz, nice to meet you. No hard feelings. I was just doing my job, understand?" Esteban responded with cool suspicion and a quick nod of acknowledgement. You spell that for me?

"E-S-T-E-B-A-N. Cruz."

"C-R-U-Z?" I can certainly spell that. Where you from?" asked Cruz.

"Ciudad Juárez, México," said Esteban.

"Tough place." Esteban shrugged his shoulders. "I'm from Colonia Juarez, California. Nice place in Orange County." Esteban remained silent as Cruz wrote on his pad. "Date of birth?"

"31 March 1990," replied Esteban off-handedly.

Steve looked at him with suspicion and gave a dubious glare; his temper flared as he realized he was being played. "Come on…"

"What?" replied Esteban.

"Smartass," snapped Cruz. "Should we try this again? You give me your right name?"

"My name is Esteban Cruz, senior." Esteban was serious. "I'm telling you the truth."

"Cruz is my last name. You're from Juarez, and I'm from Juarez. You think that's a coincidence?" snapped Steve.

"That's crazy," smiled Esteban with delight. "I must be your alter ego."

"Or you're playing with me. How'd you know that stuff about me?"

"I don't know what you're talking about."

"That's more than ironic, doncha think? I don't have time to play games, buddy."

"Run it," said Esteban with confidence. "Run my info and see for yourself."

"I'll run it! But if you're playing a game with me, and I have to come back here, it's gonna be your ass."

"My ass is grass anyway, senor. That's fine with me. You think it will change things for me?"

Cruz slowly moved away and became very staid and maintained his professional composure. "I need to get a statement from you. I'm gonna run this and be back later. 'You have the right to remain silent, anything you say can be used against you in a court of law.' Understand that?" Esteban was quiet. "I don't hear you."

"Yes," said Esteban.

"We've got you for possession, and illegal entry into the country. I'm gonna need some prints. These should be uniquely yours," quipped Cruz as he pulled out his fingerprinting machine and rolled Esteban's finger one at a time. Esteban cooperated but remained silent, and neither man could look at one another as Cruz methodically processed his information. Cruz left the room without saying goodbye.

Cruz was cussing as he returned to his desk. Someone had left a half-filled Coke can there and papers were strewn on it. He was in a bitter mood as it was. "Who the hell's using my desk?"

"Sorry, I was looking for something on file with a case you were working on," chimed a colleague in the back. Cruz guffawed.

"I don't mind that, I just mind that you didn't put things back where they're supposed to be," he said as he straightened the pile of papers and neatly placed them to the side of his desk. "It's rude," he added. His nerves calmed as he refocused and ran the check on his computer for the man he captured. As the computer loaded he was impatient as it sorted through the list of illegals. The network was slow that day and he wanted a quick answer to cure his curiosity. After a few minutes, the information flashed on the screen. It detailed Esteban Cruz's past and to Cruz's surprise it all checked out. He was spooked and stymied. The suspect was right. He was who he said he was.

11

Steve Cruz was a man of integrity and a man of his word. He was ready to eat crow over his disbelief in Esteban, so he returned the next day to meet with him. He was hoping to get a statement and learn more about him. He softly knocked on the hospital room door the next day. He was sheepish as he entered the room. He knew Esteban knew who he was and Cruz acted as if the blow up the day before never happened. His demeanor was as if he proceeded from where he left off when he was nice to the suspect. "I ran a check on you yesterday and the information you gave me checked out." Esteban shrugged and was glib with smugness, but his expression changed when he heard what Cruz said next. "I was raised to own up to my wrongs, and I want to apologize to you. I'm sorry I doubted you, but I thought you were playing a game with me, so I acted out. I hope you'll be able to forgive me."

Esteban was speechless but managed to muster a few words. "Don't sweat it. It's kind of crazy that we share the same name and stuff," he replied as he clutched his sheets tighter.

"I wanted to make it up to you. Here's a bag of candy for you when you get better. I think you can eat that."

"Gracias."

"No problem. It's an assorted bag of chocolate. I didn't know what you'd like, so I got that."

"That's very kind of you, senor," Esteban noted with sincerity and bordering on tears for his gratitude. He was grateful for the first time in a long time he had someone on his side.

Cruz was uncomfortable. "I've gotta get a statement from you. You think you can get me that?"

"Sure."

Cruz pulled up a chair. "You still have the right to remain silent and anything you say will be used against you in a court of law. I just need to let you know that before we begin. You may not be a citizen here, but you have equal protection under the law." Esteban looked off beyond Cruz and sighed. "I wanted to get your side of the story. You and your friend were trying to escape."

Esteban immediately interrupted him. "He's not my friend, senor. I want to make that perfectly clear," corrected Esteban.

"I don't understand."

"He recruited me. He is not my friend!"

Cruz paused with interest as he processed this. "Okay, we'll get to that," he said patiently and became very sincere. "I want to hear all about that, don't get me wrong. First, I need to ask you about this prior. The information I ran said you had a prior arrest for illegal immigration."

"Yes, my family and I tried to cross the border when I was young. We were caught, processed, and shipped back to Mexico. My parents saved all their money to get us here. It was our one and only chance to gain freedom. We were smuggled into the country by a *coyote*. We made it across the desert and established ourselves in Phoenix, Arizona. My father worked odd jobs to help us survive, so we could move up north, so we didn't stick out as much as we would down here. He found a job working at a tire shop. One day coming home from work, a cop took interest in him and asked to see his papers. He discovered he was here illegally. He was captured. My mother knew something was up and tried to get us away. It was hard without him. When he was captured, it wasn't hard to get us. I was just ten years old. I never thought I would be back here. I mean that."

Cruz pondered what he was saying. It wasn't unlike something he'd heard before, but it took on new meaning for him. He was able to somehow place himself in Esteban's shoes and feel sympathy. Maybe it was the uncanny fact that they shared the same last name and hailed from a town of the same name. He didn't realize that they had more in common than he thought. Not only did they share the same last name, but Esteban was the Spanish name for "Stephen." At any rate, Esteban's case captured his imagination and he listened intently as he proceeded.

"Why were you crossing the border?"

"My sister was abducted and trafficked by these guys. She was sold into slavery. I got a tip from a friend that she was trafficked by this guy to the US and I was able to arrange a meeting between us to try and get her back. He told me that she cost a great deal of money, and if I wanted to get her back, I would have to work for him as well. I thought I had no choice. As long as I had an opportunity to save her, I was going to take advantage of this situation to try and get her back. I was told that he needed me to help him in America and assist him to get to a place here."

"Do you have the name of the contact or the place you were going?"

"No, senor. I don't, but he did."

"He's dead, that's not going to do us any good now. Okay, go on," said Cruz taking copious notes.

"So we traveled to the border. He told me that we needed to transport these drugs. If we were caught transporting them we would serve some time in jail. He gave it to me in balloons and told me to swallow them. Well, he had a way of getting through the border under the fence. We got through the fence, and I felt kinda queasy…My stomach didn't feel right, it was upset, and I thought for sure one of the balloons popped. I was unsteady and not good on my feet. I was slowing him up, so he panicked and went off on his own, and I was left to fend for myself."

"Why did you transport something if you knew you could be caught and do some time?"

"Jail would supply me with food and a place to live. I have nothing. When you've got nothing, you've got nothing to lose. I thought that by taking the chance I couldn't lose. It might help me get my sister back and if it doesn't at least I could be provided for in jail." Cruz stopped taking notes and stared deeply into Esteban's eyes. "You can't know how desperate you might be until you've walked in my shoes, senor. Have you ever been hungry? Have you ever gone for any length of time without something you've desperately needed to survive? When you're desperate to connect with the ones you love. When you're desperate to satisfy the thirst for justice and hunger for righteousness. When you're desperate, you'll do anything that has the slightest chance of working. You become dead to yourself. You become dead to the fact that you know you're risking everything on a single chance of an opportunity, but you lose yourself in the game and are willing to play. It's crazy how evil it is, but desire creates a vicious cycle of nonsense thinking. When you're in the middle of chaos, it makes perfect sense to you. It's survival."

"I guess that's true," Cruz affirmed. "I can't imagine it myself, but I suppose that makes sense."

"My family is everything to me. My mother doesn't even know what's happened to me."

"Couldn't you call her?"

"We don't own a phone. Who am I going to call, senor? I have nothing." There was a long pause and Cruz worked through the true meaning of poverty in his mind. *"It could happen to any of us,"* he thought to himself. For the first time since he took the job he thought about how this man could be him. Had he been born into poverty, *he* could be facing the law in this way. He didn't know what he might have had to do to survive. He didn't know what he might have done had he been in *this* situation. He'd like to think that he would do what's right and noble, but as Esteban said, reason goes out the window when you're hungry for a fair shake.

Cruz pondered the idea of fairness. Is it fair that this man had to make an immoral decision for the sake of saving a member of his family? Is it fair that he lived in a land where such decisions were made on a daily basis? What does freedom really mean if one has to make such a decision? You're not free if you are beholden to those who determine if you live or die by making a truly immoral decision for the sake of survival.

What would the government of Mexico think? Did anyone really care? He didn't care in the past. To him, these people were just a means to an end. They were disrupters of justice in the American system and needed to be treated as such. "Law breakers," "criminals," "aliens," "illegals," and other derogatory terms that came to mind when one had just completed a tough day under the hot scorching sun and one of them had given him trouble. "One of them." It was easy to label them, because that allowed him to separate his emotions from the situation at hand. He almost wished he hadn't heard this today.

He was always able to detach and objectify the people in this situation but today was different. His hard shell of indifference was cracked and sympathy ran out of him, but he held it in as much as possible. He didn't want the suspect to see that he had touched a nerve in him.

"What is your sister's name?" Cruz asked.

"Rosa."

"How old is she?"

"She's a few years younger than me. I think she's about twenty-three. I'm twenty-seven. Yeah, she's about twenty-three. She's a special girl. My mother calls her the little 'Rose of her heart,' (La Rosa de su corazón) — but her heart has wilted since she's gone," said Esteban reflectively placing his arm over his head and looking out the window.

Cruz made a note of it. "That's good info. Thanks. I guess that's all we have. Thank you for your time. I appreciate it. Are they treating you all right here?"

"Yes. I'm grateful to them. I'm feeling much better."

"Is there anything I can get you?" Cruz asked.

"Do you know where I will be sent?"

"They'll probably send you to a local facility; after that I don't know."

"Thanks."

Cruz left the room heavy-hearted. This meeting was important for him, as something was born in him and would live with him for a long time. It was the presence of something sacred and was profound as it touched everything he did in his employment and one could venture to say, everything he did in life. It was the powerful touch of compassion. The Hebrew meaning for "compassion" is womb. Fitting that compassion would announce itself in the figure of one he viewed as a suspect, one *he* captured. It prompted him to question how a profound moment could capture and keep its hold on him. He'd never been impacted by such moments in his life. His heart seemed to escape the clutches of his experience, but this experience showed him that he was just as vulnerable as the next guy. He was afraid he was starting to feel the tug of sentimentality. How and why did it meet him here and now? Some things are left to the unexplainable; suffice it to say, he would have to chalk it up to the gift of growth in life.

12

Cruz returned to his desk and tried to run a check on Esteban's sister Rosa, but nothing came up other than the primary information he received from his first go-round. He inquired to colleagues about trafficking rings that they'd broken up in the last few months and asked for possible connections that hadn't been entered, but he came up short again.

Back at the hospital, Manning was ordered for a CAT-Scan. After the scan, orderlies wheeled Manning's bed into the room and placed it next to Stillwell's bed. Cruz knocked, said "Hello" to Manning and entered to Stillwell's section, which was stationed on the furthest wall. Stillwell was awake and groggy, but up for having a guest. Cruz drew the curtain as if that would be enough to prevent Manning from hearing and spoke in hushed tones.

"How you doing?" Cruz asked.

"I'm alright. Doctor said he got me in the chest and lost a lotta blood. Lost a lung and looks like I'm gonna be the resident pirate. Bullet grazed off a rock and got me in the eye. How's that for luck? Looks like I owe you a big thank you. Sounds like you saved my life," Stillwell said.

"Team effort. Wish I could take the credit. It's all in a day's work. Guys in the copter were great. Found a place to land, made all the difference in the world.

"Yeah, caught a few lucky breaks, I guess. Speaking of breaks, whatdya' get on our friend you took out?"

"He was a *mule* peddling drugs and part of a trafficking ring."

"You'll find that out there. Damndest thing in a place of nowhere you can still find plenty of evil floating around...buzz around the desert like bees in a hive sucking up honey and all the money they can lay their sticky fingers on."

"Yeah, well, there is that. I talked with the guy I captured."

"What'd he say?"

"Said he was recruited by the other guy."

"They all got a story."

"Yeah, but this guy's only prior was..."

"They all got a story! Can't save the world, Cruz," Stillwell asserted as he grabbed a paper to read.

"I understand that," Cruz said. He was offended but didn't want to fight back, as he knew he had the upper hand on Stillwell being of sound mind while Guy was doped up on drugs. "I understand," he calmly stated again. He looked for ways to pacify him. "I just need to understand what's going on here. I'm new." Stillwell lightened his mood during a long pause. "You know anything about the traffickers?"

"They got a house somewhere in our parts. Never really located it. Trafficking, you've got a ring of three or four people. You've got the transporter, the middle guy and the pimp. Pimp takes them and uses them for a little bit then sells them on the black market through other traffickers. Shuffle 'em around so fast, can't keep track of 'em. They take 'em from there and ship 'em off to Atlanta, Portland, LA, San Francisco or somewhere's up northeast — New York, Chicago, Milwaukee or Toledo. Best bet to break a ring is at a sporting event like the World Series or the Super Bowl. Guys come into town looking for a good time to go with their games — away from the wife and kids.

What plays in Vegas stays in Vegas kinda thing."

"We got any agents looking into that?"

"Nah, too busy down here. Don't have the money or the manpower to look into those kinds of things. Well, there's a guy I know, though. He used to work with us, took an interest in that cause after he retired, but that's about it. Don't know how busy he is or what he's doin' to fix things along that order. Guy's name is Madden — Mike Madden. Real mission guy, real hard nose…likes bustin' up prostitution rings, sex traffickers and scum like that."

"You think you can get me his number?"

"Sure, number's on my desk. Help yourself to my Rolodex. Whatcha thinkin'?"

"I don't know, I just thought I might be able to check something out."

"Whatever," whispered Stillwell. "Far be it from me to tell anyone what to do."

Stillwell saw the idealism in his young friend's eyes. He'd been around and knew that this attitude would disappear the longer he was on the force. It has a tendency to work itself out as one encounters the reality of the job. Given his circumstances, he was in no place to help anyone but himself. "Look, I'm sorry. I'll help you anyway I can."

I appreciate that," said Cruz as he reached out his hand to shake his free hand. "Lemme know whatchoo need? I'm always here. Brothers in arms…*Commilitones,"* said Cruz raising his arm in solidarity with a closed fist that resembled the black power sign.

"*Commilitones*," smiled Stillwell imitating him with his good arm. Cruz exited with optimism and returned to the office.

Stillwell pulled back the curtain to greet his new neighbor.

Manning was taken aback. "Wanted a proper introduction," Stillwell exclaimed.

"Oh, hello there. I'm Manning. Looks like we're gonna be roommates for a while."

"Yep," said Stillwell. "Nice to meet you."

"What happened to you?"

"Shot in the face and chest by a whackadoodle trafficker."

"That's messy. You gonna be all right?"

"Yeah, that's what they tell me. Thanks for asking. What are you in here for?"

"They're telling me my heart's irregular. I've been called irregular for alotta things but never for my heart. Run some stress tests on me and say it's weak. Looks like I got some blockage — put a stent in there or maybe a pacemaker…something like that, I don't know what the hell they…" his voice trailed off.

"You got a tag on your leg."

"Guess they think an old man with a bad heart is gonna escape. They had me at the facility over there." He didn't want to say much more, as he covered up the tracking device with his covers.

"Uh-huh," replied Stillwell with a suspicious hint in his voice.

"Like I said, I've been recognized as irregular for alotta things."

"I don't even wanna know," said Stillwell as if he'd heard it all before and wouldn't be surprised by anything.

"I'm not ashamed of anything," Manning said as he scratched his beard. "I'll rest fine tonight. You lemme know if you need anything. Lemme know if I'm botherin' you." Manning spit into a dish.

"Thanks. Will do," replied Stillwell.

Eleanor entered with a breeze of confidence, trying to hide her fear. Manning grabbed her tight and kissed her as she placed the flowers she was holding on the table. "Eleanor, this is my new friend, Guy. He's a good man. He's protecting our borders." She understood the subtle nod and introduced herself formally. She then attended to her husband and offered to assist Guy with anything he needed. He thanked her and waved her off politely and turned to get some sleep. The room was peaceful but a stale intensity hovered like a cloud of smoke above the beds.

Eleanor's first impression of Stillwell was that of an impudent, hard-nosed, take no prisoners, no nonsense robot, a machine of a man. She assumed his religion on Sundays was football games and drinking beer with the boys in his man cave; tossing out orders for more Tostitos and Buffalo Chicken dip to his wife, maybe some pizza, and groveling in front of the TV for fear of losing big with his Fantasy Football League. She felt as though she had a good nose for people, but her assessment of this one may have been off by a few hairs.

Her phone rang, and she answered it. It was their lawyer, Smialek, and he had some information for them regarding their case. She handed the phone to Manning who was squeamish considering a border policeman was one bed over from him. He needed to turn up the volume, so he could hear on the phone and was afraid of the information leaking through the line. Eleanor was leery, as she witnessed his uncertainty and thought how clever it was for the hospital to put Eben in a room with a border agent.

"Wait a minute," said Manning, as he increased the volume and looked over at Guy who was trying to sleep. "Go ahead."

"Is Eleanor there? I saw her when she posted bail, but didn't get to talk with her," crackled Smialek's voice from the other end.

"Yeah, she's here."

"I've got some bad news for you. The government has found the tunnel and now has critical evidence that could be used against us in a court of law. They're going to close up the tunnel and use that as a case of eminent domain for the good of safety and security of the community," stated Smialek. "They've got every right to do that, Eben. Looks like we may be stuck here on this one."

"Uh-huh. I understand," Manning replied uncomfortably. "Well, there isn't much we can do about that now. We just need to explore our options. Do we have any options?"

"We can plea bargain for a lesser sentence, but it looks like you're going to do some time either way, Eben." There was a long pause on the other end of the line as Manning was ruminating through the news. "It's solid evidence against you. We can bargain for mercy. You've been an upstanding citizen till now. You don't have any prior arrests; we can only hope that the judge will be lenient. It'll depend on who we get for our case, though. I'm sorry, Eben."

"I understand," replied Manning. The old man was grave and raised his eyebrows as to be optimistic with Eleanor present. "That's the price we pay for what we do." She knew him well enough to know that the news was not good. Although it was loud and she could hear bits and pieces, she didn't get the full story. He handed the phone back to Eleanor with a distant smile of uncertainty.

"What'd he say?" Eleanor quietly asked, disconcerted.

He looked over at the bed beside him where Stillwell resided. "Not here," he grumbled. "Not good. You may want to call him and talk with him yourself. I can't talk here. We need to consider our options." By the look on his face, Eleanor could tell that she had a sour look of concern and that it had worked its way into the frame of her body. Her air of optimism deflated, made evident by her body language. He giggled nervously to try and assure her that there was something bigger there that would look out for them like it always had. He reminded her how lucky they've been, and she nodded in agreement though she felt this time it was different. It was like she sensed the impending doom that could come from taking on a government with such civil disobedience. Eleanor considered historically what happened to people who took on the government this way. She grabbed his hand, held it tight and massaged his knuckles. It would be the beginning of a long struggle for the two of them.

Eleanor got close to him and caressed his temple and ran her fingers through his hair as she spoke. "We've been through tough things before," she whispered in his ear. "We can get through this too; long as we have each other." He agreed. She kissed him, and this managed to lighten his mood as he closed his eyes, as if he were bathing in her soothing comfort and holding it in his mind for as long as he could.

13

Cruz found the number for Agent Madden on Stillwell's Rolodex and called him. "I was referred to you by Guy Stillwell. I'm trying to track a case of a missing person. I was wondering if you might help me?"

"Sure. I don't know if I can help you. Whatcha need?"

"Well, it's a trafficking situation, may be someone who's sex trafficked. Can you tell me what you do with victims?"

"I gotta be honest with you. The chances of finding someone are next to nil — needle in a haystack when you consider how they're shuffled around and sold to other pimps. You get me some info on the trafficker, I might be able to help you take a look and see where he was going and what he was doing."

"Thanks."

"You're more than welcome to join me one of these days and see what a sting's like."

"I may take you up on that. Thanks. I'm off this weekend. You think you can hook me up?"

"Always welcome. Can always use the help," said Madden.

Cruz got to work on the other end of the equation by tracking the information of the man who tried to kill his colleague. He dug in deep by searching records of contacts and priors with lists of arrests and locations of priors. He was able to get an address in Mexico for the man and thought he'd run a trace on his behavior over there. He knew it'd be tough to get information from other officials over there, but the information he had from Border Patrol might suffice, so he went with what he had.

• • • • •

On the weekend, Steve traveled up North to where Madden lived. He met Madden in the morning at the designated location in the parking lot of a gas station. Madden's hair was a short-cropped marine cut that was high and tight. He placed his sunglasses atop his head as he introduced himself. "You must be Cruz," he said in a no-nonsense manner. Madden was a stocky guy of around fifty and had piercing eyes that had seen their fair share of danger and nefarious activity with over thirty years on the force.

Madden was tough and assertive as he spoke. "Let me make one thing perfectly clear. The government isn't concerned about attending to the issues of sex trafficking like it should. They don't fully understand the implications of what's going on. They're too concerned with the border and feel that tighter border security is the way to attack the problem. What they don't realize is that there are ways of getting people through legal means to meet the demands of johns over here. In other words, some of the women who come through here may have come through the border legally. Others are told they have jobs waiting for them, so they're duped into crossing without realizing what they're walking into. They're not supposed to be here, but they're here legally. No one seems to look at that fact when they're talking about building the wall."

"Now, lemme run you through what happens to a woman once she's here. They'll be told that they are going to their jobs as 'domestics.' In some cases that's exactly where they'll go. If a woman is young and deemed saleable, she'll be sent to a house of prostitution or a bar. They'll post ads for modeling or jobs that promise 'big money' so that's how they hook them in. After the traffickers have taken their passports and stripped them of their identities, they are usually taken to a house where they'll meet their pimps. They'll be asked to satisfy the pimp. If they refuse, they'll be beaten until they submit to the rape. They break them. Once broken, they can do whatever they want to them and make them do what they need them to do. Keep in mind that woman are disposable. They're a cheap product and cheap labor; usually enslaved so the overhead in the business is low and they can use them till they get every sap of life out of them."

Cruz listened with interest as Madden drove. "They're gonna get suspicious if they see two guys. I'm going to be on a wire and we have a camera set up. You can watch from the truck. We're going to raise a sting. I'm gonna pose as a john and see if we can't help someone. I was given a tip, and I'm trying to bust a ring. I wanna introduce you to Katrina Pritchard. Katrina's with an organization that takes care of women who've been trafficked." He adjusted his mirror. I'll need you to watch for any suspicious activity you find and take notes. A girl will be coming and I need you to tell me what kind of vehicle she comes from. Better yet, get me a plate number."

Madden pulled up to a banged up, small white van and checked his watch noting they still had "a little time." He introduced Cruz to Katrina who was dressed in khakis and a short-sleeved blouse that gave her a casual professional look. She looked tired from the heat, but it could've been burnout from her work as a social worker. Madden was quick and businesslike as he readied himself for the sting. Cruz examined the monitors and sound equipment that was set up in the van.

"You come up with me and I'll ring you when I need you," said Madden to Katrina.

Madden wired himself and Katrina turned her attention to Cruz. "You a cop too?"

"Border Patrol."

Katrina was confused. "We don't get you guys much," she said.

"I'm looking for a missing person who's been trafficked. She's a Latina and goes by the name of Rosa." Katrina was quiet as she sorted through the situation. "You been doing this long?"

"I've been helping women who've been abused for a number of years. This is just one of those places I seem to get a lot of business," she said with a sad grin and wrinkled forehead that was deeply lined with concern. Madden was ready as he put on a sharp-looking pair of glasses. Cruz looked at the monitor and saw himself and was amused.

"Where's that picture coming from?"

"It's coming from these glasses. There's a camera in here. It's go time," said Madden with a laugh. "Do me a favor and hit that record button when you see me give you the thumbs up," he said to Cruz as he bolted to the front of the van.

"Let's talk later," said Katrina. The two exited the van and Madden unlocked the door, and entered the motel on the second floor. Katrina walked along the hall and positioned herself by some vending machines on the first floor.

Cruz watched from the truck for about ten or fifteen minutes, witnessing a young woman arrive in a Cadillac Escalade and walk up to the second floor. The SUV pulled away after dropping her off, but he couldn't get the plate number from his vantage point. She walked up to the same room Madden entered. She was dressed for the heat wearing short shorts and a t-shirt. She carried a purse and looked around as she searched the door for the number. Cruz turned to the black and white monitor in the room. It was grainy but he could see Madden moving in the room and settling in for the sting. A gentle knock on the door could be heard and Madden gave the thumbs up to Cruz before he opened it. The young woman walked in and introduced herself. Madden welcomed her and told her his name was "Fred." She was reticent as she sat on the bed and was uncomfortable, and he sat on the opposite bed as they talked.

"You were sent by Renaldo?" Madden inquired.

"Yes," said the woman.

"What will you do for me?"

"I thought you talked with him," stated the young woman, confused and uncomfortable as she fixed her seat.

"I did talk with him. He said you were here to entertain me." The woman was flustered. "Isn't that why you're here?"

She took a protected stand, crossing her arms. "I guess so."

"You seem like you don't want to do this."

She placed her hand on her forehead. "No, I…." She fumbled over her words and was fidgety.

"Have you done this before? You seem new to this." She remained quiet.

"Can we just get on with this?"

"I've got the money here. I'm assuming you want this upfront." He flashed her the money and she took it. She appeared relieved.

"What if I told you you didn't have to do this? We can just talk."

"Seriously?" she replied.

"Yeah, you been doing this long?"

"About a few weeks." She broke down and crumbled inside. Madden grabbed a Kleenex box and handed it to her. "I'm not here to hurt you," said Madden. "I wanna help. I wanna help you and others. The only way I'll be able to do this is if you help me help you. You want out of this racket?"

She remained quiet. She was shaking. "Please don't play games with me," she said.

"I'm not trying to play any games," said Madden.

"I need to bring some money back or he'll kill me."

"No one's gonna kill you here. You're not going back to him. I'm a police officer," he said as he texted Katrina. He showed her his badge. "I wanna help you."

"Oh, my God," she said with a quivering voice. "I can't believe this is happening."

"It's okay. We're part of a task force to help women who've been sex trafficked. I'm not here to hurt you. I wanna introduce you to someone." Katrina entered the room and Cruz was mesmerized as he watched her take control. The girl was more at ease with another woman there and Katrina took her hand as the young woman cried. Their conversation was muffled but Cruz was riveted nonetheless. They asked if her pimp was watching and she said he was attending to someone else down the road. They moved out of the room and walked her back to the van where Cruz was located.

• • • • •

They introduced her to Cruz. Her name was Melody. She was timid and embarrassed as her auburn curls draped across her tired bloodshot eyes and mascara ran down her cheeks from crying. Her gaunt features and willowy frame revealed a half-starved vulnerability that Katrina held close to her while she escorted Melody to safety. Katrina laid out possibilities to help Melody out of her futile situation and told her about an organization that assists women who've been abused, raped and trafficked get back on their feet. She told the woman they could help her reclaim her freedom and help her establish a new life. It was clearly the best thing for her, but Melody's fear made her hesitant, and she gave every reasonable objection to help make it clear in her mind that it was the best course of action for her. "What if he finds me? What if he comes after me and hurts me? What if he hurts my family? He said he'd kill members of my family if I didn't obey him."

"That's just what we're trying to avoid. We're here to help you. Chances are he won't go near you. He won't want to jeopardize getting caught and shutting down his business. If he does try to contact you, we'll put a restraining order on him, so he can't go near you or your family. It would be better if we could get him, but that'll come with time. For now, we'll give you a place to stay to help you get back on your feet. We'll get you the help you need and bring you back to your family," said Katrina with patient calm.

"Thank you!" she said as she shook, quivered, and stuttered agreement with the plan but appeared ill at ease and confused.

"Renaldo has many girls working for him?" asked Madden.

"I live in a house with about twelve other girls."

"Do you know where it is?" he continued.

"No. I have no idea. He won't let us see where it is," she said, dabbing at her running nose.

"So there are some there against their will? Do you know if these girls have been trafficked from other countries?" Madden gently proceeded to try to get any information he could.

"There are a few from Mexico, Central America. They only spoke Spanish."

"Does he have a partner involved in this?"

"His wife helps him. She's the one who got me into it. I thought I could trust her to help me, but she used me and took advantage of my weakness just like the others. Those two prey on weakness and vulnerability. They're evil cats, man! Evil." Katrina soothed her gently, rubbing her arm and handed her a bottle of water. Melody went to her pockets and brought out the money Madden gave her earlier.

Madden's hand went up immediately. "Keep that. We need to get you a nice meal, too. You hungry?"

Melody was surprised at such kindness. "I'm starving. I only get one meal a day." She looked famished and was appreciative as Katrina handed a power bar to tide her over until they could take care of her.

"Let's get you to a safe house. You'll like it there," Madden said.

As they drove away, Cruz anticipated that this pimp could be where Rosa was. Madden agreed quietly but didn't give much credence to it at that time. He was quick to point out that it was harder to capture pimps. They had to make a bust at the actual establishment and these were hard to find. A smart pimp will have multiple sites to keep women.

They brought her to the house and Katrina walked her in to help her begin her treatment and take information. Madden and Cruz waited outside.

Katrina returned to the van and they headed back to the motel to do more good.

"What will become of that girl?" said Cruz.

"She'll be traumatized for the rest of her life. She'll need to learn to live with it and make peace with the trauma. Some people never do. When you've experienced the fallout of evil, your view of the world changes. It's hard to see good for some. It zaps the life right out of you and leaves you blind to possibility."

Cruz had heard enough. He bought in. "How are we gonna get him?"

"It's going to be hard. He's already gonna be suspicious when she doesn't come back. We need to find someone who's strong enough to lead us back to his place where we can lead a cop to his whereabouts and bust him. That woman wasn't the one. She's traumatized. We're hoping to find someone who'll wear a wire. We may be able to get him that way. It's a tough question to ask. It's not a guarantee that Renaldo's the one, but he might know of how to get onto someone else. That's the key. We wanna break the ring. These scumbags know each other. One piece of information leads to the next until the whole puzzle is completed. I'll tell you this…it's a golden ticket. If you find that young woman, she's guaranteed a visa to live in America and make a better life for herself. Unfortunately, she'll be paying a great price right now to get it. The price she pays may be the too costly to appreciate any kind of freedom she may attain, but it's something."

It was new madness for Cruz. He'd seen a lot in his short time with the patrol, but this was a new education for him. He was determined more than ever to help Esteban find his sister and return her to her rightful home of safety and security.

14

Since one of Renaldo's girls was taken out of commission and he would presumably assume that it was a bust, Madden asked the motel if he could change rooms. He lied saying that he didn't like the accommodations. The next woman who came to the motel was different. She was cold and wore a hard exterior. She wore jeans with a tiger print blouse. She masked light makeup, and had messy frizzy hair that gave her a look of someone who knew how to present an edge and play strength but maintain a pretty feminine sensibility. It was a smart approach to an unknown situation where she was vulnerable and could take charge of the unknown. She'd gained this tough shell from working in Renaldo's business for a year. She knew how to handle herself and controlled the situation methodically. She was smart and savvy. Madden was impressed by her tenacious spirit while he questioned her.

"I'm here to do what needs to be done," she said with a plaintive tone. "But you play by my rules or this conversation is over."

"Renaldo said you'd be amenable to my needs."

"I just want to be clear what the boundaries are."

"How long you been in this business?" Madden asked.

"Long enough to know that no creepster is going to take advantage of me here," she said looking around the room.

"What are you looking for?"

She walked over to the mirror and placed her finger at the mirror. She leaned in close to see. "Cameras. I'm looking to make sure this isn't a two-way mirror," she said. "If there's a space between my nail and the mirror, it's clean." She examined the mirror closely. "We're good."

"You're like a cop," Madden said.

"I know how cops work."

"You do? You been busted before?"

"Oh, yeah, it's not a pretty sight either. It sucks. I've learned the tricks of the trade, though."

"What if I told you I was a cop?"

"I'd believe you."

"Why?"

"Because you look like a hard-ass dick! That's why they call cops 'dicks.'"

Madden laughed. "You want the money?"

"Not yet," she said coyly.

"You're taking my time."

"This is all part of the process for me. I need to finish my personality profile on you. You'll get your money's worth, if I accept you."

"If you accept me," parroted Madden. "Aren't you afraid of Renaldo?"

"I can handle Renaldo."

"If you were tougher than you are, you wouldn't be working for anyone," snapped Madden cool and collected. She looked at him with disdain. He cut to the heart of the thing that irked her, and they both knew it. "Time is money," he said.

"Not my money," she said coldly and in a matter of fact manner.

"Rules are fine. I appreciate rules. I want you to know that. I'm not your average bear," retorted Madden. She smirked in disbelief. "What's so funny?"

"All men are ultimately the same. They're just animals looking for satisfaction of their needs. They all think they're not the 'average bear' when in fact that's all they are — a bear looking for satisfaction. And that's the way they need to be treated. Now, I can treat you like a grizzly bear or a teddy bear, but I'm the one holding you." She smiled smugly. "Understand? I know tricks to tame a grizzly, so don't make me assert myself and we'll be fine."

"What if I told you I wanted to spend the hour talking?"

She eased up. "It's your money. But I want the money up front and no discounts for the hour. It's what we agreed."

"Fine." He handed her the money. She walked over to the door and Madden thought she was going to leave. She watched Madden as she walked to the door. "One minute." He was confused as she slowly turned the door handle. She opened the door and checked it to make sure it wasn't jammed and locked from the inside. She closed the door, bolted the deadbolt and returned to Madden. She looked at her watch. "Just so you know, my boy's right downstairs and I keep this close if I need him." She indicated a phone. "One tap of the button and he's here." Madden was silent, squinted, looked at his own phone that was on the table and finally nodded.

"So you didn't answer my question. What is it about Renaldo that makes you stay when you've got street smarts and savvy sensibilities?"

"Security. It's easier to work through a guy."

"My sense is that you don't like the guy. I've gotta feeling if you could you'd be away from him like hot Chinese mustard sauce. He's just an accessory the business throws in."

"I don't get you," she looked at him absurdly.

"I mean, who eats that stuff? It goes right through you. I mean, it makes your nose scream and eyes hurt. You don't need it to enjoy the meal."

"I don't enjoy the meal," she said. "Food's just a means of survival."

"Then why do you do it?"

She was silent as she thought through what he was saying. "Here it comes," she laughed.

"Here comes what?"

"You're one of those holier than thou guys…you're going to be one of those righteous ones who tells me that he hates the sin and loves the sinner and then you're going to jump on my bones."

"I'm a man of my word. You said yourself you already labeled me 'dick' as in a cop. Listen…here's the point. I've got an opportunity I want to propose to you. What if I was able to get you away from this? Help you get on your feet? What would you say to that?"

"I'd be very suspect," she said crossing her arms.

"I understand that. If I asked for your help to get Renaldo, what would you say to that?"

"Get Renaldo? That scummy maggot-brained piece of slime?"

"Now we're talking."

"What's in it for me?"

"Let's negotiate that," said Madden sweetly. "By the way, I know your boy's not downstairs."

"How you know that?"

"Because I'm a cop and my friend's been casing the place. She told me when he left." She stood up as if to leave abruptly.

"Sit down, I'm not going to hurt you. What's your name?"

"Krystal," she said.

"Mike Madden." He put out his hand to shake it, and she slowly took it. "Look, you can help us. If you tell Renaldo, you blow our cover and put other girls in danger. You help us, we can help you." He called Katrina into the room and they discussed her options the same way they did with the first one. But this time it was different. Katrina and Madden managed to get her to consider taking a wire to help them track her. The tough young woman became a bit frightened and for the first time she lowered her guard and confided to them what scared her the most about doing that. They told her they could take her to a shelter, but it would guarantee that Renaldo would get suspicious and shut down the operation and blow their cover. They were hoping they could reconnect with her the next day. She could help them and they could help her. They hoped it would be a win-win for both. "I may need you to do me a favor and make a call," asked Madden to Cruz.

"Sure," said Cruz without even letting him finish."

"I need you to set up an appointment with that girl as a john. We want to get her back tomorrow."

The following day, Cruz was back to Madden's sting operation again. Madden informed him that there were new developments, and he and Katrina would be holed up in a new motel to see what they might be able to get. He prepared for the day as if the woman he talked with the day before was going to help them and work part of the sting for him. He was hoping that this woman was willing to wear a wire and lead them back to the house where Renaldo was. They would offer her some marked bills that she would bring back to her pimp and be able to help bust him. Madden utilized his connections to establish warrants that would serve their cause so they could get more information against Renaldo. Cruz was given new directions on where to meet him.

Cruz arrived that morning at Madden's makeshift office in a two-story office building in a small town that felt like it was gasping for its last breath to stay alive. A throwback to the sixties when this building was built, it reminded Cruz of his training center for the force. The stale air pumped by the small vent left a cave-like stench brooding above him, which triggered a sneeze from the olfactory senses. Cruz knocked on the door and Madden opened the door abruptly like he was waiting for him with an extended hand to shake and an invite to enter. It was only because the room was so small.

"Heard you sneeze," said Madden. "Welcome to my home. I could bring you back here, because you proved that you could be trusted," said Madden. Moving in a hurried fashion, he examined some notes and made some scribbles in a notebook. The room was replete with the all the fixings for a shoestring operation: pasty walls, no windows, a few large desks facing one another with files climbing out of old paper boxes that were decorated to look like wooden boxes, an old computer monitor and keyboard, cork bulletin boards with maps and pinpointed with tacks, ramshackle cabinets with an accordion file hanging off the side and sticky notes along with a marked up calendar, an old dry erase board detailing the finer points of his operation with contacts and numbers hastily written on them, and a small water basin with large jugs of water. The garbage can was filled with Chinese food containers.

"Yesterday was a test?" Cruz said disarmed and surprised.

"This life has made me a bit neurotic and paranoid. Cops are in on the take. Most pimps pay off cops and that's why they walk free. The cycle of violence for women is perpetuated due to big money. I knew you were okay when you told me Guy sent you. That boy scout is out to save the world in his own freakish way," laughed Madden. "Let's go."

They drove in the white van to a new motel to meet Katrina.

"How do you know you can trust her?" asked Cruz about the woman.

"Someone once told me, 'He who cannot trust, cannot be trusted.' I've become jaded and can't trust anyone in this world. That's probably why I'm divorced now. I've had my operation busted up three or four times in different places due to cops gumming up the works on what I was doing. In this business you have to use your instincts about people. I've spent years honing that instinct — sometimes it works, sometimes it doesn't. I don't know if she can be trusted, but Katrina seems to think that she can. I hope she's right. I trust Katrina. She's one of the most attuned, well-adjusted and trusting people I've ever met."

"Looks like you can trust after all," Cruz said wryly. Madden shrugged as he pulled out a piece of gum, offered it to Steve and took one for himself. "It oughta be interesting, that's for damn sure," said Madden chomping on his gum. "That's for damn sure!"

15

A confident knock echoed in the room. "There she is," Madden said. "Our star of the hour." Krystal entered but this time with a different demeanor. She maintained her confidence, but she was even more measured in restless uncertainty. They could tell that she had a rough night, and she looked fatigued as she wrestled with the proposition from yesterday.

"Well?" Madden asked seriously with his hands on his hips.

"Where's my wire," she said exasperated. "We've only got an hour." Madden was pleased snapping the money in her hand as he paid her. Further instructions were methodical: Just stay cool, calm and collected. It's going to be all right. We follow you back there. We're giving you a tracking device, but if we can follow, that's even better. We just need you to drop this chip when you step into the car. We'll have one on you and one on the car in case the car leaves, so we can follow it. Don't sweat it. Don't be obvious... You know what I mean. Now, when they get the money, that's when we got 'em. You go in there and play it as if nothing's going on. You give him the money and tell them we're paying for tonight, too. We need you to tell them that we want you back at 9 pm for a party. This lets you off the hook. They won't know it's you who called them out. We make the bust and get what we can from the house. You come back with Katrina, so you're safe and we get to work on finding the other girls so we can help them. General information. I imagine you're using pretty much the same places. If they can get a read on hotel/motel stationary or whatever, and let us know, that's good. We're going to need you to ask the other girls where they're going. Do you think you can get us that information?"

"I can try," she stated sincerely.

"Good," said Madden as he pulled out a bag with equipment.

"I needa remember it, though, 'cause I don't have any paper."

"That's okay, we can get you a little pad and a pen. Cruz, you get me that?" said Madden hurriedly. Katrina entered with the wire supplies.

"He's gone. I watched him go," she said.

He redirected his attention to Krystal. "Does he pack a gun?"

"Not when he's home…he usually leaves it locked in the kitchen cabinet safe. He's pretty careful about his guns. He's got one by his bed, too. They're all over the house. 'You can't be too sure,' he says. No one knows where they are, but he's stockpiled them around there but pretty much locked away. Just so you know, he's going to lock me in the basement with the others. That's what he does. It's not like we're roaming around free in the house. He brings us up when he needs company or to do a job, but that's about it."

"I understand. That's good to know. We have ways of getting more information. We go in tonight. This is going to be all over for you." She breathed a heavy sigh of relief.

"I'm trusting you know what you're doing."

"I've been in this business a long time. I know what I'm doing," Madden assured her.

"You give him your earnings right away?"

"Usually when we get back, so no one can see us. Sometimes in the car if we have multiple dates."

"Okay, I gotcha."

Cruz had questions of his own. "Where's the squad gonna be?"

Madden was business-like as he pulled Cruz aside. "They don't know I'm coming. I've got a friend on the inside. I let one guy know. The less they know the better. We get a squad together last minute, so they can't gum up the works on the sting. That's the only way we can do it. I need you to go down and make sure the coast is clear. If you see an Escalade SUV pull up, we're screwed in following her," he whispered in his ear. Cruz exited the room.

Krystal looked nervous but Madden in a supportive pose said, "Hey, it's going to be okay." She melted into his arms and he held her for a minute. "You all right?" She nodded and regained her composure.

"I can do this."

"Damn straight you can."

Katrina continued to check the wiring equipment.

"What if he wants me to accompany him to his room and he sees the wire?" She asked with trepidation.

"That's a good question. Can you be careful when you undress? We're going to be right there. If we hear problems, we can assemble faster if we need to. It's only going to be a few hours."

"I hope so," she said.

"No, you're going to be fine," Madden said. Madden smiled at her to inspire confidence and gave her a big hug. They both assured her, "just be yourself." Madden left them and went down to the van to ready themselves to follow the car.

The women waited as the tension of the witching hour loomed near and the hour passed quickly. Krystal let her guard down with Katrina and they were friendly with one another. "I'm a terrible actress. I can't keep a lie for long. I'm just not going to say anything." Krystal continued to try and convince herself it was all going to be okay.

"You'll be great," Katrina assured her. Be yourself."

That's the hard part. I don't know who I am anymore." The hour arrived. She primped herself in the mirror, took a deep breath and walked out the door. They listened to her as she clopped down the stairs and met Renaldo at the car. The frequency faded in and out, but they could tell that they were well away and Madden and Cruz bee-lined out of the drive following the Escalade.

"We don't want to be too obvious. These guys are always on the lookout for people following them."

"I can't imagine living a life where you have to worry about being hunted down, can you?" Cruz asked.

"That's why I left the Patrol. I was tired of being the hunter for good people. Innocent people who only wanted a better life for themselves were being treated like criminals. I remember one day an agent found a pile of water. We were told to pour it out but I never did. I don't need to tell you, water's like gold in the desert. This guy was just tossing it away. I thought about how inhumane that was. I hadn't thought about it until I saw a few of the migrants die of dehydration. That's hard to stomach." Cruz was quiet. "You've got everything on that force…knuckleheads, demagogues, fascists, power-hungry assholes who need to laud it over another person and guys who just count the hours to retirement."

"They're not all bad," Cruz said.

"Nah, there's a few good ones mixed in there trying to do some good. Sonny Phillips, Coochie, Showboat, 'Stone Cold's' a big bear, Guy, there's a few…"

"Some of those guys are gone," countered Cruz.

"Still, you've got a few idealists in there. It's like anywhere, I guess," Madden saved face.

They talked about a few of the old timers as they continued to follow. The Escalade pulled off and they lost him from view. Cruz wondered what Madden was doing. "I still got him in my sights. I don't want it to be obvious we're trailing him. I got him on the screen here." He showed him the map and the small red dot that indicated where they were. Madden pulled off. They listened as they heard them get out of the car and slam the door. Renaldo muttered some words. Madden asked Cruz to check and make sure the sound was recording, and Cruz assured him it was.

They could hear Renaldo ask for the money. Madden's eyes got big and his mouth was gaping with pride as he listened like he was watching a comedy and a smile flashed across his face when he heard her tell him, "They paid up front for later, so that's that."

"Good. I always like my money up front," said Renaldo with a Spanish accent.

"Good, I always like my money up front," said Madden imitating him and mocking him. He drove down the street and saw the Escalade parked in the driveway of a green ranch house. The red dot that was moving on the screen blinked loud and clear as they took note of the house number. "There it is," said Manning grinning from ear to ear. "There's our diamond in the rough."

They took note of the address and continued to drive, circling back around the block and posted themselves outside. Madden made a few phone calls to his friend posting the coordinates for the sting. All they could do was sit and wait. They parked the car out of sight at the end of the street and watched to make sure no one left. If he left, they'd have to take him out on their own.

• • • • •

Night arrived and the hour of the raid was getting close. Madden called his friend on the DEA and worked through their plan. They met in a parking lot and exchanged information while Steve watched the blinking red dot on the screen to make sure Renaldo wasn't trying to leave. The officer brought the proper paperwork for establishment of a search and seizure of any information pertaining to the crime that they believed had been committed.

The drive to the house was filled with excitement, measured with insecurity and abounding in a tempered realism of uncertainty. Butterflies were fluttering in Cruz's stomach. This kind of domestic situation always unnerved him. They were going into concentrated spaces that left challenging obstacles and niches for explosive battles to happen. Cruz had utilized the high stakes drama and emotional roller coaster as a form of empowerment in his life to motivate him to do better, but his trip to the house was heightened by the knowledge that the lives he was saving could lead to bigger possibilities for the victims, hopefully Esteban's family. He'd never thought of the victims he was saving quite in this way.

The sun was down and the house held a stillness that captured the night and concentrated its radiance of foreboding doom like a vortex. Madden went to the door and knocked, but there was no answer. The agents surrounded the house to ensure no one escaped out the back. "Open up… Police!" Madden proclaimed, knocking harder and harder.

"We're gonna break down this door if you don't open it," he continued. There was no answer. He kicked in the front door and police burst onto the scene in "full go" mode. A young woman had her hands up in the air begging not to be hurt and surrendered herself to them. They read her Miranda Rights while her husband Renaldo tried to escape through a hole in a bedroom that led to a crawl space in the attic. He looked silly as his feet were wiggling and dangling as he was stuck midair. A few of the police laughed as they pulled him out but stopped when he was halfway out and a gun dropped to the ground. Shouts ensued and a tumbling suspect revealed his other hand was empty. They wrestled the man to the ground and followed suit with him in minimizing his movement like they had with the woman. "You're under arrest for kidnapping," said a gleeful Madden, and he had another person read him his Miranda Rights while Madden attended to other business in the house.

The house was roused with banging and muffled talking as agents continued to filter in and search for people in every space and crevice. There was a lock in the kitchen leading to a basement downstairs. "There's more here," said Madden as he headed to the back of the house through the kitchen. "They're locked in the basement," he told another officer. Two or three more cops walked through the kitchen and there was an officer already attending to a door that was locked by two locks. Madden instructed them to get the bolt cutters to break the locks. They sliced the locks like butter.

As hot as it was upstairs, it was cold in the basement. It was the most reasonable place to keep the harem of sex slaves. Madden ducked his head as he descended the lopsided stairs. Steadying himself by leveraging his weight and placing a hand on the impenetrable crumbling walls with chipped lead paint, he ventured forth passing the only windows that provided light, two small slits on the western end of the house. The foundation of the house was crooked and dug into the square footage of the already cramped living quarters along with major cracks veined across the walls. "A rat hole," proclaimed a female officer with her hand on the buckling ceiling.

She was right. It was a dungeon of modest proportions but a "rat hole" nonetheless. At first the foul stink of rage and angst were the most pervading scents in the dank prison in which the slaves lived, but as the police penetrated the inner sanctum, they could smell human feces from a backed-up toilet, unwashed sheets and waste that was thrown in a corner. The women welcomed the police and thanked them as they were handcuffed one by one. Some women were brought against their will due to foreign abduction, others lured into the abject depravity through ignorance and a few with no consideration for anything else due to dire circumstances that left them seemingly destitute for the rest of their lives and at the mercy of a man like Renaldo to attend to their needs. Strains of mental anguish cursed them during their time there and a police raid was a welcome relief from the nagging beast of indifference that guarded them on a daily basis.

There were twelve girls down there against their will in rancid, deplorable conditions. They were prisoners, no doubt: prisoners of circumstances and mere chattel to Renaldo and his wife. Madden had one person to find and that was Krystal. He wanted to be true to his word, and take her under his care. It was dark in the basement and he called her name. He found her huddled in a corner of the room on an old stained one-inch mattress crying in disbelief. He reached out his hand like a gentleman as if was asking her to dance, and she rose to her feet and collapsed in his arms crying. He held her for a minute as a flurry of activity snowed all around them. He guided her out of the pit and up to the kitchen and out the door. Katrina was attending to another girl who was not holding up too well, but reached out her hand as Madden lead Krystal away from abject destitution.

Katrina was finally able to get away and attend to Krystal in the van. Madden emerged as Cruz watched the scene unfold outside and police led a few girls out of the house and into the paddy wagon that was waiting to be filled.

"So what happens now?" Cruz inquired as they walked back into the house.

"Time to find some evidence," a determined Madden exclaimed. "The evidence we gain here will be used to prosecute Renaldo and his wife, but it can also lead us to others if we're lucky. We need to find information that can lead us to others." He scratched his two-day beard. "It's going to be a long night for Katrina," he said. These girls will be processed at headquarters. Then they'll be charged. It's a sad reality even though they're victims. They'll probably be turned back on the street. Those who want out will be able to go home. Those who need to do it to survive will hustle again or get a new pimp. It's sad," Madden said. They're victimized and re-victimized through a vicious cycle."

"Well what about Krystal?"

"She has a special deal. Katrina will take her to the halfway house and work to get her back on her feet. It's the best we could do. When you get the force involved you have to follow procedure."

"It seems like there could be a better way to help these women," Cruz said.

"Yeah...It does," agreed Madden with a grimace. "I hate to say this, but Renaldo may be back on the streets soon when he makes bail. He'll be back to doing this again."

"With all the evidence we got with the girls?" Cruz asked.

"Even with all the evidence," Madden said like a robot and distant looking around the room. "You may want to see if any of those girls know your girl Rosa. They may be able to help you. Some of those are migrants. They'll be processed and freed. It may be your only chance."

Cruz walked through looking for any girl he could. Katrina had her arms around Krystal as she escorted her out to the van. Rosa?" asked Steve going from girl to girl. One by one he went to each girl. "¿Conoces a Rosa Cruz?" Some looked at him blankly and uttered "No," others looked at him not saying a word.

"Rosa Cruz?" said one of the girls. "She's not here."

"Rosa Cruz? You know her?"

"Yes, I know her." She said. "She used to be here, but I haven't seen her in a week or two."

"I need to question this one," Cruz professed to the officer, patting him on the back with gratitude. The officer relinquished her to him and Cruz gently pulled her aside. "Do you know where she is?

"She *was* here, but she's no longer here," she informed him.

Cruz was taken aback and moved with caution. "I know this has been a tough time for you, but do you have any information that might help me find her? Anything...Do you know where she could've gone?" The girl just shook her head. "Can you tell me what she was wearing when you last saw her?"

The girl tried to recall and placed her hand at her forehead and tapped it as if that would help her. "I think she wore a red blouse," she uttered. She had dark jeans that were ripped. I'm pretty sure she had a red blouse, though. She looked pretty in it. Renaldo gave her a green dress, too. She might be wearing that. He said he wanted her to look like a lady." Cruz took notes and asked the girl for her name in case he would be in need of her for some follow up questions.

Madden continued his quest for evidence and walked to a table in the living room, and picked up a little black book. "Cha-ching," he said. Cruz walked into the house and Madden was smiling as he saw him. "What are you so happy about?" Cruz posed.

"Usually they have their address books on them so they can have it with them at all times. In his attempt to escape, looks like he forgot this." Madden held up the little black book. "This could be a big deal. We look through it and see if we can get any matches. There were some papers there, too. We need to move on looking at this information. When other pimps hear he's been busted, they're going to want to pack up shop."

It was a fruitful night for both men. They were on to something neither one really expected. Such is the luck of righteous men with a will to serve those most vulnerable among them.

PART 3

16

The day was challenging under the heat. Travis, Father Paul and the migrants managed a few miles but found themselves meandering as they searched for new opportunities to crack the code of freedom. They were all sliding into that place where fatigue meets concern, so Father Paul ended the day with scripture. He opened his Bible to Isaiah 35 and read:

> The desert and the parched land will exult;
> the steppe will rejoice and bloom.
> They will bloom with abundant flowers,
> and rejoice with joyful song.
> The glory of Lebanon will be given to them,
> the splendor of Carmel and Sharon;
> They will see the glory of the LORD,
> the splendor of our God.
> Strengthen the hands that are feeble,
> make firm the knees that are weak,
> Say to those whose hearts are frightened:
> Be strong, fear not!
> Here is your God,
> he comes with vindication;
> With divine recompense
> he comes to save you.
> Then will the eyes of the blind be opened,
> the ears of the deaf be cleared;

Then will the lame leap like a stag,
then the tongue of the mute will sing.
Streams will burst forth in the desert,
and rivers in the steppe.
The burning sands will become pools,
and the thirsty ground, springs of water;
The abode where jackals lurk
will be a marsh for the reed and papyrus.
A highway will be there,
called the holy way;
No one unclean may pass over it,
nor fools go astray on it.
No lion will be there,
nor beast of prey go up to be met upon it.
It is for those with a journey to make,
and on it the redeemed will walk.
Those whom the LORD has ransomed will return
and enter Zion singing,
crowned with everlasting joy;
They will meet with joy and gladness,
sorrow and mourning will flee.

As they settled in for the night, there was a quiet whisper of hope singing in the camp as the verses resonated with a few of them. It soon became quiet and the night was full of stars as they went to sleep. Juanita looked to the sky, dazzled by the stars and the seeming movement of a few of them. She leveled her thumb in the air and steadied it to see if a satellite was moving away from it. She'd been told that the moving ones were satellites, and she wondered if they were taking pictures from that far up and could see exactly where she was. The others were exhausted and all fell into deep REM cycles in a short period of time, but Juanita dreamed of possibilities and fell asleep wondering how infinite the universe was.

Juanita was aroused from sleep by Father Paul in the middle of the night. "Juanita, it's time to go…it's time. We've got a chance to get out of here. Come on, let's go," he stated quickly.

She hurried and watched as the others were starting to move toward the northern edge of the boundary line where the fence was located. They were groggy, but it dissipated as the tension and anticipation revved within each one of them and awakened them each to this new possibility.

Father Paul informed them why he was waking them. "We got a call that we have a window of opportunity. They're patrolling the wall, but we have a short window if we go now. It's okay. We're going to be all right."

This particular part of the fence was a wall. It was higher than normal, but Father Paul was undaunted as he pulled out a rope from his bag that had a claw on the edge of it. He swung the claw to the top of the wall hoping it would clear the wall and hang over the side. The first throw didn't make it, but he tried again and it reached the other side. He dragged it and the cement grain was running smooth until it took hold grabbing the edge with a resonant clang and digging into it to ensure a firm hold. One by one they scaled the wall starting with Angelina and Juanita. The climb on one side felt as though they were climbing five stories and Father Paul told them not to look down and just keep climbing. Angelina seemed to be okay, but they heard her plop on the other side with a jerky crash and cry. Juanita was next. It was hard going, but she was prepared for it as their final quest for freedom loomed large and was a primary thought, aside from the delicious meal that would wait for her on the other side along with a long, hot shower. As Juanita reached the top of the wall she noticed how far up she was and panicked. Nonetheless, she flipped the rope to the other side and began her descent. Father Paul was right, she shouldn't have looked back, as it only made her more aware of just how high she was and she was frightened to death of heights. There was cover on the other side, so they hid in the weeds as soon as they were clear of the wall. Juanita met Angelina in the weeds, who was wincing in pain and holding her ankle due to turning it landing off the wall. One by one the group cleared the wall and one by one they gathered around Angelina.

Father Paul examined the sprain and there was no way she would be able to put weight on it. "Can you hop on it? Maybe we can carry you…Stay strong, Angelina, we're on the Holy Way. Put your arms around Francisco and me…we can carry you." They carried her for a few minutes and then came to the end of a road. Father Paul told them that it would be all right and they should put her down to rest. He watched and waited for a few minutes. The car that would carry them to freedom had arrived. Two men got out of the truck and Father Paul went over to meet them. He shook hands and ran back to the group. They helped Angelina to the truck, and she and Francisco piled into the back of the truck while Sancho and Juanita were invited into the cab. Paul said goodbye to them and assured them that everything was going to be all right. They thanked him and Travis. Travis was sad as he said goodbye. "I'm gonna miss you. I wish we could keep in touch. Can we keep in touch, Father?"

"That won't do them any good, Travis. It might compromise their situation and hurt them."

Juanita sat in the cab of the truck with Sancho and watched from the window of the car as Travis waved goodbye. They were relieved as they drove away. The men were nice to them. "What do you like? You hungry for something? Anything you want to eat, we'll get it for you."

"I'd like a nice steak," said Francisco from the back. Can I get that medium well?"

"Sure," laughed the man driving. "We can't get that for you now, but we'll see what we can do."

"Oh, okay," Francisco gleefully replied. "I can wait."

Each was giving their order and the men smiled as they did so. "I guess the desert has a way of making you appreciate things. Especially when you've been in the desert as long as you've been. You'll never see life the same way again when you've seen what you've seen," said the man in the passenger seat.

"That's true," Angelina confirmed. Her eyes fixed on the beautiful country and relieved to be done with the walk.

They drove to a distant place in a quiet, out of the way getaway. There was a two-story house and they brought them in through the squeaky back door. The two men escorted them into the house and directed the women to follow him upstairs, helping Angelina. "We're gonna get you a shower and some food, but first we have to take care of some business." He led them into different rooms. He directed Juanita to the end of the hall. "Go ahead in there. I'll be right in there, once I attend to helping your mother here." The room was dark and had a bed in the corner and a dresser, but for the most part was spare. She tried to turn on the light, but the bulb was burned out. After a few minutes, the man politely knocked on the door and entered the room.

"Nice and cozy," he said. "Before we get you cleaned up, I have a few questions to ask you. You ever work domestic labor before? Can you cook, clean, do things around the house?"

"Yes," said Juanita quietly.

He pulled out a piece of paper and examined it running through an itemized list. "You ever pick fruit? Pick cotton? Do any kind of farm work?" He was very businesslike in his manner.

"A little," said Juanita.

"We're gonna take you to a house. You'll be employed there and they can put you up for nothing, but the price of domestic servitude. You're gonna be all right there." He paused and looked at her in a funny way. "My God, you are a beautiful specimen...Maybe we can use you for other things, too." Her spine tingled and uncertainty tripped the wires of her calm, as he looked menacing and imposed a heightened pretension and asserted power. Juanita trembled as he walked to her, and she reached for the blanket that was on the bed. Suddenly they heard someone banging downstairs in the basement. *"They've taken the boys to the basement, and it sounds like one of them has gotten out,"* she thought to herself.

The man jumped to his feet startled, exited the room and screamed down the stairs to the other man. "What's goin' on down there? What's all the racket?"

"One of 'em has escaped."

"The man or the boy?" snapped the man in the room. "We gotta get him.

"I'm on it," proclaimed the voice from downstairs.

The man re-entered the room and put on his hat that was hanging in his pocket that said, "US Border Patrol" in big, bold letters and as resonant as a neon sign. He turned to her and said in a menacing voice, "Just when you think you're home free, your illusions get the better of you." A shot was heard in the distance. The agent slammed the door behind him and locked it. Juanita ran to the door and tried to open it but it wouldn't budge. She went to the window, but there were bars on the window. She could see the agent outside her window. He ran toward the other man but stopped. The other man was standing in a straddled position with his arms out in front of him and fired again. The small figure was hit and fell to the ground. She couldn't tell if it was Sancho or Francisco. The dark figure wasn't moving. She saw the agent break open the door, move toward the other man and yell to the man in the distance who was standing about twenty feet from the dark figure that was lying on the ground.

"You get him?" called the agent to the other man.

"Yep, I got him. I got him good." Juanita panicked and broke through the window and tried pulling at the bars.

The agent laughed. "You ain't goin' anywhere, sugar." Juanita opened her mouth to scream.

Juanita awoke with a gasp. The night was quiet and her mother heard her and woke with her. "Shhh…it's okay, baby. You were having a nightmare," Angelina said with soothing assurance as she quickly crawled over to her and took her in her arms. "I've got you. It's all right." Juanita sat up and told her mother about her nightmare. She only managed to give her the key parts she needed to hear as the vivid nature of the experience brought a chill and a faintness of heart that made her unsettled. The hope she felt listening to scripture was mingled with her mixed-up emotions of uncertainty, insecurity and expressed itself in the nightmare.

"Our thoughts get jumbled in our dreams when we're

afraid," said Angelina as she peacefully took Juanita in her arms and rocked her until she fell asleep again. Her *"little girl,"* she thought to herself. It was just like when she fell asleep holding her baby in her arms years before. Whether they were dreaming or experiencing nightmares, their circumstances had not changed. They were still caught in the malaise of Mexico hoping for freedom in the States, stranded in the lower depths between doubt and frustration.

17

Eleanor was a gumbo pot of emotions! So much was swirling around in her, so many emotions that she didn't even know where to begin. On one hand, she was worried about her boy and the guilt of sending him over there was starting to get to her since she had not heard from him. He was in his own backyard, but anything can happen even in one's own neck of the woods. She was confident that Father Paul would take care of him, as he was like family to them, and Paul took good care of everyone in his orbit. On the other hand, she was doubly worried about Eben. He was so vulnerable on so many fronts. The law was against him, time was against him and his own physical health was giving out, so his doubt played against him. It was more than she could take and she had a few good cries over the whole situation.

She attended to the ranch the best she could, and found comfort in the animals. She had one of the strangest experiences with them she'd ever had. They knew she was distraught. One day she was feeding the horses and her legs seemed to go out from under her. She sat down on the ground and the mother pushed one of the foals in her direction. She had a little feed and the baby ate from her hand. It was like the mother was sending that horse her way to give her hope. Then she thought to herself, *"That's kinda what I was doing with Travis, wasn't it? I was sending him to those folks to give them hope."*

Then the mother herself came up to her and laid her head on Eleanor's arm. It was like that horse grabbed her arm and hugged her, saying, "It's all right, Eleanor, I've been there, too." She stopped in her tracks and waited a minute. Eleanor found herself hugging that animal and crying for a good five minutes. Other horses gathered to comfort her. *"Isn't that strange? These animals know me better than I know myself,"* she thought to herself.

* * * * *

Back at the hospital, Cruz knocked on Manning's door. Manning was taken aback. "You looking for your boy Guy? He's actually out and about trying to walk to move around."

"I'm actually here to see you."

"Oh, be my guest," Manning said. "Have a seat."

Cruz pulled up a chair. "Thanks. I've been assigned to your case. They asked me to explore some questions that are unclear. Do you mind if I ask you a few questions? You have a right not to answer them, but we sure would appreciate it if you could."

"I don't know if my lawyer would be none be too happy, but I have nothing to hide."

"I guess you know that we've uncovered a tunnel that was found on your property."

"I understand that."

"I'm asking you this, because your lawyer has made clear that you are recognizing the weight of the charges that have been leveled against you. You'll be entering a plea of not guilty, is that right? You still have the right to remain silent."

"I have to abide by what my lawyer has said."

"I'm contacting you because there is a question whether there were financial considerations for the use of the tunnel by private entities. Can you fill me in on that?"

"There were no financial considerations from my end. I saw no money and received no money. Other than that you'll have to refer to my lawyer. I have nothing else to say about that."

"I understand," said Steve. "Our investigations and leads on other cases suggest that others may have used the tunnel for their own purposes. Do you care to comment on that?"

"I don't know of anyone using the tunnel. I didn't personally see anyone come up from the tunnel."

"So you just provided a means for them to enter illegally, I understand that. Our concern is that the tunnel may have been used by other traffickers who used it for illicit activity. There's been a recent conviction of a sex trafficker up North by the name of Renaldo Garcia. He states that some of the people he trafficked my have arrived through a tunnel. I'm trying to get more information on Mr. Garcia, so we can get him for that."

"I'm sorry, I can't help you there," said Manning. "I'm talking against the advice of my lawyer and you should really talk with him about this."

"I understand, sir, but I'm trying to get to the bottom of a situation."

"I'm telling you son, I was not involved in any sex trafficking. It goes against everything I stand for."

"I'm sure that's the case," said Cruz. "We are looking for any leads we can in order to prosecute this individual. If you have any knowledge that you can offer us in the prosecution of this individual, it might help you and your situation."

"Damn, I wish I could help you there. I'm a man of my word. I don't have any knowledge of a sex trafficker name Renaldo."

Cruz took notes as he spoke. He read over his notes. "Much obliged for your time. I guess that'll do that."

"Yes, sir. I appreciate it. I hope you're able to get that sombitch."

"Thanks. I hope so, too. One more thing. The school your grandson attends has marked him truant."

"That's funny, I thought my wife called him in sick."

"Can you tell me his whereabouts?"

"He's visiting some friends in Mexico."

"Got it," Cruz said.

Stillwell returned from his walk being guided by a nurse.

"Hey, there he is. The zombie awakes," said Cruz.

"Whatchoo doing here?" Stillwell asked.

"Just stopped in to talk with Mr. Manning here about some things. I've gotta get back to work."

The woman continued to guide him back into his bed. "Man, it feels nice to move. The little things we take for granted in this life. I have a new respect for those who suffer chronically."

"Yes, sir," said Manning. "I don't know if I ever tasted cookies like these. You gotta try these, Guy."

"I'm a sucker for sweets. My ex used to say the way to my heart was through my stomach. She's right."

"Take whatever you want. I can't eat anymore of the damned things."

"You've gotta keep moving. It's the one thing that keeps us from going crazy. You move and you feel like you're gone somewhere — even though you aren't. It's good for the mind."

"You said it," answered Stillwell. "You and Cruz have a nice talk?"

"Your friend there was asking for my help. I wish I could help him. I suppose you know that I was involved in some activity."

"I like you, Manning, and I don't even wanna know. The less I know the better. I don't want any part of it."

"No, I understand. It's not bad...I just like to be up front about these things. I don't like hiding things from people. I'm getting too old for secrets. Bad secrets sit in the gut and make themselves at home. Then they don't wanna leave. They get to forming all kinds of cancers."

"Yeah, I guess they do. If I've learned anything from being on the force, most people get stuck in their own lies. It's a good thing you're addressing them. I just don't need to know 'em, Manning."

"Good. What's on TV?"

"Wanna watch a game?"

"Sure."

The two men had formed a fraternity in their healing process. They liked one another and the rest of the day was spent chatting about sports and life.

18

Paul awoke early the next morning just as the early strains of sunrise were breaking through the monochrome tint of night. He stretched and saw Travis slowly rise to his feet and turned his head to mouth a "good morning" wish with a smile. They walked far enough away from the rest who were still asleep to speak but still spoke in hushed tones out of consideration for others. "Does this look familiar to you?" he asked walking a few paces and indicating the country.

"Sure. It's a lot like the other side," noted Travis as he scanned the land.

"That's not saying much," Paul quipped under his breath. "Do you know where the patrol house is on the other side?"

"I think it's about ten miles from here. There's a checkpoint and radar check about fifteen miles from here. If we keep heading this way, we should see both."

"How well do you really know this country?" Paul asked pressing Travis with the weight of the question. "That's a very important question, by the way."

Travis was quick with an answer. He wanted to make sure he could be of use to Paul. "I know it from my side. I know the back roads, side roads, crossroads, curves and bends of every mile and trek a' trail in every holler. I could tell you where you're goin' right and wrong. I can tell you when you're lost and will be found, but I've only imagined the other side. I've seen the cliffs and rocky tufts a' brush, but I only know this from what I've heard and imagined." Paul nodded and was lost in thought considering possibilities. Travis was talkative. "My grandpa told me once that we got the good land. We got the land that benefited us and that's how the boundaries were drawn. Based on what I'm seeing here, I think I understand that."

Paul was impressed and appreciated that he was articulate in letting him know. "He's right to a certain extent. The boundaries are always drawn by the needs of those hungry for power. You look at the Sudan and see there are plenty of tribal wars being fought over redrawing the boundaries. They find oil in a part and they've suddenly remembered that the land's districts need to be redrawn. They see water and the water will dictate the spoils of how things are drafted, too. America's unique 'cause its resources run from sea to shining sea. They can provide every need to survive and thrive. Other countries have to make do with what they have, but we have everything, every resource imaginable." Travis listened intently. "Beyond that mountain there it's desert far as the eye can see with a few hills and ranges. We do well to stay close to the mountainside, as it affords us more resources. But it also affords other animals what they need, too," said Paul. "Know what I mean? There's more here than meets the eye. We've got more things hiding and waiting to pounce like that lion. You make sure you keep an eye out for those things, won't you. We need good eyes now."

"Yes sir," said Travis sounding like a soldier now.

"Let's test your knowledge," Paul challenged. "Beyond this corner, what do you think is there, mountains or plain?"

"I think there's gonna be a pile a' rocks that look like piled boulders. On the other side they look like pyramids." They turned the corner and he was right. There were quasi-pyramids with huge boulders that they had to maneuver around. Paul was impressed and raised his eyebrows and feigned being shocked. From this point on, Paul tested him and saw that he knew what he was talking about. He was confident in his abilities to assess possible problems due to the land.

• • • • •

At one point they rested, and Travis saw an interesting figure emerge from behind a cliff. It was a young, wild horse. The brown foal with speckled patches of white and a blaze of white down its nose was curious and Travis knew exactly what to do. He didn't want to pose a threat, so he scrunched down into a submissive position and watched as the foal approached. The grey and white dappled mother came looking for the foal and followed behind. The little horse bowed its head close to the ground, sniffing as if it were looking for something to eat or smelling the territory. It eyed Travis who remained still. The young man slowly mirrored some of the movements of the foal. Francisco came looking for Travis and he told him to let him be for the time being as he didn't want to frighten the horse. Juanita was with Francisco as well and knew what Travis was trying to do. She too, submitted by acting in a passive way and imitated the motions as well.

The horse approached him and cautiously sniffed him. The mother realized that the humans would not pose a threat to the foal, and she gradually ventured to see what was happening and investigated herself. After a while the horse retreated through the pass and back to a band of other wild horses.

Travis was in awe of the encounter. It was exactly what he needed to help him keep his mind straight. He felt as though he'd tasted a bit of the freedom he experienced at home on the ranch. Horses were the things that kept him grounded in the world and this little gift helped him tremendously. He thought about his horses back home and how much he missed them. These horses reminded him that he was still at home in his own skin. Travis returned to the group and told them about the encounter.

They set up camp for the night, and this afforded Travis the opportunity to look into studying his newfound friends. He asked Father Paul if he could stay close to the herd. They were setting up camp about a hundred yards away, so as to not threaten the animals. Paul gave them the okay, but told him to check in before they went to sleep and to keep a safe distance. "Don't stay up too late, make sure you get your rest," Paul advised.

"I will," Travis said with enthusiasm.

"Can I come too?" Juanita asked.

"Sure. If it's okay with them." Her mother agreed.

"It'll be good to have another looking out for you," said Paul.

They kept a healthy distance but were close enough to observe the horses every move. The little foal came back to greet them and welcomed them but was called to be by its mother. The mother of the horse bobbed its head up and down as a playful greeting acknowledging their visitors. Travis said, "She likes us. We can stay here."

"Watch 'em." Travis was fascinated even though there wasn't much movement. He understood their nonverbal communication even in the subtlest form.

Juanita stayed close to Travis which appeared flirtatious but wasn't. She was insecure and innocently clung to him out of uncertainty. "What are we looking at here?" Juanita asked.

"Just look at their behavior and see if you see anything unique happening so I can take a closer look. I wanna see which one's which."

"I don't know if I understand. They all look the same," Juanita wisecracked.

"Yeah, but they're just like people. They all have their own personalities. That's what I wanna understand. Who they are as people — even though their horses," he smirked and sniffed. "See, they all have certain roles they play. There's the leader, the protector, nurturer and the sentinel among others. The leader's the one who they look to for the answers. They take on the role of helping them to find food and water. They can tell us where we need to go. I think I got a good idea a' which one is the leader.

"Yeah, which one is it?"

"I think it's that brown one over yonder."

"Oh yeah, he's very beautiful."

"Watch him. Look how he commands attention." Travis shook his head and was chagrined as he scratched his chin. "I'm thrown, he could be the protector-dominant. "See that?" pointing to something the horse was doing.

The horse didn't seem to move to Juanita, but Travis saw it. "He didn't even move," Juanita said.

"No, look how he carries himself. Watch." They watched for a few minutes and the horses all moved slowly, but she didn't see it. Travis was seeing things that Juanita couldn't see. "That's a tricky one to figure. See, every group a' horses has one who watches out for the rest of 'em. He's got leader traits, but he ain't the leader. A protector tends to be more on alert. They're the ones that if something comes along they'll push the herd away from danger. They'll break up fights.

They're misunderstood and that's where it gets confusing. People think they're leaders when they're actually protectors."

"I see," Juanita said unsure of herself with a look of confusion. She saw a horse start to preen another horse. It moved its long nose and head and waved it along its mane. "What's that one doing?"

"That's a nurturer. She's grooming the other horse. They give each other comfort through grooming. That horse is feeling scared. See how timid she is? They're intuitive creatures, boy, even more so than you or me. Dang, they're beautiful!" The horses settled down and were strewn across the sandy ground for the night. A few had dug in beds and nestled with one another to enjoy their sleep. Travis noted, "Unlike domesticated horses, these animals are free to be true to themselves out here."

"Look, that must be the leader there, no?" Juanita had a burst of excitement at the thought of having identified what they needed, and recognized that one remained standing.

"No, that's just the sentinel. The sentinel will keep watch for the night. The leader's an older one, usually a female."

"You sure do love your horses."

"I've gotten to the point where I could tell what kind of weather we're gonna have or if an earthquake's a comin'. It's strange. When they're restless, I know something strange is happening."

They paused from watching the horse and nestled in their blankets respectively.

"Did your parents teach you about horses?" Juanita asked.

"No, my parents are dead. At least my mama's dead. My daddy's dead in my heart."

"What do you mean?"

Travis spoke as if he were unsure how Juanita would take it and tried to make light of his circumstance. "We lived north a' here. My father left me and my mama when I was just a wee bitty thing. My mama died a couple years ago and left me to my grandparents."

"Lo siento. (I'm sorry.) I didn't know."

"It's okay."

"How'd she die?"

"She died a' Lou Gehrig's disease. It's a mean disease, that stuff. She slowly lost control a' all her muscles and couldn't move her arms or legs. She needed us to attend to her every need. That's when I got to studying horses. I became fascinated with their bodies and how they could move them. I loved to watch 'em run. There was something free about them. I could sit for hours and watch 'em gallop, just fly through the air like a breeze was blowing 'em along. In a strange way they became like family to me. I got to know 'em like family and friends."

"I understand that. I guess we all have moments that make us look for others. The gift is in finding the connection. You were lucky you found that."

"Yeah, I guess I was. I miss my mama something awful, though. Ain't no connection like a mother's love. Seems like that's the 'Love' of all loves if it's done right. My mama, she" — he paused as he tried to find the words — "she knew how to do it right. We were very close. I see it with the horses too. The mothers just take care a' things in a special way. They got that maternal thing that takes it to another level. My grandma told me, 'You wanna know what to do in a tough time, look to a strong woman.' She'll know what to do."

"That makes a lot of sense to me. Mi madre's been the backbone of our group. We lost some friends, and she's the one who has held us all together spiritually. Mi padre knows that too. He honors her word. I find that misfortune forces you into understanding. I understand mi mama a lot better because of this trip. She is our strength and our courage. She's had a tough life growing up, but she rose above it through her intelligence. She was a brilliant scientist who rose above due to her genius. It's very hard for a woman to do well in my country. There is the male bias. She's been able to rise above it."

"I'm gonna have to make a point a' makin' her company," Travis interjected.

"Mi padre is strong too. He's man enough to let her make hard decisions."

The horses were stirring and redirected Travis attention. What he didn't know was that back at the camp, Father Paul and the others were in trouble. They had visitors when Paul, the night watchman, accidentally fell asleep. The strangers watched them like Travis watched the horses and then made their move to capitalize on the vulnerability of the group. Paul woke up, so the stranger attended to him and quietly, but intensely poked the barrel of a gun at his head.

"Don't move, senor," said the stranger with a Spanish accent. "I don't wanna take you down," he warned as he kicked away Paul's gun to his friend.

"We're cool here," Paul said.

"You don't need to talk," the stranger assured him calmly. We don't wanna scare the others too much if we don't have to." The other stranger rummaged through his bag. The others woke up from their dead sleep.

"Hands where I can see them." Each person placed their hands over the heads and didn't move. He slowly walked from each person and unzipped their bags to ensure they weren't packing.

"Do you have any money?" asked the stranger.

"No, we're poor. We have nothing. What we have is in the bag. Take what you need, but please let us live," Francisco stated as his hands shook over his head and he sweat with fear.

"We will take what we need, senor. Gracias, senor. Your kindness is appreciated," the stranger replied with a snarky tone.

They stole the remaining food, water, sunscreen, Paul's gun and bullets most of the equipment like the burner, the flashlight, and whistle, which was used to ward off predators. They left the useless utensils that would not serve them. They were quick about their business and disappeared into the night as quickly as they came.

* * * * *

Travis and Juanita had no idea what was happening. They watched the sleeping horses and laughed as a few of them were snoring and farting in their sleep. The stars were out and the sky was vast. Travis was dozing off to sleep, but found himself aroused when he saw the horses that were in a dead sleep come to life. "Something ain't right here."

"What do you mean?"

"They're waking up prematurely. They're disturbed by something."

"What could it be?"

"I don't know. Maybe we should go back and see if the others are all right." Travis and Juanita jumped to their feet and hastened back to camp with a quick jog.

When they arrived back at camp, Paul was visibly shaken as he looked through his bag to see what the bandits stole.

"They got all the expensive items, anything they could get for money," Paul said. He threw the bag aside and kicked the ground.

"What happened?" asked Juanita.

"We were robbed by *coyotes*." Paul was serious and the others looked ill at ease. "Stay close for the rest of the night."

"They took what they wanted, Padre. They won't return," Francisco assured.

"I think you're right," Paul said with a heavy sigh.

Angelina called her children close to her and hugged them. It was a sleepless night, but they were able to eventually catch a few winks of peace and rest.

* * * * *

In the morning the group roused itself and was foggy due to the night before, but Travis was wide awake and plucky, the first one up. He visited to see the horses and saw that they too were just waking and starting to stir. He seemed invigorated by the presence of the herd.

"That herd is our ticket, Father," Travis reported to the priest. "That may be our greatest blessing in this madness."

Paul was amused but couldn't see the point of its importance. "You mean, *your* greatest blessing, don't you?"

"Ours," Travis insisted. "I got a small brainchild of an idea. Maybe we can hide in the pack. The authorities won't be expecting us there."

"So what do you propose we do?" asked Paul.

"I say we follow them and try to befriend them," said Travis.

"We don't have time to play around here, son. Those bandits took all our food," objected Paul.

"I got a feeling there's power in numbers. I just got this hankerin' deep inside to trust them, to let 'em help us."

Paul took Travis aside and had a heart to heart with him. "I don't know if you completely understand the stakes here, son. If we don't get these people into America and to sanctuary, they'll be returned as political prisoners. Political prisoners are punished by execution, sometimes beheading."

"I understand that, Father, but if we don't do something we could starve or they could die out here unless you know of someone with a tunnel around here? The only way to go is forward. We can take our chances at a crossing, I just think our chances are better if we can look to the blessings that have been given to us, sir."

Paul was intrigued by the idea but taken aback as well. He didn't want to waste time attending to a cheap trick that may not work, but he also knew that they didn't have a better plan for the time being other than climbing the fence and taking their chances being caught by the border guard.

He posed the idea to Francisco and Angelina. Francisco was agitated and grumpy. "I don't like it, senor. It is too risky. I think we have a better chance if we go over the fence."

"I think we need to give it a chance," said Angelina. "If we act too quickly now, we lose sight of the goal. We need to consider this option. We walk and see what is provided."

"We've been walking. That's all we do," countered Francisco. "I'm going batty with," his voice broke off…"No, I no think we can do this!" The veins in his neck were protruding, his eyes were searching the landscape for answers, and he trembled with fear and trepidation. His frustration was getting the better of him as he threw down his hat and kicked it a few feet. His temper was uncharacteristic of him and startled Paul and the kids, like he had assaulted them with his hurt, but it was his breaking point.

Angelina attended to the kids and they let Francisco be alone. “Come, children, help me look for wood for a fire,” she said. They knew the trick but abided by her wishes anyway.

Paul honed in directly on the pain Francisco was suffering and was present to it. “I hear you. I want you to know that,” he said. Francisco was quiet and cried in silence. He was hunched on the ground and shook his head in his knees. Paul didn’t know if he should leave him alone to have his moment or go to him. He knew it was time when Francisco spoke.

“I feel so ashamed! I can’t believe I let my children see me like this,” Francisco said with defeat, collapsing to the ground as if the weight of his circumstances couldn’t hold him any longer. He looked to the sky as his chest heaved and he moaned in anguish surrendering to it all. Paul walked over to him and got down on the ground with him.

Paul said, “It’s good your children saw it. It’s honest. They’ll respect you for your honesty. They needed to see your humanity. This is life. This is suffering. This is what we’re called to experience. You can’t experience the beauty without first seeing the ugly side of things. You can’t appreciate the light without darkness. We need both to truly experience life.”

“I’ve seen enough of both…In my country, I took on the darkness. I fought it with every ounce of my soul. And what do I get? More darkness…All I see is darkness. When will I see light again, Padre!!! When will I see light?!”

There was silence, as Paul didn’t know what to say. “I don’t know. I’m not gonna lie to you. But I know you’ll see it,” he said as he found his voice and the silence let him speak.

“I gave myself to God and he gave me the night. Why do I have to live in this darkness all the time?” I can’t see it. I just can’t see the light.”

"Well, it's always darkest before the dawn, maybe this is the turning point. Maybe this is where it all begins anew for you. I don't know…I *do* know that everyone has a point where they can't take it…Everyone. Everyone hits bottom at some point in his life. They may admit it or not admit it. If you *can* admit it, be honest with it, something new comes to you. If you can't, you live with it. It's like a sickness you carry around with you. You create a lie of the mind that will maintain you but it won't help with the climb from the bottom. It won't help you understand who or what you really are. You'll get stuck in the pity. You'll get mired in the muck of your own indulgence. And be stuck with the vicious cycle of misunderstanding and desolate, inconsolable desperation and helplessness. You'll stay right where you are and never get to see beyond the lower depths. But when you…when you relinquish and turn to the greater part of being — humility, love, gratitude for having lived…gratitude for the air you breathe right now, the love you share right now, the blessed oneness with this life — you've grasped the rope of understanding and are tied to something greater — you've arrived. And you hang on to it. And you pull yourself up with it, and you can climb to realize something more. And I climb with you…and Angelina climbs, and Sancho, Juanita and Travis. And you can get to the top and you can sit at the top…and look at the beauty and the grandeur…You can see the bountiful and the place where you've been. You can take pride that by being tethered to your honest to goodness experience of life, you've arrived and risen above. You can see the place where you once were and know that you've made the climb…wrangled with truth in your hands, your legs, your feet and most importantly your heart. You're gonna get to the other side, my friend.

One way or another with God as my witness, we're gonna get you to freedom. And you will see light! Remember this day. When you're standing in freedom, you'll remember this." Francisco's mood lightened as he thought about what the priest said. He closed his eyes as if to follow his directions. "Stay present to this. Don't forget it. You've got this idea that it's going to be different when you get over there. Look at the ground. This ground here is the same as that ground. Whatever you experience, it's up to you to make it what you want it to be. You've got it all within you. You can take it wherever you go. You can find it here as easily as you can over there. You just need to recognize it and use it to climb. Get up and climb. Keep climbing, Francisco. You can do it." Paul rose from the ground and slipped away to let him have another moment.

Francisco slowly rose from his bed of helplessness and sat up. A light wind blew and caressed his ears and he breathed it in as if to give him wind to rise to his feet. He got to his knees and gulped more air, filling his lungs. He slowly rose and picked up his hat. Paul saw him walk toward him from the corner of his eye. When he reached Paul, the priest put his arm around him and walked his newfound hope to the others.

Angelina consulted the children. Sancho stared off blankly into space not wanting to answer but Juanita agreed with the idea of following the horses. Angelina then attended to her husband and held him. She nuzzled her face in the nape of his neck and he turned his head to subtly embrace her. They said a few quiet words in Spanish. She told him she loved him. Though bashful and still ruminating, offering his new pearls of redemption, he told her he loved her, too. She gave him a delicate peck on the cheek and a soft air of light held his face as he realized *"something greater is at work here."*

Travis was witness to what Juanita had talked about the night before and marveled at the scene that unfolded. He was a bit ill at ease for having suggested the plan and inspired such tumult in the family, but something in his heart told him this was what was needed. Sancho gave in, broke his ambiguous gaze and took his mother's hand. "I want to walk with you, mama. We follow the horses, huh?" he inquired tentative and uncertain.

"We follow the horses," Angelina stated.

Francisco and Paul never verbally agreed, but it was clear that they were going to follow the herd. It was an uncertain path, but a path of conviction in the hearts of a few of the faithful — such a path is a mighty road.

19

Cruz was clued into his destiny of helping Rosa and his obsession with finding this young woman took precedence over other things in his life. His heart wasn't really into his job. He was done with foot patrol for the day and assigned to radar detection. He took over for his colleague sitting at the computer terminal that monitored infrared activity and heat seeking exposure. He looked back and forth between what he was reading and the activity at the fence he needed to monitor. His mind stayed on the case of Rosa.

Perusing the detailed notes that were sent to him by Madden to see if he could see something that Madden may have missed, he looked at a few numbers that showed up more than once. He figured these were important numbers, as the writer wanted to make sure that they were recorded. As he worked through the notes, he noticed a set of names scribbled and a date of Sept. He thought it odd that these names jumped out at him. He noticed that one of the names looked like the name "Rosa" on it but wasn't sure. The "R" looked like a "B" so he asked his colleague if he could make out if it was an "R." He confirmed that it was an "R" and Steve sat up and examined the writings on the page more closely.

At the end of his shift he jumped to his desk and made a call to follow the leads he had in Mexico and worked with a friend there to see if they could get any information on prostitution rings.

"What are you looking for?" inquired his friend from the Mexican border."

"I'm looking for any recent busts that may have connections to the United States."

"I can see if we have any, but that information is usually very well hidden. They find a way to keep that stuff under lids pretty securely."

"I'll take anything you've got," Cruz said. He hung up the phone with his colleague and called Madden.

He talked with Madden about the situation and determined that the number of the person in the black book they obtained may belong to the new pimp who was trafficking Rosa. Checking out the phone information through resources, he learned that the line belonged to Diablo Kinsey. "Diablo… what an interesting name, huh?" Cruz said.

"Why?" Cruz asked.

"That's Spanish for 'devil.' We're truly engaging with a battle against evil," Madden replied.

"Tell me about it."

Madden rifled through a list of past convictions with the name Kinsey, and was amused and immediately noted that it had to be an alias. "That can't be a real name."

"Why?"

"Because Kinsey is an institute that deals with sexual behavior. I wonder if this guy is using an assumed name. Our suspect's being cute by using that name." He checked this out with records on arrests and there was no "Diablo Kinsey" to be found. Madden who agreed to help him, mustered up a plan to consider how they might contact this person. Madden and Cruz decided one of them would play the part of a pimp and see if he could make a deal on a few women they'd just got from Mexico.

"If our suspect is being cute, how'd he get the name?" Cruz asked, thinking out loud.

"He's from up north in Indiana or Ohio," Madden posed throwing his pen against the wall like he was throwing spaghetti to see if it would stick.

"Why do you say that?"

"'Cause the Institute is in Bloomington, Indiana. They do good work there. My guess is that he's been there or knows about it and is using it as a cover. He chose to use an alter ego with an evil twang to it. One of the biggest sex trafficking centers is in Toledo, Ohio. That puts us close to that locale," Madden surmised. I've got a guy up there who's working on stings. We can check in with him and see what he knows.

Cruz spun in his chair. "Wow...unbelievable! I thought we had problems just at the border. This racket's bigger than I thought. There's a whole network of good fighting the battle of evil all across this nation."

"Damn straight there is," Madden noted. Madden dialed up his friend who informed them that he knew of Diablo Kinsey from one of the girls he was trying to help. He owned a bar, but she didn't know the name.

20

The group didn't make much of Francisco's lapse of composure, as each one of them had a bout with fear in the desert and expressed it in his or her own way. It was his turn and all seemed to quickly forget when they headed out following the horses. Francisco's poverty of spirit impacted Travis, though, as it was the first breakdown he'd seen. The weight of exile pierced his sensibilities as the smell of dust and the stink of despair penetrated every corner of his imagination. He blew his nose and black snot that clogged him up ran thick and gnarly. It seemed they ate dust, breathed dust, and became acquainted with every variety of dirt on the plain all the while serving as a feast for tens of thousands of dust mites. The dry heat coupled with the parched earth, made Travis yearn for just a splash of water for moisture — for just a little splash of wetness. What he wouldn't give for a bit of lotion. "You have any a' that sunscreen, Father?"

"We're running low. We need to be conservative."

Travis was embarrassed he asked and quickly hastened to add, "I understand. I don't wanna take anyone's portion."

"No, no, I'm just telling you," Paul quickly added as he pulled out a sample size. Those bandits took the big one."

"That's all right, I'm okay." Travis dismissed it and waved him off.

"Sure?! I don't mind giving it up. I'm good." Paul insisted as he threw it at the boy.

"I'm sure." He did think about taking a whiff to catch the scent of something different. He thought about the smell of the lotion, and how he itched for lack of a bath. Travis was starting to miss the simple pleasures of life, like a shower, a good meal, and a soft bed or even a couch. He hadn't had a good night's sleep and could never get comfortable on the hard ground. He hadn't been gone long, so he could only imagine how the family longed for these gifts.

They walked and all were getting fatigued as they hadn't eaten or drunk in a day since the *coyote* bandits took their water. Juanita was a bit cranky but tried to remain quiet. This was all new to Travis. He was hungry and thirsty. Hungry for food, yes, but even hungrier for this to be over. Hungry for the family to be safe and secure in a place that welcomed them and cultivated hope through the power of community...to be at peace in his home, enjoying one of his grandmother's delectable meals of chili or BBQ brisket, corn, salad and au gratin potatoes and corn bread. For dessert she'd have a batch of her fudge or some pralines and let him lick the bowl and spoon. He was eager to know that his instincts were right in using the horses as decoys. That he could get them to follow and help them. He was thirsty, too. Thirsty for the security of his grandparents' strength and one of his grandfather's stories about his mother, which connected him to a place of belonging. Anxious for the security of his own family and place on the ranch where his horses nurtured that innate sense of connection to the power of ineffable love.

The herd traveled across the steppe near the border but a healthy distance from the fence. It wound its way through sloping hills and craggy valleys of open land. The small foal Travis had met the day before was excited to see his friend following them. Though they travelled at a safe distance, the foal was keen to travel behind the herd, as it wanted to get closer to Travis. Its mother kept it honest, nudging it to move forward and not be distracted, staying with the herd. The group moved slowly but every now and then one of the horses would wander off out of curiosity to play and roll in the ground like an adolescent wandering from a group on a field trip and playing silly.

The mother acknowledged the group by bopping its head up and down, as if to say "hello" in typical fashion as she had done the day before. Once again it was as if she was saying, "you're welcome here." Other curious members of the pack watched them travel and Travis stopped the group when the herd stopped to keep a safe distance. At one point new members of the herd galloped over and slowly examined their new group. Travis taught each of them how to submit in order to gain their trust. They mirrored the horses' habits and chewed on hay they found as the horses chewed on hay.

Things were getting testy in the group. The conversation was slow at times. It was as if there was nothing to say and the sound of another's voice was just annoying. Paul was getting testy, too, as he saw the horses take a new route away from the fence.

"They're leading us away from the border," thought Paul. Paul was paranoid and restless as he angrily scratched his arm in agitation. "We need to head *this* way, don't we?"

Travis understood the subtext of his complaint. "Let's just follow them and see," said Travis. "We need water, and so do they. They know this land better than we do."

"But that could be miles, couldn't it?" inquired Paul a bit exasperated.

"I don't know," Travis said honestly. "I just know that they know what they need and where to get it."

The herd walked to a large mountain range and through a pass. On the other side of the pass ran a small stream, which lead to a spring. Travis was relieved at the sight and a collective sigh went up in the group. Travis likened the feeling to seeing an amusement park and the sight of his favorite rollercoaster. They broke with concern for getting too close to the horses and scurried to the watering hole. The horses didn't seem to mind as they dipped their noses into the water and sucked up the refreshment.

Travis' face hit the water and the dirt from his face dissipated into the silt all around him. He didn't care that he drank a little dirt, as it was a big part of him by now. It tasted a bit like concrete, but to him it was a sunny delight splash of ambrosia, as it nourished him and made him full. He and the others sat by this oasis drinking what they could for the better part of fifteen minutes before he even noticed the grove of trees on the other side. He and Sancho caught the sight at the same time and ran to it. The shade the trees provided quenched them as much as the water that nourished them. It was a small grove of avocados and figs. The avocados were obvious, but he had to search for the figs. Travis plucked one down, as the sticky figs stuck to his fingers and he picked the ripe ones. *"An offering,"* he thought to himself. "We have gifts to give the horses," he said to Sancho. "We need to engage them and gift them to show them that we belong with one another."

Sancho reveled in his pursuit for the perfect avocado. "We can give these avocados to the horses?"

"No, they ain't good for them, but these figs could do the trick." By now Juanita had joined the boys and Travis headed back to the adults. He took great pride in presenting them with food and Paul was impressed.

"You're quite the survivalist, Travis," said Paul.

"I'm just a Boy Scout, but I am working to be an Eagle," Travis replied.

Paul grinned and nodded glowing affirmation. "I don't doubt it. You should get a badge for this one. How about that knife, Francisco?" Francisco quickly handed it over. "Gotta be careful cutting these things," Paul quipped. "The pits are dangerous. They call these cuts 'avocado hand.'" He cut around the skin and revealed the luscious green center of the avocado. He took the knife and leveled a cut on the pit and twisted it out handing one half to Angelina and the other half to Travis. Both devoured the fruit and licked the skin clean. Sancho and Juanita brought more for the others. Travis told them his plan to feed the horses.

The horses made it to the grove and all relaxed under the trees. Travis taught them all how to offer the figs, and the horses were curious as he fed them.

"You been confirmed yet, Travis?" Paul asked.

"No, sir," he said.

Paul shrugged and slightly tilted his head as if to say it was all right. Angelina watched him for a minute. A smile played around her lips and her eyes twinkled as she arrived at an understanding she needed to share. She started to say something but thought better of it. Everyone looked to her to hear what she had to say. Then she spoke finding a better way to say what she was thinking.

"Do you know what a man is, Travis?" Angelina asked.

Travis looked off for an answer. "I don't know. My grandfather's always telling me to 'man up' and be one, though."

Paul laughed. "Yeah, that sounds like him." He reclaimed his wits and pondered deeper as he looked off and watched the horses.

Angelina took on a serious tone and spoke solemnly like she was imparting a sacred truth. "No. A man is one who is secure in himself enough to abide by what he's called to do. He's taken the lessons of learning what's right and wrong and applied them in a meaningful way. He has the innate wisdom and understanding to be full in his humanness. He knows in his heart what is right and is willing to sacrifice all he is to follow that call and take on the world with the conviction that he'll be all right. You're right there." Travis nodded and thought deeply about what she was saying.

Sancho nudged him and smiled wide, as he'd heard this from his mother before. "Welcome to the club."

Francisco was compelled to speak. "That's very true, Angelina. See, some people grow up living like children. They never find that place within themselves to understand what they're called to do. They go this way and that and they let their lives play out because they're living in fear. Yes, sir, I've seen grown men go to their graves acting like children. They never take a stand." He leveled his finger at him and jabbed it with conviction. "You, my friend. You took a stand."

"Si, you are correct. A man takes on life with the knowledge that whatever comes to him is a test and he knows the answers enough to pass it. You've passed the test," Angelina affirmed.

"Thanks."

"You don't need to thank me. It's true," she said.

Paul spoke up again. "You just need to hear it. Sometimes we need to hear it from others."

"Si, I just want you to know that. Whatever happens in life, however anyone treats you from here on out, just know that you're a man. You can sit at the table with anyone, any age and hold your own."

Travis took pride in that fact and wore it well on his sleeve as a badge of honor.

"I'm sorry I doubted you back there, senor," said Francisco.

"Don't sweat it, Francisco, I understand."

"No, no…I lost myself and was scared. I didn't know you well enough to trust you. I thought you were just a boy."

Travis excused it by saying, "Well, I know I still feel like I gotta lotta learnin' to do."

"Therein lies the wisdom, son," countered Paul.

A small lizard scampered across the sand and looked at them all. Sancho noticed the little critter and was fascinated by him. The lizard looked at him as if to smile. Sancho tiptoed and curiously leaned forward to get a closer look. The little creature shot straight away for a boulder, and made Sancho jump.

"What time is it, Padre?" Travis asked.

"It's a quarter to two."

Travis thought about school and how he was missing it. "I'd be in Trig right now," he said. *"They must be wonderin' where I am,"* he thought to himself. He only cared for a moment, though. He thought about his friends and what they were learning. Something deep in his gut told him what he was learning here was so much more important and would serve him in worldly ways he couldn't yet understand or imagine. He felt like it was something that could only be taught here in the hand to mouth wilds of nature. He was thankful for his teachers here. He knew they weren't out of the woods yet and there were more lessons on the way.

21

Back on the other side of the fence, while on patrol Cruz saw movement in the brush and identified a man in a bright orange shirt. "Freeze…Arriba!" The man was heavyset and was sweating profusely due to the desert sun. He looked Hispanic, so Steve spoke to him in Spanish. "¿Habla inglés?"

"Yeah, I speak English."

Cruz had called for backup and the second car arrived. It was the young agent who attended to Eleanor by giving her the injunction. He was in a pissy mood and wanted everyone to know it, including his colleague.

"We're Americans," said the man with his hands on his head.

"We'll be the judge of that," said the agent walking up with his gun armed and ready.

"Please don't shoot. I have friends with me. They're over there. Hey Nina," he called.

"Shut up," the disgruntled agent said.

The woman acknowledged her friend, as she emerged from behind a tree. She had a dark tan, long silken dark hair tapered at her shoulders, and bright eyes with a stunning penetrating glare. Shoulders back, she carried herself with confidence and moved like a woman who commanded an army, but walked with a glide that could be equally graceful and elegant in her manner if she chose. Realizing they were being confronted by patrol, she immediately put her hands on her head with cool detachment and slowly walked to where they were.

The woman pulled out her birth certificate from her plastic lanyard, which she wore around her neck and waved her certificate over her head like it was a white flag.

Cruz acknowledged it with a wave of the hand and wiggle of his fingers entreating her to come closer. "You're all right," Cruz assured her.

"You just keep your hands on your head and don't move them. Hear me?" scolded the officer. "You keep your hands on your head!" he screamed to her and she slowed her pace unsure of what was about to happen to her. She held her hands still on her head until she reached the officers. Then she stood with her legs spread apart, so the officer could search to see if she had any weapons.

"I got it…take it easy," Cruz said coldly to his colleague. Then he directed his attention to the man. "What are you doing out here?" Cruz asked.

"We're part of a group that searches for lost family members. Immigrants. Our job is to find missing persons who've tried to escape across the border and hopefully bring them back to safety. See?" he said sticking his beer belly out to show the lettering on his shirt that read "Search and Rescue" in big bold letters.

"Do you have papers to prove that?"

"Yes, we do. Can I go to my pocket to produce it or would you like to get it from my pocket?" asked the man. He had been here before and knew the drill.

"I'll get it," the other agent said as he dug into his pocket and produced the birth certificate and an ID badge identifying the organization he was with. The agent was aggressive as he also checked him for guns. "He's clean." Then he walked over to the woman and searched her for weapons. She shuddered as he ran his hand up her leg and closed her eyes in fear of him as if to pray. He searched her better than he did the man and dug into her short pockets as he looked for identification.

"I'm wearing my ID around my neck," she informed him.

"You just keep quiet and let me see here," the agent said.

The man continued to speak. "We knew you'd ask for them, so we all carry our birth certificates out here."

"It's getting dangerous out here. You shouldn't be out here at this time of day," he informed him talking like a father as he continued to examine the woman.

"I know, but we saw some buzzards over there and decided to follow them." Steve looked to the sky and saw the two buzzards circling. You can put your hands down. Steve asked "Where do you think this person is?

"He's over there…the man's by a tree over there."

Cruz walked over while his partner guarded the man and woman. The prisoner was situated under the tree and breathing heavy with fatigue and dehydration. He was gaunt, wide-eyed and his black eyes squinted gratitude as he heaved a heavy sigh of relief and placed his hands on his head just like the others had. Just about twenty feet away were the bones of someone who'd gone before him. Searching him for weapons, Cruz spoke to the man and let him know he was going to be all right. He brought him to his feet and led him to where the others were standing. The other officer was standing with the man and woman.

"I'll take it from here," Cruz said.

"We'd like to mark the scene. Do you mind if we mark the scene and list the coordinates, so we can have someone claim the body? Every person deserves a dignified burial."

"No." snapped the officer. "Your business is done here."

Cruz asserted himself by pulling the agent aside. "Look, this is my bust. You're here for back up. I can handle them."

"As back up, you're putting yourself in danger. I ain't gonna be responsible for you losing your life to one of them."

"They're clearly here on goodwill."

"That's what you think," asserted the officer. "Fine, rookie. Fine. You wanna take life in your own hands, that's up to you. But don't go getting me killed, understand?"

"Whatever," Cruz snapped at him. "Look, take the prisoner here, and I'll take care of these people."

"Go ahead. But I want you all outta here soon."

"Oh, yes sir, Daddy," Cruz said sarcastically under his breath. He shook his head and the man in the orange shirt half smiled. "He's not outranking anyone."

"You undermine me, boy? I ain't gonna let you undermine me. You undermine me then *they* start doing that, sombitch." He took his anger out on the prisoner as he escorted him back to his jeep.

Cruz was fed up. "Whatever. Take care of the prisoner. I'll see what we got over here."

"I've got some water for him," said the man in the orange shirt.

"He ain't gonna give him it anyway. He could care less about that guy," Cruz said. "Tell you what, I'll give you guys a ride back."

The man walked to the tree where the skeleton lay. They marked the area with a small post and tied it to the brush marking it like a crime scene with yellow tape. "It looks like this one's been gone for a number of months, said the woman.

"Yeah, replied the man nine months, maybe." They marked the coordinates and said a prayer. Cruz took off his hat while they prayed. They thanked him for his assistance and walked slowly back to the jeep.

"You got any more out here?"

"We have a group of about eight. We are in communication with each other on a regular basis. We keep tabs on each one." As they drove back to the main road, they saw their friends there and gave them a ride as well.

The woman sitting in the front seat extended her hand. "My name's Nina. Thanks for the help."

"Steve Cruz. Nice to meet you."

"You're not cross," said Nina. Steve was confused and didn't follow her. "Your name. It means 'cross.' Your friend was more cross than you." He smiled. "Your colleague loves the power. I hate to think of what's happening to that poor man he abducted. Do you think you can get me his name, so I can get word to his family that he's all right?"

"Yeah, I'll see what I can do," Cruz said.

"How much you know about search and rescue to be out there?"

"We've learned a few tricks along the way," said the man sitting behind Steve.

"I'm part Navajo and part Sioux," chimed Nina. "My people have been searching for lost souls since the beginning of time. Aside from that, I'm a pathologist and former cop."

"Yeah?" Cruz stated with curiosity.

"Yeah, I used to hunt down deadbeat dads who didn't pay their child support. I can find anything."

"Really? That's intriguing to me...so this is what you do on the weekends. Go out and look for lost people."

"This is what I do with my life. If I'm not looking for lost people, I'm looking to help people who've lost themselves, like your friend back there."

"What do you mean?"

"I mean I've made it my life's work to help people understand who they are. Given the opportunity, I can find anyone."

"It's funny I meet you. I'm looking for a lost person now."

"Oh, yeah? Aren't you agents always looking for lost people?"

"Well, yeah, but I mean, I'm looking for someone special. It's a girl from Mexico who's been trafficked. You got any advice for me in my search?"

"Trust your instincts. Most of the time people don't follow their leads. If you trust your instincts, you'll discover things you never thought you could discover. It's strange, but it's true."

"I guess it is."

"See, you're a very principled person, who's afraid of being wrong. People who are stubborn like that don't trust their instincts. You've gotta be right all the time. You've gotta see things your way. You're a reformer. You want to save the world, but you stand in the way of your goal because you don't want to be condemned by anyone."

"That's pretty good."

"You're very detail oriented which is good. You're organized and look at the world in a logical way. That's good but sometimes the world isn't logical. You need other assets to offset that."

"Oh, yeah, like what?"

"Like a heart of compassion. You don't have a lotta patience. You're working on it, but you're annoyed easily."

"You saw all that in just a matter of minutes?" Cruz asked.

"I tell you, my job is to read people. That's why I'm so good at what I do. I know the science, but I know the psychology, too. I've been around the block long enough to know."

Cruz had never had a woman be so direct with him and he was impressed with her. They arrived back at their car and they said their goodbyes. Nina pulled out a card from the lanyard and handed it to him.

"Give me a call and let me know the name of that guy. If I can help you out in any other way, I'm at your service," she added.

"Thanks," Cruz said. He was already thinking of how she might help him in tracking Rosa.

22

In Mexico, for the next few days, the group was closer to the herd and became more acquainted with one another. The horses would venture out a mile or two, but the herd always returned to this same spot for water. They met a few new ones, too. Travis took on the role of training the group to respect and honor the animals. He established trust through imitation of their action and play. He would "fun run" and the horses would "fun run." He would prance and the horses would prance. It was quite a sight to witness when Travis played dead and a horse followed suit the next day with its own rendition of the act upon seeing him. It offered a good laugh for everyone.

Juanita relished the training as much as Travis and was becoming a great trainer in her own right. She even established names for the animals to help them distinguish one from the other. They discovered that the leader in the group was a filly, and they named her Pegasus after the mythological winged horse in Greek mythology. She affectionately called her "Peggy." Pegasus was mix of gray and white with splotches of black that looked like freckles. She was a strapping, muscular animal and wise as she attempted to understand the ways of Travis with a curious turn of the head and a perceived all-knowing wink in his direction when she went along with the program and an intrepid stare when she didn't care to. Travis felt as though she was a go between like a chief and translator for the others.

He could see the respect others had for her. If he couldn't win her over, he wouldn't win over the others.

He didn't assume anything in his tutelage. Paul knew how to be kind to horses, but didn't say anything when Travis taught the others how to massage their manes and scratch them. It was Travis' show and everyone respected his knowledge enough to let him run it. Eventually, Travis established trust that would allow him the opportunity to get on the back of one of them. It was a glorious sight, a "Hallelujah" moment when Travis was able to ride Pegasus. He taught the riders manners for endearing the horses to them. Some of the horses refused to let them ride, but a few became regulars and more and more worked through their apprehension and it became fun for them.

Travis was quite the whisperer. He could see the ones who hurt and the ones who were eager to please. He honored each horse with his approach and through his gentle acceptance and understanding of the animal. This helped him establish profound relationships with the animals. Travis would not get on the back of the animal unless it first "accepted" him. He would "request" the opportunity to ride.

He did this by sitting in an elevated position and at the base of the mountain. The horse ventured close to him and only after asking and having the horse present its back, would he venture to get on its back. He did not venture to ride it right away. The trust that he was able to build would serve him and the others well. It was as if they learned the language and acceptable behavior within the community of their new friends. A ride on the back of the horse was the ultimate act of acceptance and consummate rite of passage for the friendship to mature.

The horses appreciated being fed by their newfound friends and delighted in the figs. Along the way Travis and the others would discover a few other orchards to round out their diet like apples and pears. Albeit the fruit wasn't that tasty due to the drought, especially the ones that were blighted with worms, but they still were able to get their nutrients. It was a stroke of good luck for them.

The bond between Travis and Juanita continued to grow as a result of their common love for the animals. Travis wondered what the view of camp would be like from another vantage point, so he climbed the mountain and was followed by Juanita. Sancho felt like a third wheel and stayed behind. He found some wood to carve and worked on a new piece of sculpture while they tackled the mountain and he whittled away his loneliness.

Travis paused thinking about Juanita as she made her way up the mountain. His heart was light. Every step was endowed by the notion that he was making the climb with her. He wanted to impress her. He knew he impressed her with his horsemanship, but that was nuanced in his romantic notions of the intellect. He wanted to prove to her that he was more of an athlete and protector like he did on fields of play years before when he saw a pretty girl he liked. He outplayed everyone he could in soccer and football to show his manliness. He was the cock of the walk then.

It was new for him to be with a girl. He never seriously dated, as he was too shy to ask a girl out. He always traveled with girls in groups and this was the first time he was alone with one. This girl was different. There was no grasping for topics or questioning of what he should say, or stupid second-guessing or monitoring of his words. He just spoke from the heart with her. She could've easily out-climbed Travis, but she didn't want to show him up. She liked playing the damsel.

"You seem as though you're doing all right in the wild, Travis," Juanita said breathing hard but in a flirtatious way.

"I guess I'm good at certain things and survival's one of them." Travis was out of breath, too, so he stopped, humbled by her recognition of his gift. "I'm ahead of the curve on my badges," he boasted. His long boney fingers reached for her dainty hand. It was the first time they'd touched to his knowledge and it sent a shock of realization running through him and a subtle tingle of mystery, a shudder of anxiety climbed his spine. Her bold, deep brown eyes searched his as she quietly thanked him with a look and smile.

"You wanna stop here a sec?" he asked.

"Sure," she replied.

"Seems like your momma and daddy know a thing or two about survival."

"They should. They were both from El Salvador. They were young when they escaped persecution there."

"What happened?"

"They were both very poor. El Salvador was a country at war when they were growing up. The rebels fought the government over land reforms. In a time of war, the poor are the ones who suffer the most. Government thugs would kill someone who was poor, throw them on the doorstep with a note to someone they wanted to scare and would blame it on the rebels. Rebel thugs would do the same thing; kill a poor person and blame it on the government. Who's in the middle?"

"The poor," conceded Travis under his breath.

"It became a no-win situation," Juanita continued. "They lived with death all around them and had to escape it. They went to Guatemala and it was no better there for them. It got *really* bad there, too."

"What prompted your dad to become political in Guatemala?"

"Necessity. He saw too much death and was just tired of it. He didn't do what he could've in El Salvador because he was too young and scared, so he did what he could in Guatemala. He felt he had no choice. If he wanted a better life for us, he needed to take a chance and speak up on our behalf."

"I imagine your parents have seen some horrifying things."

"We all have. When you're surrounded by death, you approach life differently. Everything speeds up when you're close to death. You get a deeper understanding of things quicker."

"What do you mean? Travis inquired.

"Remember that boy I told you about who died?" Travis nodded. "Well, there were more. We were traveling with a group. First, the father died, then the son died. When the mother lost her son, she lost hope. When she lost hope, she lost everything.

It was very interesting to witness this, though. When the mother lost her husband, she told her son as much as she could. She told him her every feeling and thought and didn't hold back. She tried to inspire him to live to carry on the name. When the child lost hope and died, everything quickened for her. She was sensitive to death, to life. She was thoughtful about the world around her, the horrors and its beauty. I knew she wouldn't make it. I could tell by listening to her that she didn't have the will to survive. She saw the world in a new way. When we lost that whole family, my parents were much more sensitive to one another. They were much more aware of being present to each other. I guess it's what helped to get us here. My mother and father would point out the beauty to us amidst the chaos and death. Love has an interesting way of expressing itself when you live close to death. You see it in bigger ways. You have to. It's the one thing that can carry you."

"I guess it would. That makes sense," Travis said stunned by her words.

"Everything in my life is faster," she continued. "In my country the poor start families and have babies at younger ages. They don't expect to live as long, so they start younger. When we buried those people, I wondered if I would make it across the desert. I wondered if I would live to have children, or kiss a boy for that matter."

Travis looked deeply into her eyes. He wanted to tell her that she could kiss him, but didn't have the nerve to say it. "You wanna climb some more?" he blurted with discomfort.

"Boys are oblivious," she thought to herself. "Okay."

They climbed again. "Dang, it sure is a different perspective from up here, ain't it?" said Travis. From the top they could see the range for miles. Below at the camp, Angelina and Francisco were blocked by the shade of trees, but he could see Sancho whittling away on his piece of wood and Father Paul could be seen reading his Bible. He pointed to some of the horses and called them by name. "See Peggy and Lightning and Daisy there…?" It was a clear day and they could see beyond the camp all the way to another range and glimpses of the fence. "Lookey there! See that over there is America." Juanita's eyes grew big as she looked down the end of his arm where his fingers were pointing. For a moment she paused in awe and he could see it glowing in her eyes.

"That's where we're going," she spoke with excitement.

"That's where we're going," he reiterated with confidence. "You like these mountains, you'd love Colorado and Utah. My grandpa used to take me up to Colorado. We'd drive along and the flowing rivers would...would..." He thought to himself, *"Cuddle right up 'gainst the nook of a mountain like a lil' child clingin' to its mother. We'd just wind our way 'round the mountain, stop and look, ponder and dream, laugh and shoot the shit outta the day with nowhere to go but each other's thoughts."* Travis couldn't get the words out and fumbled, but Juanita could see what he meant in his mixed up manner and passion for wanting to express it. "Man, those Rocky Mountains with their cliffs and beauty...They take the words right outta ya'. Make you look dumb and sound stupid like me right now."

"Take my hand, Travis. I'm afraid of heights."

"Well, why didn't ya' tell me?" She shrugged her shoulders and played coy. "I ain't gonna let anything happen to you." He took her hand and pulled her close. The message was starting to resonate with him now. "You can see everything from up here." Juanita was quiet. He pulled her close, and she curled up like it was too much for her. He pulled away to examine her face more closely and she wondered what he was looking at. She saw in his eyes that he just wanted to look into her heart. Next to the death she witnessed, it was one of the most sincere moments of her life. This was the moment she waited for, and it was worth it. They were drawn in to one another. He kissed her. It was his first kiss and hers as well, and it was an awkward kiss, as they both looked at each other while doing it. Then Juanita closed her eyes and Travis followed suit. They lost themselves in each other for a minute.

"Have you ever done that?" Juanita asked.

"Nope. Well, I kissed a girl in third grade, but that was just a nice one on the cheek. I ain't really kissed anyone on the lips before."

"Me neither."

"I think we did it right. You made me shimmy in my boots." They laughed and kissed again. The world looked different to them now. The dreamy daze of endorphins kicked in as they peered into each other's eyes and held each other close. Juanita found a connection she was longing for, a sense of security in someone.

It was merely a kiss. The kiss was just a byproduct of something deeper for the two of them. Branded in recognition of the power of love, if they never touched one another again, they had visited a secret place each could retreat to. They found a place to hold each other; that space that envelops all that comes into its orbit and inspires each to recognize comfort in connection to something greater. It was the space of healing and a balm for the suffering soul. It was a space of confidence where they knew they could get through the next episode of life having gone deeper together. It was rooted in the first love of God and a soulful recognition that there was something more to this life that was gifted in the presence of love. They unlocked the doors of the sanctified place in the heart.

Travis marveled at her beauty and worldliness as he played with her silken hair. They stayed up on the mountain for a short time, talked and laughed and became more acquainted with one another. When it was time to go, they both knew it. He didn't know when or if they would be intimate again. They both knew they had to keep it quiet for the others, as she didn't know if her parents would approve — oblivious to the fact that the others already sensed it when they trained the horses.

Descending the mountain, Travis spoke from his heart. "You've seen so much more than me. I ain't never been outta the country. Here you are, seems like you've lived two lives in one," quipped Travis as he banged a branch against a rock.

"I often thought about the world and what it's like on the other side of the ocean. I wonder if everyone lives the way we live. I guess everyone worries about their next meal. Everyone worries about finding shelter from storms, and people stealing their things. It just happens in different ways for them. Anyway, I get the feeling I don't need to go across the ocean. You've made me happy showing me this and taught me more about life since our worlds met. All I need is right here and now," she postulated.

As they were closer to the camp, they kissed one more time for good measure. Both were triumphant in their hearts and walked away from each other as if nothing happened, meeting the others at the camp.

23

It wasn't long before Cruz called Nina thinking she might be able to help him. He wanted to take her advice and trust his instincts. He called her to give the name of the man who was taken into custody, and she thanked him for that. He asked her out for dinner to discuss the case of Rosa, and she accepted. She was sincerely curious about the case, and he'd given her all his notes as she requested. After a few days, they met for dinner to discuss the next possible prospects of making inroads at helping to find the young woman. She had discovered some very interesting facts.

"Well, I think I've got a lead. You think you can get your friend to connect us with his friends up north?"

"I can sure try," said Cruz.

"We've gotta move fast. They're going to sell off these girls after the bust on Renaldo. They're probably already doing that, or making other plans in light of the new situation."

"What's the plan then?" asked Cruz.

"We need someone to go in and pose as a potential client and trafficker to see if I'm right."

"Who we gonna get to do that?" Cruz asked half knowing what was on her mind.

"I think I can handle it," said Nina.

"You sure about that?" Cruz was dubious.

"I've got a number and an address."

"That can be dangerous business. I don't know if I like the idea of you doing that."

She saw that he was genuinely concerned. "I told you this was my work before I was a forensics analyst. I can handle myself pretty well."

"I don't doubt that...I just...I don't know."

"Haven't I proven that I'm resourceful?"

"Yes, you have. Which brings me to my next question. How'd you get this information?"

"I told you I'm a master. I did what no man can do. I got inside the mind of those women."

"How'd you do that?"

She looked at him with a slow burn, and he looked back realizing it was a dumb question. She smiled and said, "I interviewed every single one of them at the pen. None of them made bail, and I asked questions. I cared and they opened up to me. Her mind went back to the interviews:

"How'd you get mixed up in all this?

They shrug their shoulders and shake their heads like they can't figure it all out, but then you ask them questions and get them talking to look for common threads.

"Where you from, sweetie?"

"Up north." One by one they all said the same thing. "I'm from Detroit, Detroit, Detroit, Detroit! Bankrupt city, struggling city, bad housing market, depressed economy," I thought to myself. Most vulnerable people live there, easy to exploit. They exploit the weakness of the poor. What else is new there? "You come down here on your own?" I asked.

The young woman said, "No, ma'am. I come down here 'cause he brought me down here."

"He" being Renaldo?

"That's right."

"You come alone or with anyone else?

"I come with other girls. He likes to do that. He brought about three others with me, but I've come back and forth between being up north and down south. It breaks things up, so it's not as obvious. He takes us where he needs to take us for the traffic flow and money."

"One of the largest sex trafficking centers in the country is Toledo. It's close to Detroit, so they can make the ride in about an hour."

"These things are like viruses. Focus in on the symptoms, isolate the problem, and go in for the kill with the right medicine. I've isolated the problem to this location up north. This suspect's got a partner and may be tied to a network. They should've busted them together. He's got some inventory to get rid of. The connections are strong and go back a number of years, so we may be able to get some old ones. Any recurring numbers on the hard drives of the computers?"

"Not yet. We're still processing those. How do you know about the old connections?" Cruz asked.

"It's an old boys network. They need to trust one another in order for this to work. They can work from state to state, so the local feds can't get a beat on them. When they do, they can work from another position. It's a shell game. It just keeps the money flowing and keeps the powers that be on their toes. I bet if you run this name on the computer, you'll find it coming up more than most."

Cruz's eyes lit up. "Running names. Sure. That makes sense," he repeated.

"Look for the ATM's and see what ones they use most, and that'll give you a locale. That's federal, so you'll have to get the FBI in on this if you want a big bust.

Anyway, they looked at job opportunities and were brought against their will when they signed on for work as models or dancers. They capitalize on the greatest weaknesses — fashion and looking good. I looked up those opportunities online and found a common number for those operations. It was a business with the local number. Tracing those numbers are easy. They need to utilize what they can to be efficient and pose as legit businesses. They can't keep changing numbers, as that would disrupt the flow of business. Keep in mind that you can learn a lot about someone from her doodles and the book has a lot of doodles. The doodles boxed in the name more than once. It was screaming for my attention. It was like there was a code in the book that kept popping up. "Pinky." Guy's obsessed with the singer, right? Wrong. Fashion line? Maybe. Guy's not a guy, but a gal.

"Pinky is a silly name," he thought to himself. "It sounds so ridiculous. This can't be."

She continued. "I asked the girls for locations that were familiar to them. It's hard to get info when you become dead to the world. You don't pay attention. But there was a common name coming up. It was a nickname…it's only mentioned once in the book, but it was there under the name of 'P. Whitlow.' The name the women told me was a nickname… 'Pinky.' The partner up north is a woman, which makes sense. Women perpetrate a majority of the crime connected to these things. Can you believe that? Women sell other women for their own financial gain. All the girls met at a particular bar. The bar was the cover for the operation. 'Swing Tango Lounge.' There's only one Swing Tango Lounge up north and it's up north in Toledo."

Cruz tried to process this. It was all so much to take in, but he was impressed by her intelligence and was taken by her.

He was intimidated by her, though, as she was smarter than he, and he played with his food as he ruminated on this fact.

"What's wrong?" It wasn't the first time she saw a man glaze over with that vague distant look, but she hated to see it on their first connection together and her eye twitched with discomfort and she frowned. Even posing as a clown, she still looked like a model, and he blushed at how cute she was to him.

"Nothing," said Cruz. "I'm just thinking…the LLC. Why would there be a Limited Liability Corporation?"

"Right?" She got excited. "One number came up as an LLC. Why would an LLC be in a pimp's book? Because by incorporating, they can hide their other businesses — subsidiary work. Just like the mob. They use beards for cover or operations to mask the seedy underside of what they're doing. I then looked at the numbers that were listed for those areas. There were common patterns in the numbers. I then looked at zip codes and deciphered what the most common codes were for them. I found that we needed to be clear about where we're going and why we need to go there before we do." She was so excited that she lost herself in what should happen next. "I'll make you a bet that the two people we're trying to capture are not men. I'll bet you a dinner they're women. They're going to know where she is and we're going to get them!"

24

The Mexican camp was growing tedious with lethargy at considering any other possible alternatives to their plan. They figured they would try to make it to the fence in the next day. They wanted to explore opportunities and weak spots that might allow them a chance to make a break. They could see possibilities in the terrain from the top of the mountain. Training continued and one by one they were able to get on the backs of the horses. It was time to consider a plan of attack. Travis would hope to lead the group of horses.

"I hope this works," said Travis as he fed Pegasus a small piece of fig and walked away carrying the rest of the fig with his arm extended so she could see it. He figured that by feeding her every twenty feet or so, she would follow him and inspire others to do the same.

Peggy was curious but uncertain at first. She looked at Travis who was walking away with the fig. She wiggled her ears and looked straight ahead. She was in front of two other horses, one horse looking at her and the other horse looking at the horse's butt. Pegasus slowly followed and the others followed her. One by one they journeyed to the fence forming a mule train. They took enough to feed themselves and the horses to feed them along the way.

The horses followed them, and more and more horses emerged from different places. It was like bands of horses rallied to support one another and a message had gone out into the horse world that help was needed. There were hundreds of them. The group walked the plains and came upon the new range of mountains that sloped along the border. The steppe was vast and one could see the radar towers in the distance. They looked like markings for oil wells and were planted sporadically throughout for a stretch of a few miles every few hundred feet or so.

"We need to explore the scope of the landscape at night," said Paul. "We need to keep a lookout for any tracking devices, though, so stay low and watch for them." They walked the perimeters to look for an opening but none were to be found. They sought any opportunity for an opening but the border was tight and opportunities seemed closed off to them.

Travis saw a gap on the hill. It looked treacherous, but he thought if they could get the horse through there, they'd have a chance. He pointed it out to Father Paul. Paul questioned whether they'd make the leap of faith.

"We could only hope," said Travis.

"It may be our *only* hope," countered Paul.

* * * * *

Francisco looked for his wife who wandered away from the group. He found her in a rock crevice looking as if she was lost in the landscape of indecision with a pained look on her face.

"What's wrong," he asked, his smile slipping away.

"I'm not feeling well..."

"What is it? your stomach?"

"My legs. I don't feel like I can move them."

"Did you do something? Francisco asked in quiet panic.

"I can't seem to move them," she uttered under her breath.

"You turn an ankle?"

"No…"

"Twist your knee?" He persisted.

"No…"

"Where is the pain?"

"Everywhere," she snapped pounding the ground. "It's everywhere. It's here," she said pointing to her heart. "It's here," indicating her mind…"It's everywhere," she said exasperated as she threw up her hands at the whole environment. "Can't we just stay back at the watering hole?" Angelina questioned as Francisco shook his head as if it were absolutely out of the question, but he remained quiet out of respect for her. She continued knowing that he wasn't going to budge. "This is an impossible situation for us. I don't know what to do. In my mind I know we need to go over there, but something is holding me back. Something is telling me that tremendous pain and suffering awaits us over there. I feel like I can't move. I'm crippled…paralyzed. I look at the gifts of the last few days and think this is the place we need to be. We have everything we need here. We have food and family and so much love."

"We need shelter," countered Francisco. "All it would take is one bad storm to take us out. Besides, you've heard Padre Paul say it would be impossible to get political asylum in any of the banana republics. Our only hope is America. We need to try and make a life…"

"I know that," she said as she shook off the impossible nature of the situation. "I know."

"There's a reason why no one is here. The land is not conducive to our survival over the long haul."

"But we have so much…these days have given me so much hope here. I'm so tired of the suffering in the desert…so tired."

"I understand, baby, we may be walking into tremendous hardship, but we need to try. You've said that we can endure anything together." She nodded and looked off knowing those words would come back to bite her when she first said them and realizing it was all coming to fruition. She hoped the next spree of frightful images she imagined herself admitting would not come to pass.

"I guess it's my turn to doubt, that's all," said Angelina.

Paul interrupted the conversation. "Francisco? Angelina? Are you all right?"

"Si, Padre. We're over here." Paul wandered over and saw the concern on both their faces as he asked if they were okay.

"We're just a little scared," said Francisco as he looked to Angelina. "She's scared about crossing over."

"I understand," said Father Paul, as he bent over and caressed her arm in understanding. "We're all a little scared. This is the time we need to rally together. If we stay here, the Mexican guards may find us. We won't have the sympathy of the Mexican government. The only thing we can do is keep moving forward and pray. As long as we're in it together, we can do this. I know we can do it. We must have faith that we're doing the right thing. We've been provided for like manna from heaven. We've been blessed with the gifts of food and water. If we don't make our move soon, we'll lose our chance to stay here. It's just as dangerous here as it is there."

"I know," Angelina said as she continued to shake her head.

"Every hope and dream is there, over that fence. Every chance for life for our children waits for us over there. We need to remember the gifts of America. It is the place where hopes and dreams come to play…it's…it's the place where justice lives and opportunity…it's the home of fortune and plenty," said Paul. She remained silent. "You're looking to dive in to the pool of the unknown. It's like jumping in a pool when you feel the water is cold. Sometimes you just need to jump in and the water will get warmer."

"I guess that's the case," said Angelina. "I can't jump in the pool. If we get caught, we may be separated. I feel secure with my family. The next step may be separation and that's what I'm afraid of…losing my family."

"I understand," Paul said, knowing he didn't need to say anything else for there were no guarantees that she was wrong.

"Please don't say anything to the children. I just need a little time to process this.

"I understand," Paul said. Francisco hugged her and held her close as she choked up. Paul let them have their time alone.

"I'm not going anywhere without you," said Francisco. "Nowhere."

"I'll be okay," she said muffled in his shirt. "I just need to be alone for a minute."

Francisco gave her one more kiss and walked away joining Paul.

"I don't know what to make of it," Francisco said. "She's been the one saying we need to do this. She's the one who's been the strength. Now she doubts."

Paul was quick to reassure him it would be all right. "It's what psychologists call a double-bind situation. She feels like we're in a no-win. She has two options and both of them stink. She has to choose the one that makes the most sense to her. She's thinking practically. You can't knock her for that."

"It's critical that we stay together, though, Padre. You said that yourself."

Paul was organizing his bag. "I know that. But think of it this way, Francisco. She's like our Mother Mary, another example of a refugee who was initially caught in a double bind. Mary was uncertain when she needed to take her leap of faith in saying, 'yes' to accepting the tremendous responsibility for giving birth to the Savior out of wedlock. There was so much against her — so much she needed to conquer in facing the horrors of the world in accepting the responsibility. That society couldn't accept a single woman having a child out of wedlock and without a husband. She could've been ostracized — or worse — stoned to death for claiming she was pregnant. The shame she felt, the shame she would impose on Joseph…All of it was problematic. It took her time to arrive at the fact that she would be all right. She needed to rise above it and elicit her faith to be true to what she was called to do. That's what Angelina is experiencing now. She needs to rise above and answer what she's called to do. Sometimes it takes a little longer when you face chaos and confusion. She's a tough woman. She'll be all right," Paul said.

"I hope so," Francisco uttered. "I hope so. I must admit, I never thought of the Holy Family as refugees.

"That's exactly what they were. They were expelled to Egypt and left to the kindness of strangers in crossing the desert. No one thinks about that when considering the issue of refugees." This gave something more for Francisco to ponder. It's funny how a simple fact can inspire courage and strength in someone. He was empowered thinking about this.

25

The kids had no idea this was going on as they were looking for more driftwood for Sancho's art. He was excited about some of the pieces he found to carve into some art and they were excited for him.

Meanwhile, a slithering cretin poked its large triangular head outside the hole near the rock at the base of the hill. Its blank elliptical eyes were set back, blending with its symmetrical diamond pattern and beautiful black and brown scales. Its pit organ was working with its slack-forked tongue sniffing vibrations and sipping danger as it hesitated and moved, hesitated and moved in a methodical and seemingly orderly fashion. It finally slithered out and glided through the pebbled sand and brush, its strong cylindrical body in tow and its button rattle shaking to fend off any possible intruders. It posted itself by the shade of brush and coiled to make itself small.

The kids were in giddy spirits as they made their way through the brush, eyeing potential harm and searching for pieces of deadwood. Sancho was laughing as he moved through the brush and stopped looking for wood for a minute to lighten the mood. He was giggling with Juanita and imitating his old principal to raise her spirits. "Juanita, what do I always say? Hmm." He spoke with a cartoon accent with his hands folded on his belly and his head downward with a fake scowl and puckered lips. He waited for her to answer and she was slow to give an answer, but smiled and encouraged him.

"I no think I know, Senor Garcia, what do jew say?" Juanita inquired, playing like a dumb cartoon character.

"I say dat jew are a berry sad girl...berry, beeeerry sad. Jew make me berry sad. Jew have no sense!" he proclaimed and Juanita laughed.

Sancho was standing just feet from the snake and was in a zone and taken with his own performance. The rattle wasn't heard. The snake vaulted forward and bit Sancho in the leg. He was distracted by his silliness as he imitated the walk of his former principal to impress her. It felt like the violent sting of a bee, but its fangs leveled a healthy dose of venom. Sancho knew right away the snake had struck him and his eyes got big and bold with fear. "Ahhhhhhhhh, snake!" Sancho screamed as he jumped back and watched the creature slither to another position in case his victim didn't get the message. The snake recoiled and watched as Sancho stumbled backwards into the arms of Travis.

"It's a rattler!" Travis exclaimed as he watched it reposition itself and heard the rattle in full maraca-like measure.

Juanita gasped and nervously shot out the first thing that came to her mind. "You okay?" desperately hoping her exclamation was true.

"I didn't even see him," proclaimed Sancho.

"Come on," Travis said as he pulled him close and protected him as they searched for more predators of the same family in the area. Sancho hopped to a clearing and Travis dragged him away as he fell to the ground. Juanita called to her mother and father. "Don't move," said Travis.

Angelina was startled to her feet. She limped along as fast as she could with a furrowed brow of concern. Father Paul and Francisco were close behind.

"Is it deep?" Paul calmly probed and examined the leg with a physician's eye.

"It pricked me," said Sancho. I'll be okay, right?" his denial evident in his frightened look.

Paul was strong and positive saying, "We gotta get it out. Juanita, run to my bag. Thank God those cretins didn't take the snake venom." Juanita ran for it but he called to her. "Nevermind, I'll get it myself. I know where to find it," Paul said but she continued on with him. Angelina held Sancho in her arms while Francisco took the knife that was on him and wiped it clean. He examined the cut and put pressure on the wound to isolate the flow of venom. We need to suck it out of him. If we had fire, we could sterilize the knife and cut the leg."

"We need to get that out of him," Angelina hastened to add. "Quick, while we can."

Francisco was deliberate and examined the leg as Paul arrived back.

"I hope this does the trick, but we may need to suck it out," said Paul.

"I'm one step ahead of you, senor," Angelina said. "Couldn't hurt to do both, could it?" Paul concurred.

"Wait a minute," Paul said as he took the water that he got from the hole and wiped clean the knife. Sterilizing it on the fly. He cut into the leg just enough to get the small area clean. Angelina sucked the blood out and spit while Sancho cried and Francisco kissed the boy's head and comforted him. Francisco took over for her and they reversed roles. Being a scientist, Angelina was the most competent in attending to him, so she injected him with the anti-venom.

"We need to keep it elevated…He can't walk on it." Paul observed.

"You'll be okay, Sancho. It's all right, buddy," Paul said with rote assurance. "We got you covered here." Francisco and Angelina traded places and she tenderly stroked his hair while Francisco bandaged the wound with his shirt. He'd cut a tourniquet from the bottom of his shirt. Sancho closed his eyes and huddled as close to his mother as he could. He grew cold and shivered with shock.

"Get him a blanket, will ya', Travis?" Paul calmly asked. "We get you across the border, we get you some nice Taquitos and some enchiladas. Won't that be nice, Sancho?" Paul posed to distract him from his plight. He searched for something to say. "Travis was telling me about his grandmother's specialty of Jambalaya. You're gonna love the Creole cooking of his grandma. She's a belle from Louisiana. She's got some down-home meals in mind for us when we get there." Travis was on it and ran to Paul's bag as fast as he could and arrived back with the blanket. Sancho lay still and closed his eyes. Francisco took over for Angelina, as he was too big for her to carry.

"I help you?" Paul inquired, but Francisco waved him off.

"We get him to camp. It's not far. I can manage. My boy," said Francisco, "my brave boy."

The snake watched this scene all unfold without so much as a rattle.

26

On the other side of the fence, the Border Patrol was keeping watch for any suspicious activity. The midnight watch arrived. Cruz sent out the pet aerial drones they named "Dragonlord" and "Cyclops" from the field office to check the area for any movement east and west of the fence. The birdlike drones with big eyes for heads and sprawling wings that mimicked the spans of vultures zipped across plantations. They swooped through craggy valleys and cavernous nooks, danger zones, hideaways and crannies of ill-fated escapes; dark landscapes which shone in the cover of a green glow of the Mexican horizon. They positioned themselves to eye culprits with a 360-degree view, but were limited in their scope to move beyond what the human eye could see. Swiftly traveling along the fence swooping and swaying like a bird in flight dipping and diving to pounce on potential prey, the night vision cameras could detect everything that was moving in the area and give them a good idea if anyone was trying to clear the fence under the cover of night.

Meanwhile, Cruz's partner was on the heat-seeking radar at the post. These two monitoring techniques would suffice in preventing any being from passing illegally. The only sign of any movement in the night was a small herd of horses gathering just over the other side of the fence in the distance. He was preoccupied as he sensed that it was unusual for animals to be moving at this hour of the night, but he moved on to other matters that were more pressing that he hadn't been able to attend to during the day.

The infrared signals indicated that there was no movement at the fence, but this was soon to change with the arrival of some animals.

27

Light has a way of opening the gates of the unknown to those who are willing to search peril for hope. The family would soon learn this lesson as there was no choice for them now but to cross the border and quickly, so they could get Sancho some help for his snakebite. The only way out was by moving forward in the cover of night. Paul looked at Sancho's leg and they initially thought he was responding well. Sancho was quiet with dread and eventually fell asleep, drifting in and out of consciousness. He was feverish and his leg was blowing up and looked jaundiced. It was determined that Travis would take Sancho with him on Pegasus. Paul feared that the anti-venom was old and not effective.

"We need to get him to a doctor who can look at him. If we can get across the border, we may get sanctuary in a church to get him help. It's the only thing I can think of. We can't take him to a hospital. They'll know he's not supposed to be there, and we risk our chances of being discovered," Paul posed.

"I know a doctor. I think she can help us. Maybe we can take him to my church just outside of town," Travis hastened to inform them.

"Good," Paul replied. "Can the doctor keep a secret?"

"I think so," Travis said.

"I agree, Padre. It's time," Francisco replied.

"Travis, you take the lead," Paul affirmed as he rubbed the back of his horse for good measure and blessed him with a hug.

They looked to the craggy cliffs, and Travis walked Pegasus to the gap, a graveled nook that opened between the ledge and a rocky three-foot jump. Erosion had played its role in the mission of the hopeful travelers and an earthquake that damaged the fence weeks earlier providentially assisted them in making the leap of faith to freedom. They carried Sancho over the fence on the back of Pegasus and Travis served as a handler for both making sure that Sancho stayed on the horse. One by one they started through the gap and the horses leaped through the gap like a gushing flow of water spouting from a sewer. What started out a band of ten became a herd of twenty then thirty, then forty and fifty or sixty horses and what seemed like a hundred crossing the border. They galloped across the field staying together and sounded like thunder as the mass of animals filled the space and galloped in a liberated pace.

28

Apprehension, disillusionment, consolation, determination and steadfast conviction were all appropriate emotions used to explain how Cruz was feeling this night, as he worked the "infrared radar analysis room." He watched as a mass of red and yellow splotches meandered into view. He couldn't quite make out what that could've been but it was slowly moving to the border.

There was a lot on his mind this night. Considering how they might make further progress on the situation with Rosa the following day, he examined potential leads brought to him by Nina that could break open the case for him. His mind raced with possibilities as he considered their plan to make a bust in the North with the help of Madden and his friend from the FBI. What could go wrong? What should we do if the plan goes awry to keep each other safe? Such questions preoccupied him for the night.

The slow red and yellow herd of animals continued to walk closer to the fence. He was more concerned with the discovery of this new evidence and perused the information with steadfast determination that Nina had written down for him. Ruminating over how he might be able to get information from the person on the other end in Mexico, he realized that was just a dead end for him. If there was any progress to be made, it would be made right there in the States.

He knew he was negligent in his responsibilities, so he attended to glimpsing at the monitor that illustrated the slow and steady movement of red and yellow as it moved closer to the area of the fence. Cruz determined it was a herd of animals that looked like cattle or horses. The infrared detected that they were moving closer and closer to the fence, so Cruz reported it to his advisor. "It's probably just a herd of horses, but you've gotta check it out." Cruz got his "war wagon" and headed down the road.

29

Travis cantered Pegasus and let her head out front to show the others where they were going. Then he guided Pegasus back to the others and tried to stay as close as he could. When he saw that his friends made it through he directed Pegasus with the angle of his body to move and the horse abided. The horses climbed through the gap and filled the space. At one point Francisco fell off his horse. *"There's no way this can work,"* he thought to himself as he felt as though his arm was out of its socket and tender in the rotator cuff. The horses circled the fallen man as if to act as a shield and cover as he reclaimed his place on the horse, Francisco managed to regain his composure and took his spot upon the horse. He winced in pain but stayed low on the horse and hugged its neck and side.

"You all right?" asked Paul and Francisco responded with a quick smile of pain and an unconvincing turn of the head. The horses packed closely together. It was as if they were serving as a trampoline should he fall again, he might land on the back of another. If he were to fall again and fall through the cracks, the blows of hooves that were moving at rapid rates and unable to stop would've crushed him. It seems preposterous but the intelligence of these animals inspired great confidence in their riders. It was as if they were secretly in on the plan to bring them to safety and they traveled at rates that were abnormal for the average bareback rider. Although Francisco and Paul fell behind, the rest the group continued to travel as far as they could at a quickened pace to reach safety. Travis along with other horses led the way relishing his role and looking back to make sure the others were staying with him. Pegasus raced another and Travis held Sancho onto the horse as best he could, preventing him from falling. It was as if they were flying and the hooves of the horse weren't touching the ground, a fluid roll on the waves of wind. At one point the other horse nudged its nose close to Pegasus to keep the boys from falling off. Travis rejoiced at riding Pegasus and the whimsical flight of fancy became merely a trot as they made their way safely away from the fence and waited for the others to catch up. He assured Sancho that everything was "all right" and the boy remained quiet as they rode off into the dark of night winding their way around mounds of brush and tufts of trees and cacti sprouting from the ground like oil geysers. They followed roads across the main road and saw a few houses outside of town. They were careful not to disturb them and draw attention to themselves, but the train made it hard and the whinnying and song of neighs resonated in the quiet.

Travis kept a watchful eye and was cautious taking the roads he thought that were the easiest to ride but the most inconspicuous. He noticed two headlights at the end of the road and decided to cross it quickly before it could spot him followed by Juanita and Angelina. They hid behind a glade of trees.

The commotion was sure to cause a stir as it was a clear night and the forecast did not call for rain or thunder. The lookout at the towers read the radar as a band of horses, but officers decided to investigate to make sure this was the case.

The horses continued to trail as the car drew closer to them. It was a large jeep and bore the insignia of the "Border Patrol."

Travis had crossed the road safely and dismounted Pegasus. Juanita and Angelina were safely in view of Travis as well, but Paul and Francisco were trapped with the band of horses caught in the mesmerism of lights of the border patrol's jeep. Quiet panic surged through Travis as his heart palpitated at frantic rates. He wanted to instruct them on what to do but held out confidence that Father Paul would manage. They dismounted and hid in the middle of the herd. Members of the herd distracted the patrol by walking to the light.

Cruz's border patrol car was stuck in the middle of the road as the horses slowly moved to the other side. He opened the door as the animals slowly passed. Cruz grew impatient, opened his door and moved closer to the animals.

Paul was tense as he heard the agent shoo them away. "Get out the way, you numb skulls. Heya! Go on, git!!" The horses nonchalantly walked away into the darkness joining the others. Paul thought for sure he had to do something, but decided to stay with the horses and low to the ground.

Travis watched as he saw the two men slowly walk between the horses. The patrol flashed its light in their direction, but due to the dismounts, all the agent saw was wild horses. He waited for the horses to cross the road and continued on his way.

"Do you think they found us?" asked Travis when he encountered Paul.

"If they'd have found us through heat sensing they'd have stopped us. I think we made it. We're not out of the woods yet," Paul assured them, "but we're good for now. How's our boy holding up?"

Sancho was awake and looked woozy as he sat atop the horse. "He held up on the ride," said Travis.

They were a few miles out from the church and ventured quietly but with careful calculated measure. Travis knew the houses that could be problems and the people who might be able to help them. As sick as Sancho was he wasn't going to engage them and jeopardize their cover. He'd just assume they take their chances and make it to the church. Travis' phone was dead, and he couldn't call his grandma. It was just as well, as she had her own concerns to deal with. They rode through the night and the early morning sun rose on the horizon.

30

"Sanctuary," Paul thought to himself. *"Sanctuary. We need to get them to sanctuary."* The thoughts repeating themselves like a mantra in his mind and kept him quiet for most of the ride. The horses made their own way and some separated from the herd and faded away into the night. "That's a lotta horse power there. I wish I could talk to these guys and thank 'em. Man, wouldn't that be nice?" Paul's voice cracked with gratitude.

"They know. They know more than you realize; things we can't begin to understand. You can see it in their eyes. They're special animals," Juanita said with tears in her eyes. "Bye, babies." She waved at them as they moseyed on to another field. A smile curled gently around Paul's lips in agreement.

They continued along the path laid out by Travis on Pegasus. The night bore glimpses of the stars that inspired possibility, but Sancho's health was problematic and weighed on the minds of everyone. The trail wound around a few low mountain hills with brambles and bushes, thickets and short woods, cacti and brush were mere shadows and dark figures to maneuver. They avoided the barbed wire of land, but Travis was extra cautious of the night challenge in tripping a line or two. The ebullient moon provided the only light and the rocks and a few fields slowed their pace, until Travis was able to find a true path he knew well and could've walked it blindfolded. The night was tricky afoot and Travis traipsed the best paths he could find in the dark. They passed a familiar house.

"We used to go on hayrides somewhere around here. My grandpa had a friend over here somewhere, I think." Travis spoke out loud to convince himself that he was traveling the right way but he wasn't sure. The pressure mounted, as he wanted to make it safely back in a timely manner and was the only one who knew the way to the church. He was relieved when they crossed a bridge that was over a dry stream. He knew exactly where they were and picked up the pace with anticipation of making up ground for the temporary uncertain meandering.

The trek was abounding with calls of coyotes and the chirp of crickets. Horses need their rest, too, so they stopped for breathers. They were running out of food and saved their water for the animals and Sancho if he needed it, but Travis felt like he needed to push through. The horses were faithfully abiding by his wishes, and the riders dismounted to make the trek easier on them. Pegasus continued to balance Sancho on her back.

* * * * *

Cow dung and hay fragranced the air giving a pungent tap on the olfactory system, penetrating every sense of Travis' being. It may seem odd to some that Travis relished the scent of manure and hay as they traveled through the country, but it made him feel at ease knowing that he was closer to home and could quite literally smell it. He was getting back into his comfort zone, but still concerned for his friends who would be challenged even more being strangers in a strange land who lived with the knowledge that they could be snatched away at any time.

For Sancho the smell may have inspired him to throw up. The clear night gave the illusion that his vomit was neon colored yellow-green and would've alarmed them if they hadn't considered that there was a black light look to the night. When they arrived at the small country church they were relieved.

The church posed like a lighthouse with a small candlelight in the upper front window of its traditional southern steeple. There was a small fountain in front of the church and a tiny stream of water dripped out of the bowl being held by an angel sculpture that seemed alive in the haunting dead of early morning as the sunrise climbed higher.

The rectory was dark, but they knocked on the door and a light came on inside. A man of about seventy-five opened the door. He donned a dusty, faded green bathrobe and was still in his crusty old pajamas. He was a clean, conservative looking man with stern nobility in his air: a pudgy nose leading to thin lips and a proud mouth. His tenure as pastor of the church had taken a toll on him and left heavy bags around his eyes and prominent sagging jowls. His gentle wisps of gray-brown hair were every which way from a restless night of tossing and turning, which gave him a rumpled and frazzled appearance. His name was Pastor Phineas, and he was thoroughly confused at the sight of one of his parishioners this early in the morning. "Is that you, Travis?" he said as he squinted through his dirty spectacles for a better look.

"Yes, sir. I need your help." The pastor was bewildered as he looked at his watch that was missing from his wrist. "I know it's late, and I'm sorry, but this is an emergency. One of my friends is ill and needs a doctor. I'm with a priest friend."

Paul stepped forward and extended his hand. "Nice to meet you, I'm sorry I know it's early and you're just getting up, but we need some help. My friends and I have come from Mexico. Their boy was bitten by a rattlesnake and is very ill. We need to get him to a doctor."

"Well, the nearest urgent care is five miles away," the pastor reasoned. "Come in, come in," waved the priest a bit agitated as he tried to wake up. The others filed in obediently led by Francisco who carried Sancho. Pastor Phineas had a look on his face like he'd tasted something sour. It was the stink of the weeks of traveling and lack of a proper shower that trailed into the rectory with them. It was palpable to him but the pastor remained polite. Paul smelled like the sheep.

"He needs a bed," continued Paul.

Travis asserted himself. "I need some juice to get my phone working again." The pastor directed Travis to an outlet and directed the others to follow him.

"I've got a room off to the right that we use for visitors. There are some washcloths and towels in the bathroom." Angelina rushed to the bathroom and wetted some towels. Francisco was grateful as he angled himself and squeezed down the hallway, carrying the lifeless boy into the room.

The room was wood paneled pine and simple with limited furniture, a dresser, a desk, a single twin bed and a few statues strategically placed in parts of the room to give it a holy ambiance. Francisco delicately laid his boy into the bed while Juanita threw back the covers with a wistful heart and a look of desperation on her face. Angelina drew a washcloth from the bathroom and wet his head. It wasn't in their character to be so bold in taking over a space, but they did it for Sancho's sake and to maximize his comfort.

"You don't have a car? How'd you get here? Travis drive you?" the pastor questioned with rapid-fire shots.

"Our rides are out back...horseback," said Paul preoccupied as he examined Francisco's concern.

"You call an ambulance?" queried the pastor.

"Well, that's a bit of a quandary. This boy isn't supposed to be here," asserted Paul. "We're hoping to get a doctor *to* him."

"That boy looks like he needs to get some fluids in him." Pastor Phineas jumped out of the room and filled a glass at the sink. "Here's some water," said the pastor as he handed Francisco a glass of water and Angelina stroked his hair. "Can he hold that down?"

Paul looked around familiarizing himself with his surroundings and honed in a on anything that would serve as a bucket. "I don't know," said Paul. "We'll see. He's just started to throw up, so we may need a bucket." The pastor navigated the crowded room and handed him a garbage can while Travis got to work on calling his grandmother.

Eleanor was at the hospital with her husband Eben when she was awakened.

"Travis, is that you?" whispered Eleanor in a sleepy trance.

"Yes, ma'am, we made it across the border."

"Oh, thank God you're all right," she said with sleepy conviction.

"I need to get a hold of Dr. Mann. I don't have her number. My friend is very sick. We're afraid to bring him to the clinic."

"I'll text it to you. I wouldn't go home right away. You're gonna need to wait it out. Don't take them back to the house. There're some troubles brewing around here. Can you call me right back?"

"Yes, ma'am. Thanks."

He hung up the phone and she managed to text him the number with help from one of the nurses who was on duty that morning. Travis attended to getting a hold of the doctor.

Sancho couldn't hold down any water and threw up into the trashcan. The pastor jutted his finger at Paul directing him to follow him outside the room. He was skeptical and spoke in hushed tones away from Francisco, Angelina and Juanita.

"You're welcome to my car if you think you need to take him into the clinic. I think that may be the best thing for him. I'm afraid he can't stay here."

"This may be a sanctuary situation, Father."

"Well, that's no good," huffed the pastor.

"Why's that?"

"'Cause the authorities 'round here don't recognize the church as a sanctuary. They're tightening the grips on things, taking matters into their own hands. They're coming down hard on the immigrants. Capture first and ask questions later."

"Yeah, but we've got the Vatican on our side.

"Nope," said the pastor shaking his head. Anger and frustration welled up in the pastor, but he was able to quietly contain it. "You don't understand. The Church may support you, but that doesn't mean you won't face the brutal consequences. There's a war between church and state. The Feds are saying that any priest who contributes to harboring an illegal is subject to prosecution. I've got too much work to do to worry myself with that. My parish needs me. We're short-handed…I can't…" he stammered, "I can't do it alone as it is. I need help. If they take me away, who will serve the community? No, they can't stay here. I can't afford it. Besides that, I'm too old to go to jail."

Paul understood this. He'd met many nuns who had gone to jail for righteous causes and suffered tremendously as a result of their convictions and their plight was branded on his mind. "I take full responsibility for them," he argued with conviction and a force even greater than before.

"It doesn't matter," countered the recalcitrant pastor. "That's not the way they see it. This is my parish. I'm responsible for what is done on these premises."

"But you can't throw them out," Paul persisted.

The pastor shook his head as if to say it wasn't him throwing them out. The refrain continued, "Sanctuary means nothing to the vile corrupted spirit that is set on it's own worldly ends. That's all there is to it. We're not playing by the ordinary rules here. We're playing by what *they* want to do. You need to take that boy into the hospital and consider what to do about his parents and sister."

Paul was disconcerted. "This is indecent, Father. What you're doing isn't right…it runs contrary to everything Jesus taught. Whatever happened to welcoming the stranger? Giving drink to the thirsty, food to the hungry?"

"I have welcomed him. I hate to be so hard," said the pastor, "but our world here calls for realistic analysis. It's a catch-22, son. You're damned if you do and damned if you don't. I'm not one to lie. What you do in your small affairs carries over into the big ones. I'm not going to start being party to something that will undermine us in the long term. I'm sorry."

"I need to get them to a church that will take them. Can you just give me some time to do that?"

"Twenty-four hours," the pastor negotiated like a salesman with a firm offer who would accept nothing less.

"I do know one thing," he said. "Fear will be the death of you. Faith conquers fear. It makes me question just how faithful a man you really are. You may want to take a look at that, Father," said Father Paul. He knew he was being too hard on the pastor, but anger got the better of him and anger always inspires rash comments.

"My Lord will be the judge of me."

"There are sins of omission, Father. They are just as great as sins of commission. How you treat the most vulnerable among us is a true test of who we are as people and a Church — not to mention a country."

"I'm glad I could help you now," the pastor said with a sharp cut and dismissive shutdown.

There was so much Paul wanted to say to him, but there were other concerns that needed attention. He felt in his heart that he was doing right by the family, but he questioned what to do next. The stress of the road caught up with him and he looked agitated and paced outside the room in the hall.

• • • • •

Travis called Eleanor and walked out to the horses as he spoke to her. She could hear them neighing in the background. When he called her, she told him that his grandfather was very sick and the government was battling hard to prosecute him. She couldn't talk, but she had been trying to figure out what to do with the refugees if they made it across. "We may need to split them up. It may be tricky to keep them all together at first." She was worried about her grandson and told him that he should get to the hospital as quick as he could or at least in a timely fashion. Travis was torn about leaving. He decided that he'd go once he knew his friend was going to be all right. He reentered the rectory.

"What's the ETA on the doctor?" asked Paul wrenching his hands and looking unusually perplexed. No sooner did the question leave his lips when there was a sudden knock at the door.

The doctor arrived and the pastor let her in. She examined Sancho and looked morose, as she shook her head. She pulled a syringe out of her bag and gave him a shot. "I don't know if there's anything we can do for him," said Dr. Mann outside the room. The others followed her out and Juanita stayed with Sancho.

"Should we take him to the hospital?" inquired a desperate Angelina knowing the answer but not wanting to accept it.

"I'm afraid it's just a matter of time. This boy's organs have shut down. I don't think there's any way of getting them to function properly. His eyes are jaundiced and the poisons in his system are taking over. Had we been able to get him help right away, we would've had a shot. I'm sorry." Angelina and Francisco hung their heads in sadness. They comforted one another and then returned into the room with Juanita and Travis who were by his side.

Father Paul confided in the doctor that she needed to keep her visit on the down low. She understood and expressed her sadness for the family.

Everything was opaque for Sancho, as the chemical imbalances in his system continued to work their magic on his senses. Violent sweats continued to drain vitamins out his pores, and the room was spinning with confusion as he tried to futilely grasp for something to hold with his right hand while his mother held onto his left hand. Francisco took the searching hand and clutched it, but Sancho was weak and didn't respond. Both parents helplessly looked on. His stomach was clenched and churned with growls of malnutrition and they spoke to the growls in Juanita's like a call and response in a song. Sancho tried to utter a few words but nothing audible could be understood. He couldn't make sense of where he was and his disorientation inspired him to accept the dreams that were presented which were a mix of his Quixotic escapes in the desert and a simpler time of semi-security of his home in Guatemala playing soccer with his friends before he knew the meaning of the madness of the world.

Paul took his turn, stepped forward and took his hand and tenderly caressed his hair with heartfelt compassion. He made the sign of the cross on his forehead and palms of his hands and spoke some Latin under his breath. Angelina cried. "Be brave, my boy," she cried to him in Spanish. "It's going to be all right. We're here for you."

Sancho was visioning the blue smoke and sat up in his bed. His words were suddenly clear and everyone understood them. "Juanita…do you see the blue smoke?" He whispered as if alarmed and mesmerized by what he had seen. Juanita looked up at her parents and looked to him. "It's right there! I can see it. I can see it." He eyed it as he lay back down. "Can you see it?"

She looked to where he was looking but couldn't see anything. She wanted to tell him that she saw it, but she didn't want to lie to him. She was stuck between telling him what he needed to hear and being honest with him. She prided herself on her honesty with him and wasn't going to stop now. "I can't see it, Sancho. I'm sorry I can't. Can you see it?" she asked. He nodded and tears welled up in his eyes.

"It's getting closer to me."

"That's all that matters," she said.

"It's beautiful…" His voice trailed off. His eyes opened wide, he opened his mouth further as if to express the awe he was seeing one more time, and he looked at the sight that was before him with a great gentle smile. He breathed a heavy sigh as if he was surprised at being given something like a gift, and he slipped away.

A heavy tension had built up in the room, an intense expression of the grief that was laden in each person present and the incredible burden of pain each had experienced on the trip. It built such an intense energy that a light bulb exploded in the lamp as Sancho's parents clutched the boy's dead body and comforted one another. Travis was taken aback when he saw the pop of the lightning flash in the bulb. He wondered if this was Sancho's soul making one last goodbye with a powerful effect; a final burst of youth expending itself on the nearest object and mischievously breaking it like a baseball shattering it, snuffing out the filament without breaking the lamp. It was as if the world couldn't hold him any longer, and he wanted to make it known. Travis looked to Paul who also noted the pop of light but was more concerned with his friends and trained his eyes on Francisco, Angelina and Juanita. The others were in too much shock to notice or didn't care to acknowledge it. Juanita reached for Paul and broke into sobs. Paul held her for a minute and her anguish was muffled in his shirt.

Travis looked out the window curious to see what Sancho was looking at when he took his last breath. He looked for the beautiful blue smoke in the sky, but all he could see was the rising sun and shadows of the horses as they slowly meandered into view. Then he saw something mysterious and wondered if this was the thing that Sancho had seen. There was a thin, low riding mist of fog on the ground that formed and slowly rose. It was a gentle lapping wave of smoke that rose forming a blanket across the field and it reminded him of the glassy reflection on the Great Salt Lake in Utah — a translucent strain that lay about knee deep now and spread out to the rest of the farm and beyond. It looked like a massive pond that stretched to the base of the mountain; it was as if it were wetting the scorching soil and the cold of night was meeting the dry hot air of the rising sun's morning, and it traveled as far as his eye could see; maybe even beyond the base of the mountain. The horses were stirring and opened out a path and seemingly watched as if they'd just been overtaken by a flood of water and were wading in it. It was if they were noting its presence, too. They looked at each other confused and Pegasus nodded as if it were saying hello or goodbye, but Travis wasn't sure if she was nodding to another horse or something else. It was the same greeting that Travis experienced when he first met the foal in Mexico that introduced him to the other horses. Another horse nodded and swatted its tail in nervous excitement and then another and another, one by one it was as if each horse was greeting it in its own way. He felt as though they were communicating with one another about it with swishing tails. Their swishing tails stirred the smoke but didn't clear it.

He thought this must be the "blue smoke" Sancho was seeing, but it looked like a low lying fog of gray and nothing more to him. Could it be that something was still there, he thought to himself or was he imagining it? It evoked something in him but not awe. It was a tender moment of awareness and presence of mind. That was it. He wondered if he perceived Sancho's mysterious sighting in his own way. He thought about what Sancho and Juanita once told him about the veil between the reality of this world and the mystery of the next. He thought about how those who are closer to death perceive a reality that is unique and their own — how they see things we can't see. Maybe that's why Juanita couldn't see it. She wasn't really looking for it, and her concern was focused completely on her brother and being present to him and easing his pain.

The tension in the room slowly dissipated and a profound hum hung in the air and stillness filled it like water filling a tank.

No one spoke. Everyone in the room moved slowly and reverently. Sancho's body of nothingness took on a qualified presence of some-thing-ness but only for a moment as the realization of the death settled in. One by one they stepped outside the room. When Travis stepped outside the room, he noticed that the fluorescent light in the kitchen shimmered and faded. Something bigger *was* happening there, Travis was certain of that now. Something beyond him was coming to pass. He didn't know if it was Sancho's soul shaking him or the weight of responsibility he now felt as a man to help the family even more. He just knew that it was profound, and it settled in his heart and inspired a few goose bumps.

Francisco followed Juanita outside the house while Angelina stayed in the room with Sancho's body. Pastor Phineas sensed something was happening. He'd just showered, changed and dressed in his priestly black, but hadn't attached his collar yet. Paul met him in the living room.

"The boy's passed on," said Father Paul to Pastor Phineas in a low subdued voice even though he was out of earshot from Angelina.

Pastor Phineas was genuinely surprised and he grew solemn. "I'm sorry," said Pastor Phineas. "I'm very sorry." Father Paul acknowledged his remarks and walked outside to attend to the family.

Francisco watched Juanita to make sure she was all right, but stopped as he saw her head to where the horses were. He knew where she needed to be and what she needed.

Travis thought about going to the hospital, but couldn't bring himself to abandon the family now. He stepped outside the house and walked around the corner of the rectory. He saw a large aluminum pail on the side of the house and a hose.

Pulling out the hose, he filled the pail with water close to where the animals were, and wandered over to Juanita who was greeting the horses and petting them. The horses responded to her grief by meeting her where she was and in their own way gave her great comfort by forming a band and surrounding her. Travis reached out to her and held her. He didn't care who saw him now.

"They're sad, too. Can you see it in them?" Travis asked.

"They know something's wrong. Look, how they're all here. They're still awake for us…attending to us. These animals carried us to freedom. I wonder where they'll go next?"

"They're free," Travis said. "They'll go where they wanna go."

"I wonder where we go. I envy their freedom…"

"You're gonna be all right." He held her for just a minute and then he left her to the horse she'd come to know who carried her across the border. It was a poetic expression of security for her, but it was fleeting.

Paul exited the rectory and sat on the porch. Francisco doubled back and met him at the porch. "I'm sorry, Francisco. It isn't fair."

Francisco was fidgety and spoke as if he needed to convince himself that it would be all right. Grief and trauma impose harsh contradictions and Francisco fell victim to grief's paradox. It was as if he was working through his grief right then and there and his eyes searched the landscape for the answers. Paul listened intently as he spoke. Francisco picked up a small twig and twisted it and bended it, as he worked through his thoughts. "Life isn't fair, senor. You were right. I thought it'd be different here than it is there. All we can do is pray that we find justice in the next life. He passed away in freedom, on free land, though. He's free now. That's all I wanted. I wanted my family to die on free soil. All I ever wanted for my family was freedom: freedom to make decisions for themselves that would grant them a better life, freedom to make a good life for themselves and others, freedom to be true to what God called them to do. He won't get to do that, but there's hope now with Juanita. Maybe she will one day have a boy like Sancho." He cried and choked on his words. "But you know... you're going to think I'm loco when I say this, but it's true... that boy...that boy was always free in his own way. I didn't think about it until I saw him in there and how brave he was. You know, he always found a way to let everyone know he was in charge. He always found a way to assert his faith that everything was going to be all right. He asserted himself like no one I've ever seen. Even in the darkest times when forces of evil were bearing down on us, he could rise above it. That's the truest expression of freedom."

"He got that from you," interjected Father Paul.

"No, this was different. He was born with something special that he gave to me. It was like he was put on this earth to teach me freedom and what it really means. He was courageous, Paul. I *learned* it from him...that boy taught me to be true. He inspired me to stand up to injustice. He inspired me to speak out. You know what? He's the reason we're here now. 'What have we got to lose, we got each other?' he would say. I never heard him complain. He took on the world unlike anyone I've ever seen. He knew that he was free. He knew that...No...he's free. Now he is free. Free from the suffering of this world." Francisco suddenly got up like he was ready to run. Pacing back and forth, Francisco worked through his deepest realization. "My boy is free!" he screamed. "My boy is free!!" He settled back down and collapsed on the ground.

"My boy is free!!!" His voice echoed in the hollow. Paul walked over to him and lifted him off the ground as he pounded the ground with his last breath of energy. He was zapped and fatigue wrangled him. His arm still bothered him, but in the process of attending to his son, he never thought to ask the doctor to look at it. "I don't know what to do with myself, Padre. I don't know what to do."

"I know. We'll figure it out. You're not in this alone. I'm right here for you."

"We couldn't do this without you, Padre. I'm not afraid anymore...I'm just angry. I just want a quiet place to call my own...to raise my family. Is that asking too much?"

"I know," Father Paul choked on his words, as he grew sadder wiping his nose from grief.

"I'm going to check in on Angelina." He clopped up the stairs and went inside.

"Good," Paul replied with a distant look as he considered his options.

This burst of emotion would cost Francisco an opportunity to bury his son properly as a neighbor was suspicious of the activity happening at the church. They would be leaving the body behind and be on the run in less than twenty-four hours. They would have to split up as a family to avoid being caught. Angelina and Juanita together and Francisco alone. Paul couldn't bring himself to keep him quiet, as he knew this is what he needed at the time. It made him uncomfortable, though, and he wriggled in his skin with uncertainty.

Travis wandered back to Paul with a heavy heart. Sancho's passing was his first experience with death of someone his age. Father Paul comforted him and consoled him. "Death is an imminent proposition that makes itself known when we least expect it. How we respond to death is how we respond to life." Travis sat up and took note of this. His eyes glistened as he realized that he was still hopeful and present to the power of the life force that surged within him having helped the family through one of its greatest struggles.

"Where is God in all this, Padre?"

Paul paused not expecting this inevitable question. "If God is the ground of our being." Pausing at his high and mighty theology, he brought it down to his level and corrected himself. "If God is in your heart, which I believe is the case, then God is right here with us. It's in our suffering and dropping of our tears; God's in our creativity and artfulness, but most importantly God is in the enduring love we have for one another. The greatest blessing God gave us is the gift of recognizing something sacred in one another, the gift of the Christ. When we recognize Christ and see Christ in another and help others see Christ in themselves, we commit to something greater than ourselves. It's hard to see it when you're so close to it." Father Paul didn't feel like he was reaching Travis. He himself was confused and tired, so he was brutally honest with the boy. "That's all I've got for you for now, 'cause I'm hurting myself. It hurts so much...does any of that make sense?" Travis was silent as tears filled his eyes. He accepted what Father Paul said. "Good. We can talk later," he continued.

"What do we do now, Father Paul?"

"We find these people a good home — a place of safety and security, something to call their own. We find them a good home and hope they don't get caught."

"How humiliating," Travis thought to himself. *"How humiliating that they would have to endure such criminal treatment all for the sake of freedom."*

31

Cruz was able to purchase plane tickets for himself and Nina and met Madden up north for the sting they planned. Nina and Cruz ran through the plan on the plane. He was a bit unsure of allowing her to go into harm's way, but thought about what Madden had said. "It was going to take a courageous individual to step forward to make something happen," and he knew in his heart she was the right person for the job. He managed to get a couple of winks sleep on the plane and was exhausted having pulled the night shift the night before. They rented a car and drove an hour north to Toledo. Madden would join them with the white van and the supplies. Katrina wasn't able to make the trip. They were on their way to meet "Pinky" at a nearby diner. So far the information was right. They told her they were interested in making a deal.

"Are we set on the plan?" asked Steve.

"I think so," Nina said thumbing a magazine and giving a smile of assurance.

"Good."

Cruz was nervous, as he said he would play the role of the trafficker. Madden just said, "It's your gig." He would wait as backup in the car. They drove in two separate cars, the van and a rental, to the Swingo Tango Lounge in a run down part of town. This part of town looked like it may have been a major hub for industry in its day, but had fallen on hard times. It was out of the way and well hidden, which prompted Cruz to wonder how it could ever even hope to have any business. Cruz and Nina walked to the front of the lounge and waited. Cruz gently guided Nina into the bar to see if he could find his new acquaintance. It was unassuming from the outside, but it was a kingly dive as far as hip majestic dive bars go. The large mirror behind the antique bar reflected a dark and dingy space that was painted in black and maroon. They tried to decorate with faux fifties décor but it just looked like a cheap chintzy tango lounge or karaoke bar that someone pulled together with knick-knacks that looked classy in their time but now were rusted and faded with age. Tinsel graced a stage to give it a timeless cheesy feel and Christmas lights adorned the perimeter of the walls. The black and white parquet floor looked like it hadn't been mopped in months, but the clean dance floor in the middle of the bar hid some uneven blemishes that come with scuffles and thirty or forty years of wear and tear. Cruz exited the bar and met Nina. She could tell from the stern look he gave that his connection wasn't there. Suddenly a woman with bleached blond hair like a Marilyn Monroe wannabe in "The Misfits," wearing a white babushka, arrived outside wearing trendy pink sunglasses and overdone pink lipstick. She was a vision of white and pink, and she sized them up as she neared the entrance. Cruz knew right away it was she as he introduced himself as "Esteban," and firmly shook her hand. He invited her inside while Nina waited outside. She introduced herself as Wilma Whitlow, but her friends called her "Pinky" because she liked pink things. She was stocky in build but made up for it in extravagant taste to distract the eye of the beholder and carried herself with bold self-assurance wearing a long white coat with pink pants and a long sleeved off white blouse. Pinky was impressed with Nina as she passed her and Cruz directed Nina to sit in the corner where he could see her. Pinky had a slight accent that sounded Ukrainian and it sauntered into her speech at times.

"Pretty girl," she said.

"I wouldn't have it any other way," Cruz replied.

They ordered and Cruz said it was on him. The woman ordered tacos, nachos and a Jack and Coke light on the ice. Cruz said he wasn't hungry and sipped a stale beer from the tap.

"What do you want from me?" Pinky asked.

"I want to see if you could take this girl off my hands. I heard about you from Renaldo."

"Yes, it's a sad thing what happened to Renaldo," she said.

"Oh, the bust, yeah…He'll be all right."

"He's been around the block, that's for sure. He'll buy his way out. You know him long?"

"Yeah, it's been awhile."

"He never mentioned your name."

"I came from down south. We've got a thing going. I met him down there."

"Uh-huh," she responded skeptically. She paused and looked away and examined herself in a small mirror. "I don't know," she said not tipping her hand. "We're laying low right now, honey. We don't have any room for her."

"Well, I'm laying low, too. I'm trying to keep product moving, so we can keep the operation up. I'm looking to make more connections, and Renaldo said you were good to go to."

"Yeah, well, we tried to contact Renaldo."

"Yeah?" Steve's mind raced at the possibility that the jig was up, but he continued in the discussion with certainty. "Then you know I'm good to go," said Cruz confidently.

"Well, we couldn't get a hold of him. We have an inside way of getting info. We hadn't heard from him. That's why I put you off. Renaldo didn't have anything to say. It was like he didn't know you."

"You kidding? No, that's not right. He knows me. Look, I've got that girl out there, do you want her or not?"

She paused a long time being coy and sighed. "We're always looking for good product, but if we take her we won't be able to use her for awhile."

"That's up to you," dismissed Cruz with a nonchalant wave of his hand. "She's a good one. She's beautiful. You don't want her, we'll send her somewhere else. It's no sweat off my back. I'm going to do fine with her. Someone's gonna make a lotta money with that girl. Look at her."

Pinky looked out the window mechanically. "She's good. No doubt about that. She's my kind of girl. We can set her up before we use her."

"Do what you want, I don't care," Cruz was nonchalant.

"What do you want for her?" asked Pinky.

"I can get a thousand easy."

"That's a little too high for us. Our girls aren't that much."

"Well, make me an offer."

"Five hundred."

Steve looked at her and shook his head as if he were insulted. "Come on."

"We can't use her for a few weeks at least. We aren't going to have a return on our investment for a long time. We have to house her, feed her…I mean, come on."

"I hear you. Let's go seven hundred."

"Six."

"Six fifty." She paused and he was uncomfortable but tried

not to show it. "I gotta move product. Maybe we can do a deal in the future. I got more like her, I'm telling you she's good."

"We give you three now and then three fifty later. We see how she works out. If she doesn't work out, it's on you. We don't do business with you again."

"How do I know you're good for it?"

She looked him in the eye. "Honey, I'm good for more than you know," she said flirtatiously.

"Is that right? I don't know about that. I just don't know," he said with a smile flirting back with her and disgusted by the thought of being with her. His mouth went dry. "I'm sorry, I need the full six fifty."

She looked at him again. "So what, we try. That's business, right?"

Steve raised his hands like his team scored a goal. "She'll be great. I want cash." Pinky went to her little pink purse and pulled out some cash. "You've got six fifty there. Count it." Steve counted the money.

"You came with more money."

"No, I always carry extra," she said.

"Sure you weren't going to go a thousand?" he laughed.

"No, I'm being fair. Seriously. It'll be good for both of us. Good for you, good for me."

"I hope so."

Her tacos arrived and they continued to talk. Steve got another beer.

"You got a lunch outta this, too," Steve informed.

"Don't worry about it. I know the owner here. He takes care of me all the time," Pinky said with no cares. She thought she met a gentleman but she was put off by this remark. He was just like all the rest.

"No problem, I'm just saying."

"You're from New York or LA?" she inquired.

"New York, why?" Steve said.

"Cause big city guys are cheap. They make you go Dutch all the time. 'You get one who buys your lunch, hang on to him,' my mother used to say."

"Oh, you're from New York?"

"Chicago via the Ukraine. Same deal. Where'd you get the girl?"

"She's from the south. We get our girls from the border towns. We got some Mexicans, too."

"They're the best workers, the Mexicans. I'll take a Mexican any day," her voice hit a higher key with excitement.

"They build the wall you'll be out of luck with them."

She laughed. "The wall. Those idiots think building a wall's going to stop us. We get them passports, we walk them right through the Customs. We get more girls from Customs than anywhere else. They're poor. They go along with it because they think they're coming to the land of milk and honey. Nothing those agents can do about it. They answer the questions, say they're visiting a relative. They lie like we tell them." Her mind went back to her original thought. "The wall…Besides, walls ain't any good if you can pay off a border agent." She laughed. "Idiots. Spend all that money, and we'll still find a new way to get them through. Mail-order brides, same thing. Fly them into Canada for all I care. We cross the mountains. Get a good girl we pay a couple of bucks for a passport and plane ticket what's it to us? Humans are the lowest overhead for a business. You can use them over and over again until they're dead. Young ones usually take a long time to die. We can use them over and over again," Pinky said with a giddy glow. Cruz was annoyed but tried not to show it and remained quiet. Evil was familiar to him now, but it always annoyed him. It annoyed him even more that he knew she was right. They would find other ways to bring their captives to the States. She scarfed down the tacos and they were ready to go. He hoped that Madden was getting all this on the camera they rigged on him as he walked her outside and said goodbye. Pinky turned to Nina. "Okay, time to go. You're coming with me, honey," Pinky kindly said to Nina. It was motherly in tone. "You come with me to my car."

"You go with her. It's okay," said Cruz to Nina. He watched as they drove away. He recorded the license plate number in his mind until he could write it down in the car and Madden was on it following from behind. It boggled his mind to think that he'd just sold Nina, the woman he was falling for, into slavery. It was unfathomable to him that these things happen on a day-to-day basis.

* * * * *

Once again Madden followed the pulsing red dot on his computer. He called his buddy with the Feds and told him where they were heading. The fall gray sadness of the town swept into the streets as Pinky's salt dusted brown Mercedes drove into town. The dusty roads of leaves kicked around as a gentle rain fell.

"You've got some clothes?" asked Pinky.

"No ma'am," Nina meekly replied and folded her arms.

"We'll get you fixed up with some clothes. Don't you worry about that."

"That's a darling coat you've got there," said Nina.

"Thank you," said Pinky with about as much enthusiasm as a sloth. "I've got a few places to go for the weekend after I drop you off and get you settled in." Nina thought to herself she had other ideas if all went as they planned.

"You lived here long?" Nina asked.

"Not too long. I'm from somewhere else. I commute."

"Where you from?"

"I told you somewhere else, didn't I?"

"Well, I just thought..."

Pinky interrupted her, "You don't need to know too much, honey. You just be nice and keep quiet for me."

Nina played dumb. "I'm sorry, I can't help myself." Nina tried to give Madden information as they drove just to be sure that he was listening and able to track them. "Tony Pacos. That's a chain?" Pinky glared at her annoyed. "Sorry," said Nina with faux shame.

They arrived at where they needed to be. It was a small complex on the outskirts of town. In front there was a sign that read "A Friendly Place To Be." The building was unassuming from the front, but inside the main yard one could see barbed wire that lined the perimeter of the fence. There was a spiraling crown of barbed wire that was bound to the perimeter of the first floor and any windows that led to small precipices on the first floor. It looked like a small security prison from the outside. Other than that, the brick building was very unassuming and quiet.

"Why the barbed wire around the building?" Nina was starting to feel the diabolical nature of the journey take hold of her.

"Oh, they get squirrels in here. Pesky things those little squirrels trying to get in the house."

She mused inside when she heard the response. "I never heard of that. Big fence for squirrels, ain't it?" stated Nina.

They walked in the building through a back door. Pinky punched in a code and the door opened. They walked down a hall and into a set of staircases. They walked the staircase to a walkway that overlooked a large shop.

"You handy with a sewing machine?" asked Pinky.

"Not really."

"You want to be in fashion, you start here from the ground up. We teach you."

"This place looks like a sweatshop," said Nina loudly into her shirt as she leaned over. "Is this place some kind of sweatshop," Nina inquired.

"It is what it is. This is where we'll house you for a while. For you it's where you'll be working. I'm going to introduce you to my friend Diablo. He'll take it from there. You're a talker, aren't you?"

"I like to talk."

"We like things quiet here, so you're going to have to mind your own with that mouth of yours. Understand? Diablo doesn't like girls to talk back. You persist and he'll get mad. I'm just telling you this for your own good," Pinky said with a sinister tone.

Madden arrived and the red blinking dot stood still. He gave Cruz the address and Cruz arrived shortly thereafter while Nina was talking with someone else.

* * * * *

The conversation was muffled and went in and out on him. Madden listened closely through the headphones when Steve arrived in the truck. Things got a bit testy and they couldn't quite make out what was happening. It sounded as if the man was interviewing Nina, but they weren't sure what he was saying. The next lines generated from the conversation alarmed them. They overheard her saying.

"Where are you taking me?" cried Nina. "Leave me alone... she screamed and muffled sounds resounded over the crackling line. Don't hurt me...you'll be sorry," she warned. "You have no idea!"

"Shut up!!" said the man. The sound of thuds, cracks and the clatter of boards and glass breaking pierced the sound waves and a pitiful screech of horror from Nina. Silence broke into the signal and captured the line. The bad breath of a long moment loomed over them, and rancid indecision sliced the crease in Madden's furrowed brow. It left a bad taste, as Madden looked sick and confused about what to do next. He didn't want to go in without backup and feared doing so would play against them. He looked around as if to find a button that he could press to make it all right.

"What's going on?" exclaimed Cruz.

"We can't go in. We need back up," Madden leveled in plain assertion. It was the first time Cruz had witnessed him scared and an uneasy crawl of horror climbed Cruz's spine leaving his wits to stand on end as he reclaimed his momentary loss of his reasoning.

"Well, we...we need to do something! We can't wait. We told her...We'd be there for her. She needs us...she needs us now. We've gotta go now. We've gotta help her," said Cruz.

Pricked with a sudden burst of conviction, Madden jumped to his feet. "Let's go," Madden said as he grabbed the wire cutters and bolted out the door. "You're right, we can't wait for the rest of them." Madden called his friend. "Pete, this is Madden. We're you at? We've gotta go. Our principal player, she's being hurt. They've taken her hostage. We need to break this up now! You hear me? Now. We're going in!" They looked along the side of the fence and Madden gave Cruz the cutters, cut through and collapsed the five-foot corrugated metal like aluminum foil. There was a small faded sign that said "electric fence" that neither one of them saw at first sight, and Cruz just gave a bemused lucky look at Madden as they both climbed through safely to the other side. There were sharp-pronged stakes of barbed wire crowned at basement level. It ran through Cruz's mind that they were hell bent on keeping whatever they had in that building.

They fired shots at the door handle and lock, crashed through the door and a stale air of mold flooded out the door and rushed into the coldness. A bell sounded and whooping arpeggio of an alarm that also cranked out a high-pitched squeal deafening them. Down they went to the stairs of the basement. Shepherding a resounding force of anger and contempt, Madden broke through the next door armed and loaded for what may lay around the corner. The next door was barricaded but the door swung open as someone ran into the arms of the waiting Madden. He ushered her back into the room. "Police! Get back in there. Stay calm."

Shrill cries of concern poisoned the room and wailing gasps of anxiety with choking tears of gratitude from a few that knew their harrowing nightmare would soon be over when they saw the two men enter with guns. One woman was wailing terror and other shrieks of uncertainty as she reached out to others for help. Panic and fear clamping down, down on every last person who was lost in confusion as a woman and man directed a few to the exits in the back but halted due to the prompting of Madden and Cruz — both screamed curt and bellowing cries of "Don't move, don't move. Freeze, police! Freeze, police!!!" Madden held his badge up high for all to see.

"What's your twenty?" Madden called to his friend on the radio.

"We're here — over," said the voice on the other end. "We've got it surrounded. Over. I'm coming in."

Machines were buzzing and the shanty lights lit the way. A loud radiant booming hum hung over the room but generated no air for the inhabitants. Sweat and bone chilling heat saturated every pore of the room and being within it. The sweltering room was cooled only by large fans positioned at both ends of the shop facing each other caddy corner. There were rows and rows of sewing machines. People cowered in submission to the authorities while their emotions were tottering between tremendous relief and knee buckling, crippling panic. A loud beep suddenly rang throughout the hall punctuating the moment and alarming people who were not expecting it.

Twelve officers in all assumed various positions throughout the massive shop. Two went up to the catwalk and the rest stayed low. A few were positioned outside in case there was anyone trying to leave the building. The workers raised hands even higher as they stayed on the ground and raised their shocked faces to see more police storming through the doors armed. One by one the police searched for weapons, but found none on anyone.

Cruz looked around for a door. There were a few of them. "Where's the girl? Where's the main office?" An Asian man with his hands on his head directed him to the door on the far right. "Show me." The man scurried to his feet and nervously opened the door. He led him down the hallway, where a fight was continuing to ensue. The hallways were a series of rooms that were dorms for the workers and housed the overworked staff. Steve ran full speed to the end of the hall and busted through the door followed by Madden.

Cruz broke into the room only to find a man taking on Nina. Both were engaged in a full out brawl of magnificent proportions. She was trying to hold her own, but bloodied up pretty bad until Cruz and Madden were able to apprehend the man with a few shots of their own to the face and stomach. Cruz reached out for Nina.

Nina was shaking, but got to her feet and held Cruz close. "It's okay. It's over. I'm sorry we lost communication. We lost sound." She was shivering but pulled away to attend to her bleeding nose and the bruises on her face. They stopped at a bathroom down the hall to help clean her up. She was still in shock. "This place is sinister... Boy, am I glad to see you."

"You okay?" asked Cruz.

She affirmed that she was all right. We need to see if she's here. They walked into the main shop where the police were dealing with the workers one by one. They positioned themselves at the top of the catwalk and were armed to shoot should there be any problems.

One by one they walked through the large factory yelling out the name "Rosa Cruz?" A woman raised her hand for them to come over there. She was standing in the back by one of the large fans. Steve saw her, acknowledged her, called to Nina and darted to the back to find a woman in the arms of another being gently rocked back and forth while she was crying. "Rosa Cruz?" The woman nodded and the fear filled young woman slowly reached out her hand to Cruz. He took her in his arms, and she quivered and radiated fear like a booming amplifier. He assured her, "It's okay now. I'm here on behalf of your brother Esteban. Is that your brother?"

She nodded and cried louder. "You're from Juarez, Mexico? It's going to be all right." Nina comforted her by putting her arms around her and took over for Cruz in holding her. Cruz saw Madden as they were processing people and one of the officers had Pinky in handcuffs. She looked at him horrified, and he just guffawed with delight as he passed her. "You look pretty in pink, but you'll look even prettier in stripes." He'd heard that line from an old Batman show and delighted in the fact that he was able to use it on her.

"We'll see about that," quipped Pinky back at him as he pulled Madden aside.

"What are we gonna do now?" asked Cruz.

"I don't know where we take these people," Madden said. "There's nowhere to take them."

"Can we get them some food?"

Madden shrugged. "There's no beds; nowhere to house them. Maybe we can call one of the Missions. Katrina says we're 'full up' down south."

Nina interrupted them. "I know a man down south who may be able to help Rosa and any others who might be from Mexico. He's hard to reach, but he comes and goes from the States and we may be able to contact him. His name is Father Paul."

"Can you get me a number?" asked Cruz.

"Yes. He's a good man. He may be able to direct you and give some help.

Cruz and Madden gathered their wits and drank a bottle of water to calm themselves. "I'm still shaking," said Madden. "Look at that." He said raising his hand with a slight tremor.

"Adrenalin," said Cruz. "I'm feeling it, too. Nothing like the rush of doing good, is there?" Madden was quiet as he downed another bottle and walked back inside to see his friend. They led Rosa away who was wrapped in a blanket and wore it like a shawl. One of the greatest horrors of her life was over for now.

Nina would call Father Paul and he would redirect them to someone who might be able to take her in as houseguest, so she could recover.

32

At the hospital, morning dawned and both men were awake but in the groggy phase of waking and hadn't spoken to one another. Manning was awaiting Eleanor to arrive before his surgery. The nurse entered and administered some drugs into Manning's system, and he looked over and saw that Stillwell was moving. They greeted each other with a "good morning."

"How you doing today?" asked Manning.

"I'm still so sore."

"Yeah, I hear you. You gotta suffer a little bit before it gets better."

"It's a big day for you, isn't it?" stated Stillwell plainly.

"May be bigger than I realize. I don't know…"

"What do you mean?"

"Something tells me that my days are numbered. I don't know if I'm gonna make it out of this surgery. I could be wrong. It's just a thought that's coming to me. I guess those thoughts are more frequent the older I get. I can be making something outta nothin'."

"Yeah, we all do that.

"Funny phrase, 'making something out of nothing.' Can we *really* make something out of nothing?" I mean something's something right?"

Stillwell laughed. "It's too early for me to think about that. Everything is something. This damned place makes you think. That's all you do is make something out of nothing…

You consider those things, and you go round and round and round and round."

"I don't mean to get too deep on you. I guess that's what happens to an old man. You get to start thinking of your life and the meaning that much more when your days are numbered."

"Old man? I've been thinking about that since my situation happened. I'm a young guy. That's the nature of the beast of mortality. This whole thing I've experienced has made me think about life in a new way."

"That's good."

"Yeah, I guess."

"You guys on the border face some tough stuff."

"Yeah, I wonder if it's worth it for me. I'm thinking about my wife and kids," Stillwell said reflectively.

The two men paused as they reflected on their own situations. Then Manning spoke up. "Lemme ask you something… you ever wonder about the people you're taking in? You ever think about their circumstances and why they're coming here to America?"

"I don't need to wonder about the guy who shot me in the face," snapped Stillwell defensively. He had heard this question before and always hated it.

"I understand that. That's a clear case of someone who shouldn't be here. I'm talking about the ones who can't help their circumstances."

"Everyone can help their circumstances. We make choices to do right or wrong every day. Those who make a choice to abide by the law, have a good life. Those who don't, well, that's their decision. They've gotta suffer the consequences. They wanna do right to help someone make a better life, they're gonna suffer. They should ask themselves if that other person would go out on a limb and sacrifice their comfort for them. Nine times out of ten, I don't think they would."

"Come on, you think it's just black and white? You think right is right and wrong is wrong?"

"America's the greatest place on the face of the earth. I don't need to ask. We've got a court system to handle that and fix it."

"And every case that's determined is right? There are no innocents in prison? If we didn't have civil disobedience, we wouldn't have civil rights. Martin Luther King was jailed over thirty times for his nonviolent protests," said Manning.

Guy didn't bat an eye. "Laws are made to protect people. They ain't perfect, but that's why we have leaders to help make that right. They see an unjust law, they can fix it with a better one. We on the border just do what we're called to do. It ain't my job to make a new law, that's someone else's job. It's my job to carry the law out."

Manning was persistent. "No, I understand that, but who inspires the politician to see the injustice? — those who act out against the law that's unjust? Lemme put it another way. You ever consider why these people would risk bringing their children and risking their lives in a truck, on a boat or in the desert?"

"Sure. I thought about it...you can't look into the eyes of a child and not wonder every now and then what they're thinking. I'm a human being. I have kids of my own. All I know is I wouldn't do it. Those people need to get their house in order in their own countries. Make life better for their own kin. It's not my job to do that. My job is to protect people. It's a very dangerous thing. I've saved a lotta lives. I gave an eye and a lung protecting my country. Ain't nobody gonna undermine what I do. Ain't nobody gonna tell me that what I'm doing isn't for the good of others," said Stillwell very defensively.

"Yeah, you have helped. Nothing wrong with saving lives. It wouldn't be right. All I'm saying is…" He leaned over as he suddenly became very serious and intentional. "It doesn't matter what you or I do. If someone wants freedom, they're gonna make it happen for themselves. People kill for it. I've seen it in war. They'll do whatever it takes, even if it means death. And there ain't a damned thing you or me can do to stop it." He could see that he got to him and pressed it. "I'm sorry, but it's true. You're willing to put your life on the line, you must really know what you're fighting for to be willing to do that," he exclaimed.

Stillwell waved him off as if to say no one ever thinks about that. "Thankless people. Man…" snapped Stillwell shaking his head.

"I fought for my country, too. I'm not thankless. I just knew what I was willing to die for. You willing to die to stand in the way of another person gaining freedom?"

"I have nothing to say about that, Manning! Nothing."

"Well, nothing is something, right?" It was a pointed joke. You got stuck with a guy with strong opinions. That can be a man's worst nightmare, especially in a hospital."

"You can say that again!" Stillwell was irritated and his voice got louder.

"I ain't sayin' anything that ain't true, and if it's getting to you, you need to consider why that is, my friend."

"It's getting to me 'cause you and half the assholes who criticize us don't know what we do. They don't know what it's like to sit and fry like an egg in the sun for the sake of someone trying to be somewhere they ain't supposed to be.

They don't know what it's like to see dead children wrapped in their mother's arms and smell the stink of hopelessness in their shit-stained clothes and the puke of malnutrition...or to pull your friend out of a river where he got caught in the middle of a flood looking for illegals in the weeds. They don't know what it's like when you try to help and get nothing but bureaucratic aggravation and some fuckin' pissant who ain't got a clue about what to do about a problem but tells ya' to follow orders anyway 'cause he's worried about the suits in Washington coming down on him. They ain't got a clue that you're trying to do right by someone when everything else around you is pointing to the fact that it's wrong. They don't know that some of us actually care and are stuck in a no good goddamned situation that's never gonna change!" There was a profound pause that sliced a sliver into the anger.

"I'm sorry, Guy. My feet are swollen and I can't walk — it makes me cranky."

"Ah...Everyone thinks they know...I'm sick and tired of it!!" He punched his pillow and looked to the ceiling.

It inspired Manning to look at his point in a new way. "There was a man...He fought his whole life trying to do what was right. He paid his taxes, he raised a family, and he contributed to his society...He did all he could to do right by others. He saw a circumstance that wasn't being fixed by the law. Another person's life depended on him trying to be helped. He saw it in his mind that it was his duty to save a life, but he had to break the law to do it. What does he do? He let the law work its magic and lose the life or does he do what he's called to do and save the life? Does he take matters into his own hands?" Stillwell slowly leaned over in interest. "A couple of other people happened to get involved due to this man's involvement. As a result of this man's involvement, others take advantage of it. Others he's not aware of. They exploit the situation. Lemme ask you this, who's to blame? The man who tries to save a life or the society that created the injustice to begin with?"

"The road is paved with good intentions. That person may bring more harm to the country and not even know it."

"Then again, his action may help the country," said Manning stubbornly. "Well, I guess that's the messy nature of life. We never know how our good intentions can help a cause and how it might hurt it. For the most part, if the values are there, the virtues have been cultivated, a well-formed conscience is present…then our good intentions have a way of working it all out…They seem to win out in life. Then again, we never really see the fruits of the seeds we sow. I'm an old man and I've seen that enough to know."

"I'll take your word for it," Stillwell replied.

Manning continued to think out loud. "Does my action bring more life or does it bring destruction? That's the ethic I lived by."

Stillwell paused and thought about it for a minute. "That's not a bad way of looking at it," said Stillwell. "I haven't thought about it that way."

Manning was still stuck in his thought. "As I look back on my life, as I look back at history, the ones who understood what was right in their hearts were the ones who were on the right side of history.

"Hitler, Bin Laden they thought they were right in their heart of hearts."

"I'm talking about the people who tried to build the world, not destroy it…I'm talking about the Kings, the Mandelas, the Yunuses, the Wangari Matthais, the Mother Teresas and the Malalas of the world.

"Oh, those people," replied Stillwell not interested.

"Those people who created…those people with visions to make this world a better place through nonviolence, creativity, ingenuity and imagination. Those people who didn't need to destroy things to make things happen. Not the dopes who were stuck in their own egos and created things for the betterment of themselves through destruction…I'm talking about the visionaries. There's always been that person who knew in his bones what he needed to do for the sake of the common good. I'm talking about noble people. When I went to war in WWII, the rest of the world and I just knew that what we were doing was right. You felt it in your bones. In hindsight we were right. Love is always on the right side of history. That's all I'm saying. You've got your whole life to test that theory, and I challenge you to test it."

"Okay," Stillwell laughed. "I'll see what I can do about that."

"Guy?" said Manning pensively. "There's a battle being waged between the heart and head every day. We ain't even conscious of it, but it comes out in everything we do." Manning was reflective as he continued on. "It's a strange situation. I don't know if I'm gonna make it out this surgery alive. Something's tellin' me this may be it. I've given my whole life to doing what's right…I used my mental faculties to make it through this world, and trusted my heart when those faculties failed me. I always come out all right. I fought for this country and was willing to die for it myself…willing to die for freedom and liberty, willing to die for justice and rights…die for something bigger than myself in the name of what was right. Other people in other countries were willing to do that, too. I look at this world and I see such madness. I look at what I do to contribute to the madness and what I do to quell it, make it right. When I'm dead and buried the madness continues. Never ending, I guess. I do know this, though...those who are suffering need to be addressed. I've done what I could to take away that suffering, so my soul's right with the world. We're all made in the image of God. You wouldn't know it by looking at the way we treat each other, but for my money that's worth more than anything. We treat one another with the dignity we deserve. We abide by something greater, something bigger than any law. We listen to the heart, take the way of love, we come out all right."

"I guess we're both right. Neither one of us is going to see what the other is experiencing until we experience it for ourselves. I guess that's half the problem, isn't it?"

The meds kicked in and Manning felt light-headed. There was so much more to say but he couldn't find the words. He thought, *"Absolutes...they're nasty...that's nasty business. The letter of the law ain't perfect and neither is the spirit of the law... the conscience will always give you a good wrestling match."* He muttered, "I don't feel bad about what I done to help this world. On the other hand, I've brought my wife into things she didn't necessarily want to be a part of. I muddied the waters for her and now she's gonna live with her decision in how she responded to right and wrong. It's a messy business this life."

"Yes it is. It's a messy world. All we can do is try to make it right for our children."

"Amen to that." Manning paused. "I like you Guy. You're a good man. I know you believe that in your heart."

"Thanks. I guess that's the common ground we've found. What do we do for the children?"

"Yes sir." The room fell quiet. Manning looked off and stared at the wall and looked as though he penetrated his thoughts beyond the wall. "No regrets," he said quietly. There was some movement outside his room and a few people passed by. Suddenly there was a beeping outside the room and it startled him and brought him back from allowing his imagination to wander. "What's that?"

"I don't know," said Stillwell. "They'll let us know if it's something we should worry about."

"Huh," said Manning. "I hope so." He listened to the beep's slow and steady pulse, and meditated on the beep and what it could mean. He heard someone outside the room call to another. "Hey, can you help me here?" said the nurse. The beep suddenly stopped and the nurse wheeled it away to another part of the ward. He heard the sound of a siren far off in the distance.

Manning's mind wandered to his mortality. He thought about his marriage and the wonderful years together with Eleanor; the days on the ranch and their travels to Europe and kissing on the Rhine; his romantic exploits on cool nights as they took in a concert at the town square; his daughter who gave life to their house and planted her soul there when she passed; Travis' and his thumping around the house and the laughter that imbued the place with an unrivaled spirit of joy. Then his thoughts turned to his obligations and the concerns for Eleanor. He knew companies that were doing business on his land had pulled out. They didn't want to be associated with them due to the present circumstances in any way that might jeopardize their business prospects. He would lose a major source of the income as a result of that. He wondered what Eleanor would do for income when he was gone. Legal bills were starting to mount as a result of his actions. Would the social security check be enough to help with Travis? Would he be okay for going to college or would they have to dip into that rainy day fund they set aside? He wondered what might become of his grandson's future? It's all about them," he thought to himself. "It's always been about them — or so he thought."

Eleanor entered the room as hopefully as she could, her nerves tempered with optimism. She went straight to her husband's bed. "You're awake."

"About as awake as I can be," Manning said.

"Did you sleep?" she asked as she massaged his temples to relax him.

"A little," replied Manning still agitated by his thoughts.

She looked over and saw that Stillwell was awake. "Hello, Guy," she called to the next bed.

"Hey, Eleanor," said Stillwell half out of it.

She redirected her attention to her husband. "You look a little unsettled. You'll be all right. The doctor's performed thousands of these," she said to him.

"I don't know. I don't know if this heart has too many more pumps left. The pump's been primed and it's starting to fail. I just gotta get used to that fact. We both do."

She leaned in and kissed him. "Well, your heart is my heart. And if your heart sees fit to go, my heart will be with you. Let's not think any more about that. Let's look for a few more years."

"Always the optimist. That's why I fell in love with you. It's been a good life, though, hasn't it?"

"It sure has."

"I'm sorry if I've caused you any harm. You know, I didn't mean any harm toward you."

"Stop that. You've given me a life I never thought I could have. I cherish those sweet memories of yesterday. I look for the simple gifts of today and tomorrow will offer new treasures for us — whatever they may be. I'm confident of that."

The nurse entered the room. "We've gotta move you to another room, Mr. Manning, so we can prep you," as she grabbed his IV and prepared to move him from the bed. "You ready to go?"

"As ready as I'll ever be," said Manning, as she ushered him into a wheelchair. "Hey, wheel me over to my friend over there." Stillwell turned to him as Manning extended his hand. "I want you to know you're in my prayers, my friend."

"Thanks. I'll be thinking about you today." The two men shook hands. "It's gonna be all right, Eben."

"I'll see you on the other side," said Manning seriously.

"Wherever that is," replied Stillwell with a smile and a wink. "Don't make something out of nothing.'"

"You kidding? That's all I ever do," said Manning with a wink.

This conversation weighed heavy on Guy, and he confided in Cruz when Steve came for a visit later in the day. The men reflected on whether or not they would reveal the content of this dialogue to the higher ups. If they didn't tell them and the authorities found out what the men knew, it could be their necks. Both men would lose sleep over this information and turned over in their minds what to do next.

33

Eleanor was distant and moved in slow motion. The ranch house seemed vacant like an empty church even though she and Travis were together again. The occupants were as lost and distant to one another as the prairie land that separated their house from their neighbor's house about ten or fifteen football fields away. Rolling clouds were menacing as a cloudburst was waiting to explode. A light drizzle fell. The workers played chicken with the weather trying to get as much work done as they could, loading solar panels onto the truck as fast as they could before the cloudburst. Lightning streaks darted veined branches across the sky and the punch of rolling thunder punctuated the gift of the spectacle. Eleanor watched from the windows mesmerized with the laborious action of the workers for some reason. The death of Eben took her to another place — it was the fact that she was still moving and life was going on when she wanted it all to stop. Death has a way of stopping the world for a time for those who are grieving, but she knew all too painfully well that it must move on. It didn't mean much to her the taking away of the solar panels, but it was significant at the same time as part of her income was being taken away.

The cloudburst dumped its load and the workers were caught. They scampered into the cab of the truck looking like frightened chickens being chased by a dog. One of them stayed under one of the panels, but decided to make a break for the truck, and his friends let him in on the driver's side. Another character was waving his arms up and down like a jokester trying to find his toolbelt in the heavy downpour and was playing the fool. His friends just laughed as he squawked to "lemme in, lemme in." Keeping the doors locked as he pulled at the door, the man banged on the door and after a good bucket of rain drenched him, they finally let him in. *"That's Eben,"* she thought. *"He's sending a little burst to keep 'em on their toes."*

"Grandma?" Travis asked quietly but she didn't answer, so he asked again. The fog of grief was filling her bones like it filled the house. "Grandma?" Travis was waving his arms while sitting at the table with his computer trying to get her attention. She looked over as if to acknowledge him, but looked out the window again. Travis spoke anyway. "Father Paul sent a note: 'What do you think for a reading?'" he asked. "Father Paul said to look at the ones he sent. He wrote, "I like the call to Joshua, Joshua 1:6-9, the call to carry on…'Be strong and courageous.' I also like Matthew 25 for the Gospel — 'The Judgment of Nations' or maybe the Beatitudes. 'Blessed are the poor in spirit, for theirs is the Kingdom of God.' What do you think?"

"Yes, that's fine," Eleanor said.

"No, I want you to look at the choices." Travis paused and understood, but still gazed at his computer and doodled around on it and clicked on a few things just to distract himself like she was distracting herself. He realized that he was getting distant, too, so he closed his computer. Looking over at her, he asked, "Are you all right?"

"I'm looking for our guests. It looks like the panels are coming down pretty easy. I'm just watching them take a portion of our income away. Eben's gone. It's ironic, dontcha think? He's gone and they're taking away the very thing that gives us energy and life. This whole thing was his damned idea."

Travis was quiet but then spoke up. "We'll be all right." He impetuously walked over to her and hugged her.

"Oh, I know," Eleanor responded as she patted his head gently and ran her fingers through his mussed up hair. "Have you heard anything from our friends?"

Travis looked up at her and smiled. He did not want to tell her a second time that he'd received a note from Father Paul, so he handled her with gentleness and managed her dignity. "They made it north. They're on their way. It looks like they're trying to make it to Ohio. Father Paul has some friends up there. Looks like a church is gonna take them in."

"Father Paul has friends everywhere," said Eleanor. "The man's like a saint."

Travis thought about Sancho and how they had to leave him abruptly without giving him a proper burial. "I wanna do Grandpa's funeral up right. I wanna make it special for you."

"You have some thoughts? Do you want to say a few words?" she asked.

"I think so. I think I understand him better."

"Me too. He did things his way and as odd as they were I know in my heart he was a righteous man. He took a stand with his life. You make sure you mention that in your eulogy."

"I will."

"If it's too much, you don't have to do it. I only want you to speak if it'll help you. Father Paul should be back to do the Mass. He'll do right by him, too."

"Thank you. I think I'll be all right. I think I need to say something."

"He was proud of you. You always made him see the world in fresh ways. You brought him tremendous hope for the future." Travis didn't know what to say to that. "Think of a funny story to make them laugh. He'll want some laughter in the house. You can pick any number of stories, can't you?" Travis, who was attentive now to a possibility or two, smiled and sniffled, as she hugged him again.

The house held a pale scent of sadness and gloom as grief from the night before slept with the two of them and was still heavy with sleep. The scent of death hung in the dust-ridden belongings of Eben that had been cleared out of an extra bedroom. The forgotten un-watered plants that were dying due to neglect and preoccupation added to the mist of foreboding uncertainty until the presence of a new life found its way up the long drive.

The Border Patrol car pulled up and the hum of the engine coming to a stop and clanking of a door disturbed the profound silence that beat between them. The rain had ceased for now, and Cruz waited as Rosa lunged to the back seat for a small bag and slowly exited the car.

"They're here," said Eleanor with resounding clarity. She went out to the front porch to greet them followed by Travis. "Welcome," she called from the porch. "We've been expecting you." Rosa's bright eyes relented and carried a half-lit fire and glint of promise in her as she put on a positive face, but her heavy heart slowed her step and her shoulders drooped in defeat as she moved onto the steps and a light breeze blew her knee high chocolate colored dress and revealed her black spandex leggings and spindly legs. It was her natural way to bring a spirit of happiness with her wherever she went. The resonant strains of habit mustered every bit of energy in her bones to carry her forward, as she grabbed the small bag with a few items that had been given to her by Nina.

"I'm Steve Cruz. This is my friend Rosa. Rosa Cruz."

"Well, hello, folks. Come on in and sit down," said Eleanor.

"I can't stay. I'm on my way into work. I just want to introduce you to your new tenant."

"Rosa, it's a pleasure to meet you. I'm Eleanor Manning and this is my grandson, Travis."

"It's nice to meet you," said Rosa meekly. She managed a slight smile. "Thank you for letting me stay here."

As sad as she was she tried not to show it, and Eleanor beamed with hospitality as best she could. "Travis why don't you show Rosa around the house. Our home is your home. The first drink we offer you and then the refrigerator is open for your needs whenever you want. Don't be shy or you'll starve. You just help yourself to anything you want."

"Thank you, ma'am," said Rosa.

"Travis, why don't you take her in and show her to her room. You get her something to drink, too. Would you like something to drink, Steve?"

"No, I better be getting on." The house was stoked with new energy as they ventured inside, and Travis proceeded to show her the lay of the land. He was filled with new purpose again. Cruz and Eleanor waited outside and spoke in hushed tones on the porch, as the light rain stopped and the workers continued to disassemble the solar panels. "I just want to thank you for making room for Rosa."

"It's what we do around here. Our home is always open," said Eleanor.

"I was sorry to hear about the passing of your husband. I'm good friends with Guy Stillwell, and he passed along the news."

"Thanks, I appreciate that," she said with tempered good will.

"Guy liked your husband a lot."

"Well, he liked Guy."

"Listen, Eleanor, Guy related some information to me that he'd heard from your husband just before he went into surgery."

"Oh, he did, huh?" Eleanor grew cold and uncertain.

"My understanding is that you've had some problems with us over a tunnel that was built." She remained silent and a breeze chilled her to the bone as he spoke. She was waiting for more dread to come her way. Cruz looked for the words he wanted to say and discomfort hung in the spaces between. "He said that tunnel was all his idea...your husband's there...He felt a ton of guilt for what he'd done. I guess what I'm trying to say is...I just hope you and your grandson there can find some peace. It sounds to me like you didn't have much to do with it. I sure do hope his passing will end your legal problems and you can put that behind you, ma'am." He gave an awkward glance with an absurd grin and grew uncomfortable as he looked around to see if anyone had heard him, as if there were agents around. He wasn't one for sentiment and she sensed it, so she looked away as if she didn't notice his awkwardness.

"I hope so, too," she said lightening her tense demeanor with a voice of relief. "It's been hard going, that's for sure, and it'll be harder for awhile."

Cruz traced a half circle with his foot in the wet sand. He noticed a baseball and picked it up, rubbing the dirt off it and holding it like he was holding it tight for security. "I'm not a stranger to that, that's for sure. I don't know if any of us are. That poor girl...She's crippled with fear. She's very quiet... that's what trauma does to you. It's gonna take a while for her to get any kinda normalcy back — if she gets it. That poor girl in there's been through a lot. Our sense is that she doesn't even wanna be here. I wanna make her feel as comfortable as possible."

"I imagine she'd want to just be with her momma in the comforts of her own home and comforts of her own environment," said Eleanor.

"Well, I hope we can help her out and get her momma here for a visit. Get that family on a path to have a better life."

"That's..." Eleanor grinned widely now as she searched for her words. "That's what we're all looking for." She spoke with tender wisdom and crisp certainty. She just knew with every ounce of her being.

"Well, I must be going. I'd like to stop back with my friend Nina at some point. I was hoping we might be able to check on Rosa as she settles in."

"You're always welcome here. Our home is your home. Maybe I can have a welcome dinner at some point."

"That'd be real nice." Cruz tossed the baseball to the porch, walked back to his car and shouted. "You have a nice day now. Enjoy this rain. We sure needed it."

"Yes, we did. You too," she called back.

The ground was steaming and the coolness of the rain refreshed the scene leaving a breath of new life; birthing itself in the waters of renewal like a nice bath and the fresh smell of salty vigor; the blue-smoked mountains in the distance cased an ashen pall as a muggy film of sanctity clung to them and humidity moistened the skin. Travis and Rosa walked out onto the porch with drinks as Steve's car pulled away and they waved goodbye. The pink lemonade was sour and bitter but it tasted sweet and sugary to them. They'd both been deprived of a simple delight such as this and it took on new importance to their newfound sense of taste.

Travis, who was forlorn for most of the day, had a sudden burst of energy at the thought of entertaining his new guest, and his placid manner was aroused with newfound enthusiasm. A flood of thoughts burst forth, "Come on to the stable and see my horses. You like horses? That's a dumb question, everybody likes horses, I guess. They're magical animals. We sure can learn a lot from 'em." Eleanor smiled as they walked to the paddock, and Travis ran ahead and led a dappled gray horse with black spots out of the stall and into the ring that was strewn with hay and patches of wet grass.

Eleanor could still climb the whitewashed fence — spryly even and whispers of yesteryear seemed to take hold of her. She felt a gentle tap of the past on her shoulder as she recalled a date with Eben at a rodeo and sitting on the hard bleachers watching the show and the magnificent turns of bravery as riders dazzled and demonstrated sparkling fits of poetry in motion between man and animal. Now the presence of a horse sauntering gracefully into a pasture was enough for her to kindle a reset of perspective. She stretched out her hand. "Come on up here and sit with me. Unless you don't want to get that pretty dress wet and dirty," she said cleaning off a spot for her. Rosa climbed the sturdy fence and sat alongside her. Rosa dabbed at the small wet-dusted white rail and made a smiley face on it but erased it as Travis led the horse over to her. The horse greeted Rosa as kindly as Travis had. Travis gave her some oats to feed.

"She likes you," said Eleanor. *"Animals are funny that way,"* she thought to herself. *"They seem to know who needs their presence the most and what to do to put your mind at ease."*

The sun peaked out every now and then, but the clouds were prominent and it looked as if another rainstorm appeared on the horizon as thunder rolled in. A second cloudburst was filling its pail of bluster and the workers hurried, watching it again and attending to their business. The sun itself had bursts of radiance and retreated behind the clouds like the cloudburst before it.

Travis pulled some tricks out of the horse as he looked to the sky. Rosa, marveling at what he could get the horse to do, watched as the horse reared back on her hind legs and lifted her front legs into the air. She held her pose and looked like a statue of glory. "We better be quick. Looks like it's gonna rain again," Travis said. Then he noticed something in the distance coming his way. It was a few horses. They meandered onto the farm and had appeared as if they were lost and looking for a new way to go. Travis stopped in his tracks in awe as he did in the presence of all horses. "That looks like Peggy!"

"What?" Eleanor inquired as she awakened to his excitement.

"Pegasus!! One a' the horses I was telling you about." Astonished, he hopped the fence and ran to them. The horses didn't appear to be frightened. It was as if they knew him. They were like old friends who paid a surprise visit. They were, in fact, old friends. Prancing up to him were a few horses that carried him and the family to freedom with Pegasus in the lead. "I'll be damned, you found your way back to me. You're even smarter than I thought you were," he stated with glee, as the horses returned his greeting with neighs and wagging tails. Eleanor was coming back to life.

"I guess they wanted to meet you, Grandma. They wanted to meet my family. Have I got a story to tell you about these guys," Travis said to Rosa.

"Grandma, can we keep 'em?"

"Now hold on there…that's a bit premature now."

"They were looking for me."

"I guess. The least we could do is get them some feed. Give them some shelter from this storm.

"Dag blammit, I had a feeling I'd meet you again! I had a strange feeling we were meant to meet. Ain't that something, Grandma?" He said as he scratched them and beamed with joy.

"It sure is. But Travis, these horses are meant for the wild. They're meant to roam free."

"I know that, Grandma, I just want you to consider it."

"Where would we put them?"

"Well, you said yourself, there's 'always room at the inn.'" Eleanor looked at Rosa and gave a wide-eyed face of silly regret knowing that those very words would one day haunt her. "It's almost like we were meant to be friends forever." He turned to Rosa, "Boy, do I have a story to tell you about these guys. They're Mexicans, Rosa. Talk to 'em in Spanish."

"Hola," Rosa laughed slightly and uncomfortably as she tried to feel out her new companions and wondered if she was doing right by appeasing the boy.

"See," said Travis. "They understand you. They're from your country," he joked. Rosa felt more at home.

Eleanor was thrown for a loop, but the joy she saw in Travis' and Rosa's hearts inspired her to consider the guests for a little while, even if it did cost some money. She felt like she owed it to them for bringing back her boy in one piece and protecting him. They led the horses away to the barn and housed them just in time for the next batch of rain to explode.

It would rain for days on end right through the funeral ceremony for Eben. The mourners were drenched standing at the burial place of Eben and next to him the fresh newly seeded gravesite of Travis' friend Sancho, but they didn't mind. In fact, they had a moment where everyone put down their umbrellas and let the rain fall on their faces, so they could soak it all in and relish its all encompassing beauty.

Father Paul waved the thurible over the casket three times. The chains clanged as blue-smoke rose and dissipated thus leaving a fragrant hue of incense in the mourners to savor, mingling with the blooming jacaranda trees. "Ashes to ashes, dust to dust...rain to rain, soul to soul," said Father Paul as he blessed the scene, splashing holy water on the casket. He wasn't supposed to say those last words, but he did anyway. Nobody minded and Eleanor eased back thinking *"How appropriate"* with a smile.

As a result of all the rain, streams would burst forth, bringing water to the arid desert and rivers in the steppe. The burning sands became pools and the thirsty ground, springs of water. The way they tread became a holy way for Travis. He wondered why the land was redeemed. He also thought, *"Right now someone's being fed by that rain. Someone in the desert is getting a taste of a little gift from nature that he's been denied."* It was an insight that was lost on him before his journey over the fence. Every time he walked the fence he wondered who was over there in Mexico and what challenge they may be encountering. Every time he walked that ground by the church and the graves, he felt the hallowed nature of its presence.

He had learned the sacred meaning of *respect*. He'd learned the value of looking deeper at the world around him and venturing to see the simple gifts of life by taking another look at things. He found a new place for himself in this life. He could never look at this life the same way. The wilds of life and the shards of death held a mystery to him that made him pause, look deeper. Travis learned at an early age the stinging reality of mortality and the limits of fear in the human condition, but he also tasted the sanctity of boundless wonder and infinite grace. He peeked behind the veil of another world, and a new horizon dawned for him.

It took on a new depth of meaning, this land he inhabited. The new understanding was equaled only by his new breadth of awareness of the precious nature of life that he witnessed in those around him; those who lived in safety and security working the land for the good of all, and those who cherished every moment though tormented by challenges of adversity and their poverty — and especially the lives of the hunted and the saved…rising on the road to freedom.

THE END

ACKNOWLEDGEMENTS

I am grateful to everyone who was instrumental in helping me on this journey. This book would not have been possible without the help of giving souls who have shared their talents and insights in unique and profound ways.

Thank you to Shana Kelly, Dan Coyle, Connie Schultz, Glenna Edwards and Mike Pophal for their professional guidance and open heartedness in helping me along the way. They welcomed my requests and pointed me to where I needed to go, and I am grateful to them for their suggestions to help me move forward and make things happen.

To Christine Gerety for championing this work early on and her gentle support of me throughout the process. Chris read an early draft and encouraged me to see more. She stayed and watched it all unfold and was there to question, wonder and laugh with me right up until the last sentences.

To Julie Christiano and Nancy LaFever for their exceptional editorial skills. Their dedication to this work, wisdom, critical eyes and all-important encouragement were instrumental in seeing more.

To Dan Ertle and Amie Kosberg for the Spanish translations. They made the voices real and helped characters come alive and be authentic.

To my teacher and mentor Joe Garry, Jr. for teaching me the value of social justice in art and helping me cultivate my art through the power of theater. Joe introduced me to the art of writing through theater and taught me that an author must "see the image, and live the image before he can project it."

To Sr. Mary Genino and the RSHM for introducing me to this topic and inspiring me to bring this issue to a greater audience "so that all may have life to the full." They brought me in and nurtured my spirit and introduced me to an "extended family."

To Kerry Kennedy, Mary McCoy, Karen Robinson and the folks at the RFK Center for Human Rights for expanding my horizons in seeing more possibilities in human rights for the classroom and challenging me to go deeper in seeing those "Defenders" who are helping those on the margins.

To Lasan Darboe, Nika Soon-Shiong and Michele Chan Soon-Shiong for their belief and encouragement of me and my work when I needed it most, and their heartfelt commitment to engage in transformational change for the betterment of our world.

To Andrew Demeter for broadening my horizons to consider bigger options, and Deb Robison for her marketing advice. Kevin Gorman for his marketing savvy and his undying dedication to helping me share my work with others.

To Mosie Trewhitt and "Annie" at Liberty Horsemanship whose expertise was critical in helping me understand more about horses and their magic.

To David Braughler for his belief in my work, his wise insights and his professionalism in putting the book together. And the folks at Braughler Books for employing their gifts and artfulness. Special thanks to Craig Ramsdell for his adroit cover and interior art.

To my students and colleagues who have challenged me to go deeper and inspire greater awareness in the joy of bringing more light to this world. My family and friends who supported me through this powerful odyssey and continue to empower through their tender expressions of ineffable love – especially Susie Klein for her unconditional support and belief in what I was doing, and for letting me use her house as an office.

Last but not least, to Jimmy Klein, and Art Miccio for their belief in me and reading every word I've ever written and giving it to me straight. They are responsible for shaping my inner vocabulary and recognizing the power of spirit to conquer. (WITS)

ABOUT THE AUTHOR

William Klein hails from Buffalo, New York, and was raised in Cleveland, Ohio. Both a spiritual director and a teacher, William has taught social justice and human trafficking since 2004, and has served as a faculty member at colleges and preparatory schools in California and Ohio. His global travels have inspired his quest to bring the simple wisdom of world mythologies and sacred teachings to a greater audience. His reflections and essays are available at spiritbeat.net.

CPSIA information can be obtained
at www.ICGtesting.com
Printed in the USA
FSHW010733030420
68763FS